SILENT MAYHEM

THE MAYHEM SERIES, BOOK THREE

SUE COLETTA

Tirgearr Publishing

Published by Tirgearr Publishing Ireland www.tirgearrpublishing.com

ISBN 978-1-910234-38-9

A CIP catalogue record for this book is available from the British Library.

10 9 8 7 6 5 4 3 2 1

Some things in life defy comprehension, but that doesn't make them any less real. Or deadly.

When a familiar crow drops a cryptic scroll at Shawnee Daniels' feet, she's compelled to open it, even though everything in her power warns her not to. Mr. Mayhem—the most prolific serial killer the North Shore has ever known—claims her life is in danger. He "claims" he wants to help her, but just last year he threatened to murder everyone she loves.

While Mayhem taunts her with oddly-placed feathers, like The Creator left at his crime scenes, an interstate killing spree rocks Massachusetts and New Hampshire. A madman is decapitating men and women, dumping their headless corpses on two area beaches. But what Shawnee soon uncovers shatters all she's ever known, her memories shredded, the whispers of the past in shambles on the ground.

Can she find the strength to move forward, or will the truth destroy her?

To my readers, who continue to humble me with your enthusiasm of my work, and to the amazing folks in my community, both online and in person…

May the stars carry your sadness away.
May the flowers fill your heart with beauty.
May hope forever wipe away your tears.
And, above all, may silence make you strong.

ACKNOWLEDGMENTS

Thank you to my best friend and husband, Bob, for your endless support and encouragement. I wouldn't want to continue this amazing journey without you. Hugs & kisses to Bobby, Kathy, Berlyn, Scarlet, Joey, and Dad. I love you all so much. xo

Special thanks to Detective (Ret.) Danny R. Smith for your help with getting Shawnee out of a particular sticky situation in a plausible way.

Huge hugs to Devin, Pat, and Taylor at The Other Guy's Tattoo Shop. Not only did you allow me to use your shop in Silent Mayhem, but one of you even offered to die a merciless death. You're awesome!

The beautiful quote in the dedication is from Chief Dan George. Thanks for your words of wisdom, Chief.

A quick shout-out to my awesome editor, Sharon Pickrel, and the rest of my amazing, supportive crew at Tirgearr Publishing. You rock!

Last but not least, thank you, God, for blessing my life in unimaginable ways.

SILENT MAYHEM
Mayhem Series, book three
Sue Coletta

PROLOGUE

"Do not depend on anyone too much in this world,
for even your shadow leaves you when you are in darkness."
- Ibn Taymiyyah

Monday
Midnight

"A s you take your final breath, let the tears rain down from the heavens, a silent mayhem whispering the sins of the past." In the bunker, an ornate lair several feet below ground, Mr. Mayhem leaned toward Mary Rowlandson's face, her bloody nose an inch away from his. Gazing into her watery eyes, he listed his head to one side. "Will you scream for me? Oh, how I miss the sound of raw emotion."

She screeched, "Why are you doing this?"

"You don't know?" He jerked away from her, laying splayed gloved-fingers to his chest. "My apologies. I was under the impression that you'd been fully informed." His gaze fled over his shoulder to Chayton, his protégé. "Is there some reason you withheld the truth from Ms. Rowlandson?"

1

Chayton bowed his head, staring at the concrete floor.

"By doing so, you've missed the mark, my dear boy. Look at me." He waited for the young executioner to look up. "This message is important. She needs to know...to understand...she must feel her shame."

With an intent stare into Chayton's eyes, he strode toward him. "Listen to the wind, it talks. Listen to the silence, it speaks. Listen to your heart..."

"It knows," replied Chayton.

"Indeed, it does."

He gave a knowing nod, and young Chayton swung the sword.

In one swift motion, Mayhem snagged a fistful of Ms. Rowlandson's fair hair before her decapitated body crumpled to the concrete. Raising the severed head toward the dome ceiling, he proclaimed, "With this one brave act, the tears shall fall. Your reign has begun, my son. Make us proud."

CHAPTER ONE

Two weeks later
Tuesday
7:00 p.m.

Things weren't all that bad till he showed up and tossed a hand-grenade through my life, shattering my memories, everything I believed in pieces on the ground.

It all started when I left work on Tuesday. One lone crow circled above my head, his wings in a constant flutter. The flapping created a wind tunnel that blew back my hair and shuffled my bangs. Sunlight shimmered off precision-placed feathers, black and gleaming. I stopped dead in the middle of the Revere Police Department parking lot.

Motionless, my time spent imprisoned in an underground bunker clawed at my mind, body, and spirit. In a soft tone, I said, "Poe?" Nah. Couldn't be. Could it? Mayhem fled months ago. Why would he risk returning to the area? Besides, it's not like blackbirds avoided urban areas. Revere had more than its fair share—learned that little tidbit the hard way.

When the crow dipped even closer, I curled my forearms

around my face. Peeking through the crack between my forearms, a thin and shaded sliver of space, Poe's gold ankle band collided with the sunlight, and shot a beam straight in my eye. Almost being blinded was probably the highlight of my day. Because if the crow was, in fact, Poe, then Mayhem couldn't be far behind.

With a quick turn of the head, I scanned the parking lot for the black Caddy, my pulse keeping pace with Poe's fluttering wings. I'd had run-ins with him before, and I sure as hell wasn't in a hurry to do it again.

Hovering a mere six inches above me, his talons opened in slow motion and out dropped a scroll, striking the toe of my right motorcycle boot. A direct hit.

Time thudded to a stop.

Every bone in my body screamed for me to step over Mayhem's note, and that's exactly what I should've done. But I didn't. God forbid Shawnee Daniels drove down Easy Street. I also should've never pulled the twine bow that held the scroll together.

Ivory stationery unfurled, revealing the message inside.

Dearest Cat,

You are in grave danger. Meet me at that quaint diner you like so much. One hour. Please remember, it's rude and unbecoming to arrive late. I would hate for you to miss what I have to say. It might save your life.

Hugs & Kisses,
Mr. M

Save my life? He had some balls, considering he's the only one who'd threatened me over the last year, not counting his merry band of psychos. Zings ricocheted head to toe. Was he stalking me again? If so, why? Maybe he's the danger I should avoid. Either that, or he used the excuse as a ruse to get me to show. Mayhem wasn't stupid.

I pulled back my shoulders. But neither am I. Two could play this game. All I had to do was scope things out. What choice did I have? That's exactly why he left the note vague.

Nicely played, asshole.

Within fifteen minutes, my knee bouncing with excess energy, I raced through the entrance of the parking lot to the Lone Range-R, one of my favorite diners. The gas pedal tangoed with the car mat, and I leaned sideways, my hand groping for a way to untangle the two. By the time I straightened, my jeep was sailing straight for the dumpster. I jerked the wheel to the left, tires screeching across the asphalt, Ol' Bessie's rear-end fishtailing in leftover sand from the snow plows last winter.

With both feet, I slammed the brakes. The jeep bucked, jumped, and then stalled. Admittedly, I'd made classier entrances.

Ego bruised but not broken, I turned the key.

Tick, tick, tick, tick, tick.

"Dammit. Not now." I twisted the key a second time.

Tick, tick, tick, tick, tick.

"You bitch!" In the hopes of appealing to one of my jeep's multiple personalities, I rubbed the dash. "I didn't mean that. C'mon, girl, you can do it. We only need to go another ten feet."

Tick, tick, tick, tick, tick.

"Screw it. You win." I got out, slammed the driver's door, and spit at the tire. "Hope someone hits your sorry ass." The bitch would probably make me pay for that comment at the worst possible moment.

Scanning the lot, my head swiveling faster than a ceiling fan on high, I searched for Mayhem's black Cadillac CTS, but couldn't find it anywhere. Had he changed vehicles? In the far corner of the lot sat a gold Hummer. On its roof, three crows perched on the utility rack. Standing shoulder-to-shoulder, they cocked their heads as I strode by, six beady black eyes glaring straight at me.

Super, he brought his freaky pets, too. Lucky me.

Hand trembling, I tugged open the thick glass door of the Lone Range-R and held my head high as I strutted inside, even though nothing about this situation was what I'd call normal. The hostess grabbed a menu from the wooden slat on the side of the podium. "Will anyone be joining you today?"

"Yeah. There's two of us, but I think he might already be here. I saw his vehicle in the parking lot." In case I never made it out of here alive, or some poor schmuck discovered my remains in a nearby ditch, I offered her a few details to remember for when Levaughn interviewed her after my death. "See that gold Hummer out there? It's the one with crows perched on top."

Obviously, she didn't give a rat's ass, because she never bothered to look. Bitch. Instead, all she said was, "Name?"

What name did he use? His moniker, Mr. Mayhem, would sound bizarre at best. Unless he just used Mr. M. Wavering back and forth, I guessed, "Umm, Daniels?"

The hostess ran her finger down the page in an appointment book. "Shawnee Daniels?"

I spread my arms wide, shaking jazz hands as though an unknown entity had entered my body. "In the flesh."

Where the hell did that come from? Get a grip, Daniels. If you're not at the top of your game, Mayhem will crush you.

She stared at me as though I'd lost my friggin' mind. Sadly, she wasn't wrong.

"Alrighty then," she said, her tone placating. "Your party arrived fifteen minutes ago." She swept her arm in the direction of a room full of tables. "Right this way please."

Mute, my lips glued to one another, I followed her past families and couples who laughed together, having a great time while I, on the other hand, neared the most vicious serial killer the North Shore had ever known. Too bad no one knew that but me.

Regardless of how anyone judged my decision to keep Mr. Mayhem's identity secret, I still held firm. Fact was, the day I ratted him out was the day everyone I loved died in unfathomable ways. Mayhem wasn't the type of dude to screw with, even on his best days.

As the hostess and I approached the booth in the back, Mr. Mayhem rose, his black fedora pressed to his chest. "Ms. Daniels—" he smiled, his freaky eyes soft and inviting— "how nice of you to join me." He swept a hand toward the bench across the table from him. "Please, after you..."

Sprinting toward the exit wasn't an option at this point, so I slid into the booth, my mind racing with endless scenarios of how this covert meeting might play out.

"I'll send your waitress right over after you've had a chance to look at the menu," the hostess told us. "In the meantime, can I get you something to drink?"

Mayhem grinned, and my fingers balled into a fist; I'd had just about enough of the niceties already. "Ladies first," he said, the grin morphing into a sly smirk.

I glanced up at the hostess. "Nothing for me, thanks."

From across the table, Mayhem shot me the concerned parent look, and I didn't buy the charade for a second. He'd have to up his game to con me into lowering my guard.

"Aw, don't be like that." He faked a pout. "We have a lot to discuss."

"Fine." Anything to get this over with faster. "I'll have a hot chocolate with marshmallow."

He rubbed his palms together. "Ooh, sounds delightful. I'll have the same please."

"Two hot chocolates coming right up." With a curl of the fingers, the hostess swept her hair around the largest turquoise earring on the planet. Okay, maybe it wasn't big enough to break a record or anything, but it had to weigh at least a quarter pound, her ear lobes stretching to her jawline.

"Thank you kindly—" Mr. Mayhem glanced at the nameplate above her heart— "Alicia. Beautiful name."

She tittered, and I almost puked. How could anyone buy his nicey-nicey act?

Once Alicia strolled out of earshot, I crossed my arms and legs, my foot involuntarily swinging back and forth. "What's all this about?" Thinning my eyes, I jerked forward. "I don't like being summoned by your psychotic crow."

He winced. "Poe, I assure you, is no more psychotic than I am. His feelings are much like yours and mine. The intricacies of a crow's brain are really quite fascinating."

I resisted the urge to roll my eyes…barely. "Yeah. Great. Whatever."

"Perhaps you'll feel better if you allow me to explain why I sent Poe."

Leaning back, I re-crossed my arms. "Go for it, hotshot."

"The reason I contacted you the way I did was to lessen your level of distress." He weaved his long fingers together, resting his hands on the table—the same hands that ended the lives of so many, over the years—his black leather gloves stacked beside them. "Had I knocked on your door, for example, you may have reacted impulsively and without forethought. This way, you had a chance to prepare yourself. Did you not appreciate the advanced notice?"

"It's fine, whatever." My right knee bounced in anticipation. "Tell me why I'm here."

He glanced in the mirror above my head. "Let's wait for Alicia to deliver our drink order. In the meantime—" he rested his chin in an open hand, mesmerizing almost-translucent eyes drilling a hole straight through me— "what's going on in your life?"

"Meh. Same shit, different day." I leaned across the table, lowering my voice, my tone cold, calculating. "A better question might be, what's happening in yours? Murder anyone recently, Mister Mayhem?"

As if I'd said nothing at all, he shook out the linen napkin and spread it across his lap. He folded his hands in front of him on the table again and then leaned back against the booth's maroon pleather. Then, out of the blue, he asked, "Are you aware of your heritage?"

And my head almost snapped off my neck. "Excuse me?"

"You worked The Creator case, did you not?"

How could he possibly know that? "Yeah," I said, hesitant. "I work on a lotta cases. What's your point?"

"In fact, one could say you had a personal stake in the outcome of that case. Correct?" His eyes flickered toward the mirror; this dude took cautious to a whole new level. "Hold that thought a moment."

The hostess set our drinks on the table.

"You are too kind, Alicia." He gave her a quick wink, and she blushed. "Thank you."

If she only knew what he was capable of, she'd take off and never look back.

Once Mayhem's new admirer left, he puckered his lips, blowing steam off his hot chocolate, as if he hadn't just tossed a grenade through my cool façade. "You were saying, Shawnee? Pardon. Do you mind if I call you by your first name?"

I half-shrugged. "Hey, why not? Apparently, you think you know everything about me anyway."

"*Au contraire.* If I were cognizant of all things, there would be no need for this conversation." He gestured with his hand, urging me to drink. "Your cocoa is getting cold, dear."

The only reason I'd ordered the damn thing was to shut him up. I could care less if it rose up and danced a jig. Hm. Actually, that might be kinda cool.

My mind snapped back to reality. Whatever possessed me to open that damn scroll?

To force Mr. Mayhem to pay attention I leaned forward, my gaze transfixed on his unflinching stare. "What was your involvement in The Creator case? Were you helping Jack Delsin, is that it?"

All innocent-like, he rested an opened hand to his heart as though appalled by my question. "Goodness, no. Although, I did admire his creativity. Even you have to admit, the wings were an ingenious touch."

"What? No, I don't." A bitter tang engulfed my mouth, my voice rising in intensity. "Lives were lost, and for what?" Huffing out a breath, I clawed a hand through my hair. "Look who I'm talkin' to. Enough!" I slapped the table, a wave of anger shooting through me, threatening to give Mayhem the advantage. "Tell me why I'm here."

Cool as ice, he dabbed his lips with the napkin. "Jack was a powerful man. Were you aware of that?"

"'Powerful' would not be my description of Jack Delsin, but whatever. Make your point."

He scanned the room, then lowered his voice to almost a whisper. "I assume by your earlier reaction that your parents passed away before teaching you about your roots. Is that a fair assessment?"

"I have no idea what in the hell you're talkin' about. Is this why you brought me here, to dig through my childhood?" I rose halfway, rooted through my pocket for cash. "Save it, pal. I'm outta here."

Mayhem reached across the table and latched onto my forearm, his grip firm, and threatening. "Please, Ms. Daniels. I have never lied to you. Listen to what I have to say. It could save your life."

I lowered my gaze to his vice-grip around my arm, and he let go. "You've got five minutes." I tapped the gold watch that I'd procured from a power couple a few years back. "And those five minutes start now."

"Not here." He skimmed the restaurant. "As it is, I shouldn't even be discussing this matter, especially in public." He swigged his cocoa, dabbed his lips with the napkin, and rose. From his front pocket, he withdrew a gold Ferragamo money clip and slapped a twenty-dollar bill on the table. "Join me for a stroll outside."

I flashed both palms. "Whoa. I'm not goin' anywhere with you, pal."

"Pal." He smirked. "Love your style, I really do." Pausing, his unblinking stare lasered into my soul. "Last chance. Are you sure you won't reconsider my offer?"

"Positive."

"What a shame. Well—" he sighed — "I gave it the ol' college try." With no further explanation, he set his fedora on his head, tipped the hat toward me, turned, and soldiered out the exit.

I collapsed against the booth, my arms hung by my sides. What the hell just happened?

At the glass door, I waited for the Hummer to drive out of the parking lot before hustling to my jeep. A black feather laid against the windshield. Had Poe dropped it on purpose?

I leaned in to study the white ring around its base. The opaque quill snuggled under the driver's side windshield wiper. It's impossible to land that way. But why would Mayhem leave me a feather?

CHAPTER TWO

Tuesday
8:00 p.m.

The call came in at twenty-hundred hours. Lovers found a corpse on a secluded section of Revere Beach, but the particulars weren't clear. On the drive over, Detective Levaughn Samuels called Officer Franklin Langley, Jr., the first responder to the scene.

"Langley," he answered, his voice shaky, nervous.

"Hey, it's Levaughn. You all right? Callin' to tell you I'm en route."

"The bastard cut his head off!" His scream vibrated the hands-free speakers in the Crown Vic. "There's blood all over the sand! Oh my God." His tone turned grave, ill. "I'm gonna be sick."

"Breathe, Langley. I need you to stay with me." Levaughn's grip tightened around the wheel. The integrity of the crime scene took priority over a rookie's weak stomach. "Are the staging lights setup yet? Sunset's in a half hour."

"Patrol's doing it now. Please hurry. It's bad, Levaughn. Real bad." He gagged. "I don't know how much longer I can stay here. The smell is…" The gagging morphed into dry heaves. At this rate, it was only a matter of time before he contaminated the entire crime scene. "Oh, shit. Gotta go."

The line went dead.

"Dammit." Drumming the wheel, Levaughn gunned the gas, the car launching into high gear, blue lights tumbling onto the dusky road. By the time he hit Revere Beach Boulevard, the blazing siren pounded his eardrums, a steady beat that morphed into dull aches at the temples.

Next to the sea wall, he pulled curbside, then rummaged through the glove compartment for over-the-counter migraine medicine. Only one tab left in the travel bottle. It'd have to do for now. Every civilian in the area came to witness this victim's headless corpse. Somehow, he needed to preserve the integrity of the scene.

In front of the police tape, he shot a glare at two uniformed officers, standing around doing nothing. "Crowd control—now." His voice boomed. "And video the onlookers. If the suspect likes to watch, we might catch a peek at 'im." Levaughn ducked under the police tape, strolling toward the remains.

Dr. Juan Chavez hunched over the remains of a Caucasian nude male, approximately thirty to thirty-five years of age. With the Medical Examiner blocking half the body he couldn't tell much more than that, but when he rose, the full impact of the brutality caught Levaughn off-guard, and he rocked back on his heels, his jaw slacked in disbelief.

"Whoa." He inched closer. "Is decapitation the cause of death, Doc?"

"As far as I can tell, yes. Death didn't come quickly, either."

Staring at the remains, he tried to weigh the level of hatred for someone to decapitate another human being, but he kept coming up empty. "Whaddaya mean by that?"

"Well—" Chavez rolled off his latex gloves— "contrary to

belief, even if decapitation is swift, as it appears here, the mind can remain conscious for up to ten seconds. Which is plenty of time for the victim to feel pain, terror, grief. He could even glance down at his detached body."

Levaughn's lips twisted. "You're not serious."

"Actually, I am. The phenomenon's been documented."

"With what, a chicken?"

"A chicken," echoed Chavez. "Men." He shook his head as if he weren't a card-carrying member of the gender, even though he played for a different team. "You want examples? Fine. In nineteen-eighty-nine, an Army veteran was involved in a fatal automobile accident with a friend. At the accident scene, he reported that his friend's decapitated head changed facial expressions, and I quote, 'First of shock or confusion, then to terror or grief.'"

For some reason, Chavez withdrew his cell phone, his eyes still focused on Levaughn. "Perhaps the most notable study occurred in nineteen-oh-five by Dr. Beaurieux. After the execution of convicted murderer Henri Languille, over the course of twenty-five to thirty seconds of observation, Beaurieux recorded being able to communicate with Languille by getting him to open his eyes and focus on the doctor by calling Languille's name." He flashed one finger, then another. "Not once but twice."

Head shaking ever so slightly, he waited for Chavez to wink or smile, but the doctor remained stone-faced. Guess he wasn't fooling around. "Yeah, I find that a little hard to believe. Sorry. What he probably saw was the body's reaction to the trauma. Nerves will twitch when they're severed."

"Levaughn, my boy, you can be so closed-minded at times."

Levaughn's head ached, throbbed. Just once, could they get through the initial examination without all the usual bullshit? There wasn't enough coffee in the world to brighten this day.

Staring at his phone, Chavez said, "Here's Doctor Beaurieux's journal entry from that day, and I quote, '*Here, then, is what I was able to note immediately after the decapitation. The eyelids and lips of the guillotined man worked in irregularly rhythmic contractions for about five or six seconds. This phenomenon has been remarked by all those finding themselves in the same conditions as myself for observing what happens after the severing of the neck.*'"

Levaughn tongued the inside of his cheek. "Like I said, Doc, the body reacted on its own."

"You didn't let me finish. Typical man." Chavez tsked his tongue. "He goes on to state, '*I waited for several seconds. The spasmodic movements ceased.*'" He emphasized the last sentence for Levaughn's benefit, as though it proved his outlandish theory. "'*The face relaxed, the lids half-closed on the eyeballs, leaving only the white of the conjunctive visible, exactly as in the dying whom we have occasion to see every day in the exercise of our profession, or as in those just dead. It was then that I called in a strong, sharp voice, 'Languille!' I saw the eyelids slowly lift up, without any spasmodic contractions—I insist advisedly on this peculiarity—but with an even movement, quite distinct and normal, such as happens in everyday life, with people awakened or torn from their thoughts.*'"

The doctor cleared his throat. "Pardon the archaic language, but I'm reading the text verbatim."

Lowering his gaze to the cell phone, Chavez turned his attention back to the online journal entry. "'*Next, Languille's eyes very definitely fixed themselves on mine with the pupils focused themselves. I was not, then, dealing with the sort of vague, dull look without any expression, that can be observed any day in dying people to whom one speaks; I was dealing with undeniably living eyes which were looking at me. After several seconds, the eyelids closed again, slowly and evenly, and the head took on the same appearance as it had before I called out.*'"

To verify the article was, indeed, on a science-based website, Levaughn peered over the doctor's shoulder as he read the last paragraph. It's not that he didn't trust him, but a good investigator didn't take anyone's word at face value.

With a quick glance back at Levaughn, Chavez continued reading. *"It was at that point that I called out again and, once more, without any spasm, slowly, the eyelids lifted, and undeniably living eyes fixed themselves on mine with perhaps even more penetration than the first time. Then there was a further closing of the eyelids, but not less complete. I attempted the effect of a third call; there was no further movement—and the eyes took on the glazed look which they have in the dead."* Both finely-waxed eyebrows arched at Levaughn. "Now do you believe me?"

"Yup. Looks like your facts are spot on, Doc." He would've said anything to stop the history lesson. Forcing a quick grin, he squatted next to the disembodied head. The mouth gaped open in a silent scream, the eyelids at half-mast. "So, lemme get this straight. You're sayin' this horrified expression occurred post-decapitation?"

"It's entirely possible." Chavez knelt beside him. "You see, the main factor in consciousness after decapitation is the mental and physical state of the victim prior to dismemberment. The killer would need to take the victim by surprise for the facial expressions to occur post-decapitation. Because if the victim feared the impending strike, then blood would release from the brain a lot sooner. Typically, oxygenated blood in the brain lasts about ten seconds. However, fear would cause the heart to pump faster."

Chavez rose and slid his cell phone into the inside pocket of his burgundy suit jacket. Levaughn eyed him up and down. An ivory shirt and burgundy tie, brown-and-ivory spectator shoes. Latinos were nothing if not stylish, especially gay males.

"In the case of the guillotined convict," he continued, and Levaughn couldn't wait till he hopped off this particular soapbox so they could get back to work, "the prisoner showed extraordinary sangfroid, even courage, from the moment he was told that his last hour had come, until the moment when he walked to the scaffold. Perhaps that's why his head remained conscious for such a long period of time. In all honesty, the twenty-five to thirty second period is highly unusual. Most last about ten seconds, fifteen max."

Then why the hell did he bother reading the journal entry? He dropped his throbbing forehead in his palm. "Okay, let's say your theory's correct. Even if we use the ten second period, this strange phenomenon means the suspect attacked from behind, if that's where this incredibly gruesome look came from. That's what you're sayin', right?"

"I said, it's possible."

"Fine. Then why are the eyeballs bulging from the sockets?"

"It's called racooning," Chavez said as if Levaughn should have known. "The head acts as a vacuum. When the pressure is released, it causes the eyeballs to protrude."

Levaughn leaned closer to the severed head in an attempt to examine the point of decapitation, but he couldn't determine much from this angle. "Does your preliminary examination align with the neck being severed from behind?"

Chavez slipped his thin fingers into a fresh pair of gloves and then rolled the severed head onto its face. "See the smooth striation mark? That only occurs with one swift blow. No hesitation. And the blade would need to be extremely sharp."

Out of nowhere, Special Agent Odin Barrett leaned into the conversation, and Levaughn jumped. Who invited the FBI?

"The UNSUB used a sword," he said as if he doubled as Master of the Universe. "I've been investigating a series of similar homicides on Weirs beach in New Hampshire. If you roll the head back a little, you'll notice the vic was also scalped at the crown."

In an instant, Chavez turned on the stereotypical gay man routine. "Hey, blondie. Fancy meeting you here." He slipped off one glove. Pinky extended, he held a limp wrist toward Odin.

Odin's gaze shifted between Levaughn and Chavez. When neither responded—Levaughn stifling a snigger—Odin shook only the pinky finger. Which, obviously, wasn't what Chavez had in mind.

This day might finally be looking up.

The ME hovered his bony forefinger inches away from Odin's chest, tracing his body up and down. "You look as scrumptious as ever."

The special agent went into a protective stance, wrapping his arms around his midsection, recoiling as if being visually raped by a lifer in prison.

Watching the two of them never got old. "Okay, leave blondie alone now. We've had our fun." He leaned over the top of the severed head. "Was he really scalped?"

"Afraid so."

"When'd you plan to tell me, Doc?" To not give Odin the satisfaction of out-shining him at a crime scene, he dialed back the rage and flipped open his notepad. "No harm done. Got TOD for me?"

"Not yet," said Chavez. "I'll have more information once I get him back to the morgue."

Odin raised a stiff finger. "If I may interject a moment, the body's still in full rigor, so wouldn't that indicate between eight-to-ten hours post-mortem?"

"Not necessarily," said Chavez, indignant about Odin's blatant overstep. "Lots of things go into determining the time of death, including whether or not the vic had drugs in his system."

"Sorry, my mistake." Odin backed away. "The heat and humidity must be getting to me."

Chavez flung a fist to his narrow hip. "Well, why don't you try loosening the tie for a change." Again, his gaze traced him from head to toe. "Feds...no sense of style."

Folding his lips around his teeth, Levaughn swallowed a snicker. After all the crap he pulled with Shawnee, he deserved this kind of treatment, and so much more. A switch clicked in his brain, snapping him back to the task at hand, and he waved over Officer Langley, who'd been hugging the sea wall ever since Levaughn parked the car.

The young officer jogged across the sand, to the crime scene. "Yes, sir?"

"Did you interview the witnesses yet?"

"Witnesses?" His eyebrows V'd. "What witnesses?"

Why'd he always have to spell out each step? Damn rookies. "Canvass every house in a one-mile radius and tell those two wastes of skin—" he jutted a thumb toward the officers he'd told to control the scene— "to question every individual in the crowd. Someone must've seen something."

"I'm on it." Langley spun on his heels and took off, probably dying to get as far away from the remains as possible.

Meanwhile, Odin hiked his pantlegs and squatted. "A couple of these tattoos look fresh, which also aligns with the previous victims. See the two sevens?" He pointed to the lower abdomen, above the right hip joint, where a bold, black seven marred the skin. Then hovered his gloved hands over the outline of an inverted seven tattooed below, on the upper thigh, like a mirrored image.

"Maybe they're someone's initials." Levaughn shrugged. "Using the alphabet as a cipher, the two sevens could stand for G.G."

"You could be right," said Chavez. "The victim is a father, after all." Tears filled his dark eyes, his chin dipping to his chest. "See the child's handprints tattooed on his wrist?" His Adam's apple rose and fell. "Sometimes I really hate this job."

Dwelling on the victim's family was never a good idea, nor was it productive, but Dr. Juan Chavez was a kindhearted soul. A lead detective like Levaughn blocked out that aspect of a homicide. If he didn't, the death investigation might stall. But it wasn't always an easy thing to do. After all, he's still human, with family, friends, and a woman who drove him crazy.

"What about the D on the left shoulder and the C on the right?" Levaughn turned toward Odin. "Is that consistent with the New Hampshire vics?"

"Not at all. If you study the D and C tattoos, I think you'll find they've been there for a while. The double sevens, however, do align with previous homicides. We've been running down tattoo shops, looking for leads. Thus far, nothing's panned out."

Levaughn's gaze widened. "We?"

"Lieutenant Holt didn't inform you yet?" Visibly uncomfortable, he chewed his lower lip. "We've setup an interagency task force of sorts. I thought he told you."

An explosion went off inside his head. "Really," he said in a matter-of-fact tone. "At whose instruction?"

"Mine."

"Yours?" He choked on his own spit. "So, the FBI's runnin' the show now?"

With a hidden smirk lurking just below the surface, Odin claimed he was only here to consult, but he'd been down this road with him before.

"Uh-ha," Levaughn said, glib. Let's see how long that lasts. Special Agent Barrett didn't possess enough restraint to allow mere detectives the time they needed to fully investigate serial murder.

CHAPTER THREE

*"My face is a mask I order to say nothing
about the fragile feelings hiding in my soul."*
- Glenn Lazore (Mohawk)

9 p.m.

Behind Mayhem's beautiful wife, the sweet aroma of honeysuckle rising through his senses, he brushed the ends of Kimi's long, dark hair—a few silver strands nestled in between—with a handmade porcupine quill brush that had been in the family for centuries, the top beaded in bands of alternating cobalt, pink, and magenta. Nurse Poe nuzzled his head under Kimi's chin, his talons latched ever so gently on her delicate shoulder. The Black Crowes' "She Talks to Angels" played in the background. Kimi had always loved this song.

"Why don't we take the electrode cap off now, darling?" Mayhem set the antique brush on the bedside table and kneaded her shoulders, her muscles stiff, unforgiving. "It's getting late. You must be exhausted."

Across the computer screen, the BCI technology typed Kimi's thoughts. "Is she safe?"

"Whom, my love?"

"Cat."

Eyes wide, Poe glanced back at him as if to say, "Uh-oh."

"Ms. Daniels? I told you, my love, she refused my assistance. What more could I do?"

Kimi stared at the computer. "Protect her" typed across the screen.

He heaved a sigh. "How can you ask that of me when you know the predicament I am in?"

"I vowed + U owe her." Often Kimi used abbreviations because concentrating on each letter took a great deal of effort with ALS.

When Poe's head spun this time, he tossed Mayhem a spiteful glare.

"All right, all right." He raised his hands in surrender. "Why is everyone so concerned about Ms. Daniels? She's already proven that she can take care of herself."

Across the screen, his beautiful wife mentally typed, "Not this time."

Closing his eyes, he pinched the bridge of his nose. "I agree that the situation may not be easy to discern, but she's smart. Eventually, she will figure it out."

Kimi added an exclamation point to "Not this time!"

"But, honey—"

"Watch him," she wrote. "Protect Cat."

Poe hopped onto the bed, spread his magnificent wings, and bounced on his knees. Flapping in slow motion, he bellowed a deep *ca-caw, ca-caw, ca-caw,* his tone thundering through the room. Magnificent creature.

Mayhem bent down to admire the twinkle in his loving wife's eyes. Glory and pride exuded off every inch of her flawless skin. So, as usual, he relented. "You win. I doubt Chayton's involved, but I will track his movements; however, that is all I am willing to do unless Ms. Daniels specifically asks me to intervene."

"Thnx. Luv U."

He kissed her soft lips. "I love you, too, sweetheart." He turned back to Poe and stroked his chest feathers with a hooked forefinger. "Mom can do no wrong in your eyes, huh, buddy?" Lowering his voice, he leaned aside, hushed, "Don't think for a moment that I will forget who you sided with tonight."

Behind him, Kimi grunted her disapproval, and he whirled around.

"What?" His shoulders sprang to his ears. "He knows I'm joking." He hooked an arm at their beloved crow companion. "Come now, Nurse Poe. If we must start tracking Chayton's movements, we better get the patient settled before we depart. Start working your magic while I get the bed ready."

Nurse Poe flew to Kimi's shoulder, nuzzling his cheek against hers, an outpouring of love exuding from every feather. Kimi's eyelids melted closed.

"Good boy," he crooned. "The patient is nice and relaxed." He slipped off the electrode cap and disconnected the wires. With an arm under his beloved wife's back and another under her knees, he lifted her out of the desk chair and carried her to the hospital bed, where he gently laid her on the cool, cotton sheets. He fluffed the pillow around her head, stroked her cheek. "You mean everything to me, my darling. I do hope you know that."

Her eyelids closed and reopened, confirming she did.

"We'll be back as soon as we can." With the back of his fingers, he caressed her cheek. "I'll instruct Yaz to check in on you in case you need anything while we're gone."

Fala Yazza Locklear—known fondly as Yaz—worked as Kimi's home health aide. She also grew up with Cheyenne, their daughter, so Kimi enjoyed having her around. Mayhem did too because Yaz never questioned his late night rendezvouses, her impeccable couth near-impossible to find elsewhere.

After a quick whistle for Poe, who promptly flew to his shoulder, he closed the bedroom door. Smirking, he whispered out the side of his mouth, "Ready for a little fun?"

Poe cawed his acceptance.

In return, Mayhem winked. "Let's go find our boy."

CHAPTER FOUR

Wednesday
8:10 a.m.

Two hours into my shift at the Revere Police Department, and I found all kinds of information about feathers. Talk about déjà vu. I'd walked this particular road before, with Jack Delsin—aka The Creator, who left one black feather at each crime scene—and in laymen's terms, it sucked. I certainly wasn't in a rush to relive the terror of almost being skinned alive over a stupid box.

What's Mayhem trying to tell me? Was our entire conversation a ploy to get me alone and eliminate the one person who could identify him? Or had he really tried to warn me that my life was in danger?

Levaughn poked his head into the computer lab, and all my muscles jumped at once. "Find anything on the vic's phone?"

As if I'd been hard at work the whole morning, my fingers raced over the keys. Complete bullshit. Other than finding the victim's contact information, I hadn't gotten far. But Levaughn didn't need to know that. "Yup. His name is Patrick Couturier, a tattoo artist and co-owner of The Other Guys Tattoo Shop in Laconia, New Hampshire."

"Laconia?" Levaughn approached my desk with his unmistakable sexy swagger, his navy suit pants fitted around toned thighs. Mm-mmm. "Shawnee?"

"Huh?" I ran the back of my hand across my bottom lip, drying a spot of drool. "Laconia, right. Yeah, it's kinda freaky that he lives so close to your sister, right?"

"That's not it." His tongue toyed with the corner of his mouth. "I probably shoulda told you sooner, but...uh...Odin's back in town."

Adrenaline surged through my system. "He's...what? Why?"

"He's linked a series of murders on Lake Winnipesauke and Weirs Beach, both in the Laconia area, to the vic found in Revere. It looks like the homicides are connected somehow."

For some godforsaken reason, I blurted out, "Did you find a feather at the crime scene?"

"A feather?" His head jerked backward. "Y'mean, like Jack Delsin's MO? No. Why?"

"Never mind." I swatted my shaky hand. "Forget I said anythin'."

"Shawnee, you don't ask questions for no reason." He slid onto the corner of my desk. "Talk to me. Do you think these murders are connected to The Creator case in some way?"

"No." I left it at that. Without more to go on, the less said, the better. "Anyway, Patrick Couturier's phone is filled with photos of three kids, two boys and one girl. I'm guessing they're his."

"Yeah." Frowning, his eyes tilted downward. "Chavez figured as much. He had a child's handprints tattooed on his wrist."

An invisible fist gut-punched me. "Shit."

"I know. Kids make death notifications even harder." Deep

sadness tugged on the corners of his full lips. "Do me a favor and look into the tattoo shop."

"Whaddaya lookin' for exactly?"

"Not sure yet. All the vics had fresh tattoos of two sevens."

That's new. Maybe these murders aren't connected to Jack Delsin. "Ya think the killer tattooed 'em before death or after?"

"Probably antemortem. Tattoos need blood-flow to heal."

"Then he must be keeping them for a few days."

"Wow." He sucked in a quick breath, jolted to his feet. "I didn't even consider that." Pacing in circles, he rubbed the back of his neck as if it'd been a long ass night. I could relate. Finally, he stopped and whirled toward me. "What if someone beat him at his own game?" He leveled a finger at my computer, his gaze focused, determined. "Dig into Couturier's background, his social media, anything you can find out online. If we've got a copycat, we need all the ammunition we can get."

"Y'mean, the victim could be the New Hampshire killer? Wow. Okay. Consider it done." On my computer, I opened a new window. When Levaughn hovered, I hinted for him to leave. "Anythin' else?"

"Oh. No. Sorry, just mulling over the case. I'll let you get back to work." He sauntered toward the door—*I could watch that man walk all day, every day, and never get bored of the view*—then stopped and turned back. "Dinner tonight?"

"Sure," slipped out my mouth. "I mean, I'll text ya later. Nadine said somethin' about wanting to hook up after work. Sounds like her and Christopher are havin' problems again."

"Uh-oh."

"Right?" I tossed a sarcastic smirk. "She'll never learn. Once a dog always a dog."

As usual, my unbiased man refused to comment.

After he left, I brought my research back up. Before I could concentrate on work, I needed to erase the niggling sensation nipping at my side. The feather Mayhem left for me had meaning. To figure out what that might be, I flooded my screen with various blog post links. If I could determine why he left the feather, maybe I could get a bead on what he was planning.

I clicked an article entitled, "Ancient Symbol of Prophecy." The article stated that a crow was the keeper of Sacred Law, ancient magic, and divination. Nothing escaped a crow's keen eyesight, both in the physical and metaphysical worlds. A Native American totem, the crow's a messenger of foretelling, which included warnings.

Huh. Maybe Mayhem really was trying to warn me. About what, though? The only recent disruption to my life was him and his psychotic fowl.

I lowered my gaze to the article...

When a crow appears, it's beckoning for you to use your second sight, your sixth sense, the gift of clairvoyance. The crow sees our soul, and his call echoes deep within us.

Not sure if I agreed with that last part. The only thing Poe aroused in me was dread, but I continued reading anyway.

As the custodian of ancient magical laws and wisdom, when the crow calls, we experience a flash of our authentic self.

Funny, I don't remember that happening when Poe and his murderous compadres tormented me last summer. Quite the opposite, in fact. I screamed like a little girl, flapping my hands like hummingbird wings, trying to get the frickin' birds as far away from me as possible. Not that I'd want that to get around. Trust me, it wasn't a good look.

Not only does a crow have the ability to peer into the spirit world, he's a significant messenger of omens. The omens could be a spiritual blessing or warning; through his gift, the crow teaches us how to read the signs.

Gulp. This article couldn't be headed anywhere good.

The crow has powerful knowledge of the changes in the cycles of life and death. He's also the omen of death.

And there it was. My ultimate fear typed in black and white across the flat-screen. Hesitant, my nerves sizzling like carbonation on a child's tongue, I scrolled down the page.

When the crow caws, pay attention to the message.

Did I miss something? What the hell's the damn message?

I backed out of the page and clicked a new article entitled "Crow Symbolism" since Mayhem got off on that shit.

Associated with life's mysteries...blah, blah, blah. *The power of this bird as totem and spirit guide*...blah, blah, blah. *Sign of luck. Also associated with the archetype of the trickster; beware of deceiving appearances.*

Finally, something that made sense. How could I ever believe, even for a second, that Mayhem was genuine? The dude's a frickin' serial killer!

And as for his "associates"...throughout history, the crow's been associated with both positive and negative symbolic meanings, such as life magic, the mystery of creation, destiny, personal transformation, alchemy, intelligence, a higher perspective, being fearless, audacious, flexibility, adaptability, trickster, and manipulative mischief. The negative list included bad omen, death, and dark witchcraft. Poe obviously relished in his dark side, regardless of how many times Mayhem claimed otherwise.

Before abandoning this idea, I read one more passage...

The crow also carries the power of prophetic insight and symbolizes the void or core of creation.

As in, The Creator? Even though my heart sped up, pumping faster than a bullet left its chamber, I managed to shove that notion aside for a moment. None of this mattered if the feather wasn't from a crow. What other bird could it be, though? Mayhem surrounded himself with black birds. Could it be a raven feather?

For shits and giggles, I clicked images to compare the feather on my windshield against ravens and crows.

Endless photos of feathers filled the screen. Scrolling through them one by one, none had a tuft of white near its quill. Except for a magpie, but they weren't indigenous to the east coast.

Frickin' perfect. Now what?

CHAPTER FIVE

9:33 a.m.

L evaughn strolled into the morgue to gather details of the deceased's injuries, time of death, and hopefully a clue to help narrow down the suspect pool. The Medical Examiner had confirmed that the victim found on Revere Beach was, in fact, Patrick Couturier. Oddly enough, Odin had already put Couturier at the top of his suspect list, due to his profession as a tattoo artist and shop owner, but he certainly hadn't chopped off his own head.

If Patrick Couturier lived and worked in New Hampshire, how did his remains wind up in Levaughn's jurisdiction? Perhaps his copycat theory held merit. 'Course, it wouldn't be the first time sleep deprivation overshadowed logic.

As the headless body lay supine on the stainless-steel table, Dr. Chavez examined the neck wound more closely. "Decapitation is not an easy endeavor," he explained. "In order to sever a head, the killer needed to cut the thyroid gland, trachea, esophagus, cervical vertebra, spinal cord, and spinous process, never mind the inferior thyroid artery and vein, internal carotid artery and jugular vein, recurrent laryngeal nerve, as well as the vagus nerve, external jugular, stellate ganglion, accessory nerve, anterior tubercle of transverse process, and vertebral artery and vein."

Even though medical terminology was not Levaughn's forte, it was easier to nod than argue. Who cares which arteries and veins the suspect severed? A detective needed cold, hard facts. End results, without all the rigmarole. "Does any of this help to pinpoint the time of death?"

"Not really." Quick shrug. "I just found it interesting, is all."

Levaughn squeezed his forehead. After this visit, he'd need to double-up on the migraine meds. "How 'bout we just stick to the facts that can help us." That wasn't a question. "Were you able to narrow the death window?"

"I measured the core temperature via rectal thermometer at the scene and compared it to the ambient temperature to determine algor mortis. The ambient temp is usually higher on the beach, though, due to the blazing summer sun, so we need to adjust for that. I also found whiskey in the deceased's stomach contents. Alcohol raises a person's core temperature."

Did he answer the question? Let's try something easier. "Were you able to determine how long the remains were on the beach? I'm having a hard time believing that no one saw a headless corpse or the scumbag who dumped it."

"Well, judging by how quickly sand absorbs blood, as well as a cursory examination of the surrounding area, I'd say the remains were found almost immediately. But you make a good point."

Found almost immediately. Now we're getting somewhere. "Maybe there's an eyewitness who's afraid to come forward." He scribbled a note to check on Kilroy's progress with the canvass. "Sorry, didn't mean to interrupt. Go on."

"Where was I?"

"Time of death."

"Actually, I was figuring out algor mortis." Chavez peeled off his latex gloves and withdrew his cell phone from his pocket. Staring at the screen, he muttered to himself, his index finger punching key after key. "If the body cools at one-point-four degrees Fahrenheit per hour for the first twelve hours, and point-seven degrees for every hour after that, then within the first twelve hours we'd expect to see the temperature at around eighty-one-point-eight-degrees Fahrenheit. However, the core body temperature read seventy-three-point-two-three-degrees Fahrenheit on the beach."

Using the calculator app, the doctor's complete attention was on that screen. "So, if we deduct seventy-three-point-two-three from a normal temperature of ninety-eight-point-six, that equals twenty-five-point-three-seven-degrees of total heat loss. Using our equation, the victim lost sixteen-point-eight-degrees in the first twelve hours after death. We then take the difference between a normal body temperature of ninety-eight-point-six and deduct the first twelve-hour period of heat loss, which is sixteen-point-eight. That leaves us with thirteen-point-three-seven-degrees. Then we take that number and divide it by point-seven to get our subsequent hours of cooling."

He flashed the screen at Levaughn. "By my calculations, that gives us a cooling rate of about nineteen-point-one hours, give or take."

"Wow, Doc. You couldn't've just said the vic died nineteen hours prior to discovery?" Wagging his head side to side, he jotted the time in his notebook. "You examined the vic around eight p.m. Nineteen hours earlier puts TOD at about 1 a.m. yesterday. Correct?"

"Well, like I said, alcohol and the heat also played a role, as does the amount of body fat and clothing. Factoring in environmental concerns in addition to body mass, let's say the time of death occurred somewhere between eleven p.m. Monday night and four a.m. Tuesday morning."

Finally, a definitive answer. "Thank you." In addition to jotting down the time, he scrawled a note: *Find out what time Patrick Couturier's tattoo shop closed Monday night.* Raising his gaze to the Medical Examiner, his eyeballs creaked open, his sleepless night wearing him down. "Anything else I should know?"

"I sent the tox screen to the lab. I can tell you, however, the amount of alcohol in his system made abduction a lot easier."

"Abduction? But I thought you said the decapitation had to be done via blitz attack in order for the facial expression to change."

Chavez exaggerated an exhale. "And I stand by my initial theory. The surprise attack didn't occur on the beach. If it did, I'd expect to see castoff spray on the sand. You didn't find blood spatter elsewhere, did you?"

"As of yet, no." He wrote *beach is secondary crime scene.* "Now we're on the same page. Did you find any trace evidence, fibers, or residue to indicate how the suspect may've wrapped the body for transport?"

"Step into my office." Chavez swung his arm toward the microscope, where glass slides squeezed red fibers. Peering through the lenses, he said, "These look like carpet fibers from a vehicle. I found two of these beauties in the victim's hair." He turned his attention to Levaughn. "Wanna take a look?"

Head down, he scribbled the information in his notebook. "I'll take your word for it, thanks."

"Until the lab runs the fibers through the mass spectrometer, I won't be able to give you an exact make or model, but keep your eyes peeled for a vehicle with a red interior."

That's something, at least. "Great job." Levaughn patted his back in solidarity. "The trace will help weed out the crazies."

Many high-profile cases attracted attention-seekers to voluntarily confess to crimes they didn't commit. By withholding evidence that only the killer would know allowed them to test the validity of those false confessions.

"I also found two dog hairs in the neck wound," Chavez added, "which I sent out for testing. The lab should be able to determine the exact breed."

"Which is useless if the hair came from Patrick Couturier's dog," Levaughn pointed out. "Do we know if New Hampshire detectives found red fibers or dog hair at the previous crime scenes? I haven't had a chance to check the files yet."

"I guess someone needs to speak with blondie, then." He flung his hands to his narrow hips. "What is your problem with him, anyway? The tension at the crime scene was almost palpable."

"Story for another time, Doc." He stuffed his notebook into the inner pocket of his blazer. "Right now, I need to find Shawnee and convince her to do something she won't want to do."

Laughing, Chavez snorted as Levaughn strode toward the door. "And you wonder why I prefer men."

Outside in the hall, he thumbed Shawnee's cell phone number. The call went straight to voicemail. Was she still pissed off about Odin? He waited for the beep. "Hey, you. It's me. Need to ask a favor." *Damn. That's not what he meant to say.* "Umm, call me back." *Super. Now he sounded desperate.* "I mean, I was thinkin' about driving up to see my sister. Wanted to know if you wanna take the ride." He paused as if she'd magically answer the call. "Okay, well, I'll wait to hear from you."

A dial tone hummed in his ear.

Did the message go through?

CHAPTER SIX

"When you were born, you cried, and the world rejoiced.
Live your life so when you die, the world cries, and you rejoice."
- Cherokee Proverb

10:33 p.m.

Mayhem drove through the entrance of Lynn Woods, the headlights smoldering cylindrical spheres across the dirt road, tree bark illuminated in its edges. Months had passed since authorities had raided the bunker. No one would expect him to return. Ms. Daniels made sure of that. Which, actually, worked out rather well. With Kimi's very existence dependent on his return, he rarely took chances anymore.

As he exited the Caddy, giant wings swooped out of a nearby tree. Amid a hunt, a Great Horned Owl hurtled toward Poe, Edgar, and Allan's usual path.

Framing his mouth with both hands, he warned, "Watch out!"

The mighty hunter vanished into the treetops. Silent, Poe

and Edgar glided—single file—through the opened driver's door, skidding to a stop on the leather bucket seats.

Under the crescent moon's meager light, Mayhem reclined his head, his eyes searching the darkened sky. He leaned in through the door. "Where, pray tell, is Allan?"

Poe's chest feathers heaved in and out.

In a battle that dated back centuries, before even American Indian feet walked this great land, crows and owls had been at war with each other due to a genetically imprinted, intense dislike. Without ever seeing an owl, even a fledgling crow instinctually, aggressively, comprehended its ingrained hatred.

"Please tell me you did not leave your brother behind again."

Head hung in shame, Poe stared at his gold ankle band.

"You know how dangerous this area is at night. How could you be so careless?"

If this exact scenario played out during the day, Mayhem might be more apt to step aside and let his precious companions mob their enemy. But the innate darkness gave the owl an unfair advantage. Because a Great Horned Owl had crow on its menu —the species a crow's most dangerous predator, with its large eyes, wide-opening pupils, and retinas that contained many rod cells for stellar night vision—Poe and Edgar's lack in judgement could cause the death of their brother.

His stomach sank. Thanks in part to facial disc feathers that directed sound waves to its ears, their opponent also possessed remarkable hearing.

Dropping his beak to his chest, Edgar hopped closer for forgiveness.

The American Crow could out fly, out climb, and out turn most owls, but that gave him little comfort. Despite an owl's sharp, hooked talons and meat-tearing beak, its feathers boasted soft edges, which aided them in nocturnal stealth and homing in on live prey. Although, those same feathers were an impairment when it came to speed. Crows, however, encompassed strong, stiff feathers, which made them accomplished aerialists, but he wouldn't want to bet Allan's life on it.

"I see that you are both cognizant and apologetic of the wrongdoing you've committed tonight. We still need to locate Allan. If that Great Horned Owl finds him first—" Gazing at the sorrowful faces before him, he didn't have the heart to drive the point home. "Well, I am certain you understand the stakes. Come now. Let's go rescue your brother."

It wasn't easy loving wildlife. Nature could be so cruel at times.

From the trunk, he withdrew a high-powered flashlight. Spotlighting the menacing intruder's nightly activity was a sure-fire way to scare him out of the area. "Boys, call Allan. We do not want Mr. Owl to think he's easy prey."

A menagerie of caws echoed through the treetops as Poe and Edgar soared into the darkness. The Great Horned owl hooted, barked. Branches in a nearby oak shook—fierce and hard, leaves raining down to the dirt path. Edgar's intense *ca-caw* bellowed deep in his throat. Moments later, the owl catapulted out of the tree, with Poe and Edgar on his tailfeathers.

Allan lagged behind.

Mayhem cupped his mouth in his hands, ordered, "Poe— that's enough." Normally he steered clear of wildlife matters, but they had a job to do. If he was unable to soothe Kimi's fears, his homecoming would not be welcomed. That he couldn't allow. Kimi's happiness was all that mattered. The ALS had taken too much time from them already. He would not let anything, or anyone, steal another second.

His loyal crew glided toward him, with Poe in the lead, looking especially proud.

As each one landed on the roof of the Caddy, he tipped his fedora. "Poe, Edgar. Nice of you to join us, Allan." Grinning to show that he wasn't angry, he killed the flashlight for their benefit. The interior light would suffice. "Now, if you boys are done fooling around, perhaps we could complete our mission." He held out a straight arm, and Poe flew to his forearm.

With a quick peck on the forehead, he guided Poe to his shoulder, then turned back to Edgar and Allan, still perched on the roof—eager stares awaiting direction. "Come now. But stay close, please. We cannot risk anymore delays."

CHAPTER SEVEN

Chasing psychos was not my idea of fun. Rather than hacking a confiscated hard drive—standard procedure in the white-collar cases I normally worked—I did as Levaughn asked and searched Patrick Couturier's social media for clues. It's amazing how much personal information folks released to the public. Every family photo contained metadata, which revealed the exact location of where the amateur photographer took the shot. Private messages could also easily be hacked with any number of online spy apps.

Parents might be shocked to learn the statistics applicable to their children.

Fifty-five percent of minors shared information with the public. Meaning, anyone in the world could view a play-by-play of that child's life. One in four teens posted rumors, videos, or racy photos on Facebook to harm others. Three out of ten teenagers in the United States have been stalked online by strangers, including pedophiles. Sixteen percent of all online stalking occurred on Facebook. That number might not seem like a lot but considering all the social media sites out there today, it's a huge percentage.

The National Center for Victims of Crime reported over one-million women and almost four-hundred-thousand men were stalked online each year in the US. In my work at RPD, it wasn't unusual for me to read private messages. From drug deals to sexting, users believed they had privacy. Not true. Facebook stored records, lots of records, records they had no business keeping. Came in handy for me, though.

As for Couturier, all I uncovered was his undying love for his wife and kids. He had the Messenger app installed on his cell phone, so I didn't even need to crack the ol' knuckles to hack his private communications. Other than chatting with friends, the only unusual message was from Amanda Orme, mid-thirties, Facebook profile stated "Single. Not in a relationship." No red flags to indicate she used a fake account. In the chat box, Pat and Amanda discussed a meeting on Weirs beach.

Was she dead, too?

Or maybe Levaughn's right. If Couturier's the scumbag responsible for the New Hampshire homicides, then could Amanda Orme be the copycat? If so, how did she transport Couturier's body across state lines? A drive from Laconia, New Hampshire to Revere, Massachusetts took over two hours with minimal traffic. Transporting a body via an automobile was a risky move. Or maybe they weren't involved, and two unknown homicidal maniacs worked as partners, one killer working on the North Shore of Massachusetts while the other roamed the rural streets of New Hampshire. Two killers working in tandem made sense, but before I shared my theory with Levaughn, I needed proof.

Or, could Amanda Orme be Patrick Couturier's partner?

Maybe he'd double-crossed her in some way, and she sought revenge. Nonetheless, if they were, in fact, dual serial killers, they must've had a way to communicate, especially with such an odd yet precise MO.

My fingers raced over the keys one last time before I had to meet Nadine.

If Amanda's Facebook posts were any indication, she had a dark sense of humor. Most of her posts leaned toward the morbid side. Whereas Pat, as friends called him, showcased family photos and videos of tattoos. A talented artist, too.

I logged off and locked the door to the computer lab behind me. If I didn't, Chuck would go through my shit two seconds after I left the building. Brown-nosed bastard.

Fifteen minutes later, I drove through the parking lot of Kowloon Restaurant, my favorite Chinese place. As I climbed the stairs to the entrance, I glanced over each shoulder, scanning the lot, but I couldn't locate Nadine's car anywhere.

With the restaurant's roofline scalloped in gold, an enormous triangle shaped the front entrance, and a massive clay-colored Tiki totem stood above four glass doors. I swung open the right and gave my name to the hostess.

"I'll be outside," I said. "You can still page me out there, right?"

A blank expression stared back at me. Did she speak English?

Not two seconds after I sat on the green-carpeted front steps someone grabbed my shoulder from behind, and I jolted to my feet, a closed fist aimed straight at Nadine's face. "Are you outta your frickin' mind? Never—ever—sneak up on me. You should know that by now."

She quailed back. "I'm just playin' around. Geesh. You don't need to bite my head off."

"Sorry." My stiff posture eased. "Guess I'm a little jumpy.

There's this case I'm workin' on..." Perhaps I shouldn't finish that sentence. After what Nadine endured with The Creator, she's paranoid enough.

Over the loudspeaker, a woman spoke in broken English. "Daniels, party of two. Your table is ready."

Dodged that bullet. Perfect timing.

Blended aromas of fried rice, teriyaki, and soy fragranced the air as the hostess escorted us to our table. Kowloon Restaurant had the widest variety of Chinese food anywhere in the area. They even served Maine lobster. The ornate building itself featured waterfalls, games, and a live stage for stand-up comedians, singers, and bands. Much like Las Vegas, the place rocked night and day.

The hostess sat us in the ship, an actual ship inside the restaurant. Cool spot but overcrowded. Definitely not the place to discuss anything personal, never mind murder. With any luck, Nadine would forget about my earlier slip.

"So—" Nadine sipped her water, ice crackling in the glass— "you gonna tell me why we're here?"

"Whattaya mean? Lunch was your idea."

She reached across the table, and I slapped her hand away. "You sent me a text. Don't you remember?"

"What the hell are you smokin'? You're the one who texted me."

"Shawn," she said, and my upper lip twitched in defiance, "we both know you're too cheap to spring for lunch unless you want something." She shook out the red-linen napkin, the material floating across her lap. "So, you might as well tell me what that is."

Nothing in her tone or expression indicated deception. Nadine believed every word. Who would want us together in this specific restaurant, at this exact time? Oh, my effin' head— Mayhem! I closed the menu, slid the ice water toward me, the cubes popping, cracking. While I scoured every inch of the restaurant, my gaze tunneling on face after face, my lips rested on the rim of the tumbler. Water was nowhere near strong enough, so I motioned for the waitress, pocketing her tip two tables over.

When her gaze connected with mine, she hustled over. "Are you ready to order?"

At least, I think that's what she said. Who the hell knows with her non-native tongue. She might've told me to go fuck myself, and I returned a smile. "I'll have the buffet, please."

"Make that two."

"Also, a shot of Schnapps. Peppermint, if you've got it. Actually, make it a double."

"Hard liquor at lunchtime?" Tossing me a cutting glare, Nadine's lips smoothed to a straight line. "Don't listen to her. We'll have two ginger fizz beers, please."

I snarled. "Who died and made you boss?"

A fake smile plastered the waitress' face, her head nodding in a continuous motion, her vacant gaze bouncing between us. Clueless. To her, our conversation probably sounded like complete gibberish. Anyone who dared to venture beyond the menu took their chances at Chinese restaurants. Learned that little tidbit the hard way. To this day, even the mention of raw octopus activated an army of stomach acids and saliva glands.

"Fine, Nay," I conceded. "You win. I'll drink your weak-ass beer."

The waitress tucked the leather-bound check pad in her apron pocket and strolled away.

While I waited for the first in a long line of alcoholic beverages, my knee jackhammered on its own. Why would Mayhem arrange this meeting? And what the hell did he want with my best friend?

"What's that noise?" Nadine ducked her head under the

tablecloth. Grimacing, she straightened, her lips pursing at me. "You better spill. I mean it. I'm not kiddin'."

As I skimmed the surrounding tables, I chewed the inside of my cheek. Forks clanged against china plates, other patrons fumbled with chopsticks, and couples slurped the last remaining drops of a shared Scorpion Bowl. No one was looking in our direction, except a pre-teen boy, knuckle-deep in his own nostril.

Nasty. My stomach rolled forward, then back.

"Well?" prompted Nadine. "Got somethin' to tell me?"

I stayed silent.

"I am so sick of this ship." She balled her napkin in both hands and tossed it on the table. "You never tell me anything."

"The word's shit. You're so sick of this shit, not ship. If you're gonna swear, do it right for chrissakes." The tendons in my neck tightened, heat pouring into my face. "And while we're on the subject, where do you get off tellin' Levaughn I got home late the other night?"

"If you've got nothin' to hide, why's it matter?" Her accusatory tone ignited a fire within me. "Unless you're out catting again."

"How many times do I have to tell you, I'm done with that life? Man, you must have a wicked view from that ivory tower."

Tears welling in her eyes, she looked away.

The waitress returned and set the two fizzy beers, or whatever the hell they're called, in front of us. "You can go to the buffet whenever you're ready."

Nadine continued to stare at the wall. Something was bothering her. She wouldn't be this upset over my remark; we'd been friends almost our entire lives.

"Great. Thanks." After the waitress left, I took a belt off the beer. Bogus shit, if you ask me, but I kept that to myself. "You were right, Nay. This fuzzy beer is the nuts."

She giggled. "It's fizzy, not fuzzy."

"Oh. Right." I winked. "Hey, about what I said earlier…"

"It's not that."

"Then what's wrong?"

Twirling one strand of hair around her finger, her aqua eyes tilted downward, the tears pooling even more.

"Whatever's botherin' you, you can tell me." I kept my tone soft, non-judgmental. "You know that, right? Maybe I can help."

"Christopher's having an affair," she cried out, bawling into her napkin. "What am I gonna do?" She cried harder and harder, her heaving chest ruffling her blouse, buttoned to the chin.

Did Mayhem know Christopher was cheating on her? After all, he'd arranged this lunch. But why would he even care?

"Did you hear me?"

I stalled. "What makes you think that?" Not that I doubted it for a second.

"Huh?"

"Did you ask him if he's havin' an affair?" I mumbled under my breath, "Again." How could she think an ol' dog could be housebroken? And I don't mean a dog of the furry variety.

"Didn't have to. When I was loading his jeans into the washer, a phone number fell out of his pocket."

"And…?"

"And I called it." Blue eyeliner streaked lines down the sides of her face. "Some girl answered. Her voice sounded familiar, too. Unless I imagined it. Not sure about anythin' anymore."

"Did you confront her?" Stupid question. She wouldn't have the balls for fear of learning the truth. To Nadine, denial was a happy place.

"No. I hung up."

"Wait, what?" Reclining my head, I guzzled half the beer. "That's it? End of story. You didn't say anythin'?"

"No."

I flung out my hands. "Why the hell not?"

"'Cuz."

"That's your big reveal, 'cuz?"

"When the girl answered she said, 'I was just thinkin' about you, handsome.' So, obviously, she recognized our phone number."

Oh, man. Not good. As much as I longed to say, 'What'd you expect? The dude screwed your aunt!' I couldn't. Besides, she was beginning to cause a scene with her non-stop blubbering. Instead, I went with, "Maybe Christopher wrote the number down wrong."

"What if he loves her, Shawnee? What am I gonna do?"

As far as problems went, hers was a lot easier to solve than mine. Just sayin'.

"Gimme the damn number." I stuck out a flat hand. "I'll deal with it."

"But…what are you gonna do?"

"I'm gonna have a little chat with this pig. In the meantime, don't sleep with Christopher. God only knows what he picked up. In fact, why don't you come stay with me for a while? Gaining some distance might be just the thing you need."

Nodding, she blew her nose into the napkin—*bet the waitress will appreciate that*—and then rummaged around in her bag for the phone number, finally finding it in the change purse. "You sure?"

"Positive. I don't want you to worry about this anymore, 'kay?"

Her bottom lip pouted, and I raised my so-called beer in the hopes of cheering her up. "To one last dog in the world."

She didn't find the toast as comical as I did, evident by the way her chin dimpled. Oh, well. So much for that idea.

Twenty minutes later, I dragged the napkin across my lips, broken chips of Crab Rangoon, a puddle of duck sauce, and chicken teriyaki sticks scattered across my plate.

After paying the tab—yeah, I got stuck with the bill—I waved goodbye to Nadine and strutted out to my jeep. A half-black/half-white feather blew in the breeze, the windshield wiper anchoring it to my windshield. My gaze shot to the sky, blood sluicing through my veins. Three crows flapped away from the parking lot, a reverberating *caw, caw, caw* echoing through the blazing horns of route one.

What did Mayhem want from me?

CHAPTER EIGHT

2:30 p.m.

With no return call from Shawnee, Levaughn poked his head into the computer lab. She wasn't at her desk. Where was she? And why wasn't she calling him back?

On his way back to the bullpen, Odin cut him off in the hall. "There's been another murder on Weirs Beach. Decapitated female, approximately thirty years old, same double-seven tattoos. I'm heading to the crime scene now. Want to tag along?"

"Tag along?" Baring his teeth, he sneered. "You say that like you're doing me a favor."

"That's not what I meant, and you know it. Honestly, Levaughn, you really need to let things go. How I feel about your girlfriend has no bearing on this case."

"Unless, y'know, you add her to another suspect list." Done with his bullshit, he headed toward the bullpen. Over his head, he tossed, "I'm not the one with the problem, Agent Barrett."

"That's Special Agent!"

Swinging open the door, he smirked a satisfied grin.

"Wait—" Odin clomped toward him. "I need the file on the Couturier homicide. Since I'm headed to New Hampshire anyway, I'll swing by the tattoo shop and interview his business partner."

A sharp pang shot to his temples, and he whipped his head around, his back molars clenching against suppressed rage. "No, you won't. Patrick Couturier's remains were found in my jurisdiction. You're here to consult, not to trample all over my investigation."

"I...I..."

"I already planned to visit the shop. In fact, I'm waiting for a call back as we speak."

Odin seemed to startle. "From who?"

"You let me worry about that. In the meantime, I still need your psychological profile of the killer. Rather than play detective, do your job." He stepped through the doorway, letting the door swing closed behind him, but Odin still didn't take the hint.

"Wait."

Stopping mid-stride, he rotated toward him. "What now?"

"Can't we put our differences aside? It wasn't that long ago that we were friends."

"A lot's happened since then." A musical trill emanated from his suit pocket. The caller ID read Shawnee Daniels. "I've gotta take this." He hustled back out to the hall and over to the window at the end. Once out of earshot, he thumbed the green "accept" button. "Hey, good lookin'. I was just thinkin' about you."

"You were?" She seemed surprised. "Why?"

Sometimes chivalry was lost on his girl. "Did you get my message? I wasn't sure if it went through."

"I got it."

"And...whattaya think? You up for taking a ride?"

"Yeah, I dunno. Lieutenant Holt dumped a ton of work on my desk."

"I could talk to him, tell him I need your help."

"Do you? 'Cause the message said you were driving up to see Austyn. Which is odd, considering the Weirs Beach crime scenes are around the corner from her house."

Aw, shit. This conversation wasn't going as planned. Maybe she'd be more amenable in person. "Are you in the computer lab?"

"No." She didn't offer any more details. Classic Shawnee. That woman took mysterious to a whole new level.

His instincts told him not to push, but the words fell out of his mouth much faster than he could stop them. "Where are you?" He cringed. She did not like anyone prying into her business, including him. One would think after dating for a couple years, he'd earned the right to ask for her whereabouts, but Shawnee's strong mind and street smarts ruled her heart. To her, the mere question likened to an interrogation.

To avoid her calling foul, he backpedaled. "What I mean is, can you meet me somewhere?"

"Can't right now. I'll buzz ya back in a few."

Before she hung up, he came clean. "Okay. You're right. I'm heading to New Hampshire to check out the crime scenes and interview a potential witness, but afterward, I thought we'd swing by Austyn's. Make a day of it. Don'tcha wanna see Maggie?" When she didn't respond right away, he resorted to good ol' fashion begging. "Please, babe, I need your help. Won't you at least think about it?"

Long pause.

With a breathy voice, she said, "When are you leavin'?"

"Tonight or tomorrow morning." He tried to remain upbeat. "Whatever works best for you."

"Fine. I'll think about it."

"Great. Thanks." Another moment of silence hung between them. "We're good, right?"

"Yep." Again, she didn't offer more. Only this time, he was smart enough not to push the issue. "I gotta go."

"Okay, babe. I'll buzz you—"

A dial tone flatlined.

Did she hang up on me?

CHAPTER NINE

12:30 p.m.

After Levaughn called, I dialed the number Nadine gave me. By posing as a UPS driver who couldn't find the house, Christopher's bimbo gave me directions to her door. Stupid bitch.

Within minutes I was standing on the front stoop of her split-level home—paid for by a sugar daddy, no doubt—with a cardboard box that'd rolled around the back of my jeep for the last two weeks. Long story. Let's just say I wouldn't run out of mace canisters anytime soon.

I thumbed the doorbell.

A bleach-blonde about twenty-two answered the door, wearing nothing but a peek-a-boo teddy and high-heeled slippers, tufts of ivory feathers on her toes. "For me?" Her voice pitched so high my skull fissured in ten places.

Rather than answer, I pushed past her, purposefully slamming my shoulder into hers. "Where's Christopher?" I scouted in and out of every room on the main level before heading downstairs.

"Hey!" The bitch actually had the balls to grab my arm. "He's not here. Who the hell are you?" She kicked off her come-fuck-me slippers and veered around me. With stiff hands on either wall, she blocked the stairs to the lower level.

Big mistake. In one swift motion, I ran my fingers up the back of her neck, grabbed a handful of hair, and twisted the brittle strands around my wrist. With one firm tug, I jerked her head backward and then down by my side, dragging her down the stairs with me, her nails clawing at my wrists. I ignored her pitiful attempt to break free. Some chicks should really hit the gym once in a while. I could wipe the floor with this home-wrecker.

"Christopher, get the hell out here, or I'll kick the livin' shit outta your whore!"

The coward crawled out from behind the sectional sofa. "Let her go, Shawnee. I'm warning you…"

I threw my head back and jeered. "Or you'll what, tough guy?"

"Let her go." His pleading tone made him look even more desperate. "This is between me and Nadine. It's not even your business."

From below, the chick muttered, "Shawnee Daniels?"

I ignored the bimbo, her head somewhere around my thigh, still clawing at my arm with her fake press-on nails. "Seriously, Christopher? Who do ya think sent me?" I yanked the bitch's face up to mine, our noses almost touching. "Did you know he's engaged or didn't it matter to you?"

"Ow." She swung a sloppy right hook but missed.

That's when I slammed her face-first into the sheetrock. "Answer the question! Did you know?"

Blood swirled across her hot-pink lipstick. "Does it matter? Obviously, she can't satisfy him like I can."

Blinded by rage, I threw an uppercut to her gut and tossed

her on the floor, ramming her face into the hardwood by the back of her head, her hair tangling around my fingers.

Trying to be the hero, Christopher yelled, "Stop—you're gonna kill her!"

Nadine was so hurt—heartbroken, really—and it was all because of this bitch who didn't give two shits about whose home she gutted. I glowered at Christopher. "If I were you, pal, I'd run. I'm comin' for you next."

"Stop—you don't understand! That's Chelsea, Nadine's sister!" He clawed both hands through his sandy-brown hair. "There, I said it."

I released the bloody bimbo and rose. "What the hell is it with you and the Couture family? You're sick, you know that? First her Aunt Patti, now her sister."

"You slept with my Aunt Patti?" Chelsea slapped him across the face. The imprint of her hand left a red blotch on his cheek. "You pig!" The spaghetti straps on her peek-a-boo teddy dangled off both shoulders, blood saturating the lace bodice, dripping down her bare legs.

Ain't that ironic? The sexy outfit she wore to entice her sister's fiancé now displayed her betrayal like a scarlet letter.

Waving praying hands, she pleaded with me. "Please don't tell Nadine I'm in town."

"Ya mean, she doesn't know?" When Nadine first heard her sister ran away from home, she was out of her mind with worry. For five years, she had no idea where she'd gone. And now, Chelsea expected me to keep her secret? She had some balls, I'll give her that.

"I came back a few months ago."

"And this is what, your way of surprising her?"

"You're right." Shoulders slumped, she hung her bleeding face. "She doesn't deserve this. I don't know what I was think-ing. I hated my parents for moving me to Florida." With rage in her eyes, she spun back to Christopher and slapped him again. "Aunt Patti's my favorite aunt, you prick!"

"Look. You were five when you moved down there. It's not like they pulled you outta high school for chrissakes." Swallowing hard, I tried to slow the surge of adrenaline pumping through my system. "Do your parents know you're safe?"

"Yeah. They're paying my rent."

"And no one bothered to tell Nadine?" Nostrils flared, spittle flew from my mouth. "What is wrong with you people?"

"I made them promise." Her whole body begged me to understand. "I told them I'd run away again if they told."

Wow. What could I say to that? I hadn't seen Chelsea since she was in kindergarten. Quickly doing the math in my head, my heart sunk. "How old are you?"

"Eighteen."

"Eighteen!" Energy surged within me. "You're practically jailbait!"

Palms out, Christopher took a step toward me, then hesitated as if approaching a wild animal in the forest. "Shawnee, please, just listen. Chelsea called the house when she got into town. We met for a drink to discuss the best way to tell Nadine. One thing led to another and—"

I jabbed my finger in his face. "Do not finish that sentence."

Christopher's gaze flitted around the room, searching for a safe place to land. "What're you gonna do?"

"I have no idea. You both really screwed the pooch this time, I'll tell ya." I rubbed my forehead between my fingertips, trying to ward off a headache that was lingering all day. Sitting on the stairs, my boots planted on the tread below, I rested my elbows on bent knees.

I stared at Chelsea, my mind whirling with unanswerable questions. *How do I even begin to explain this type of betrayal? This affair will crush Nadine. Would it be worse to let her find out on her own?*

If Levaughn pulled this crap, I'd wanna know. What's the best way to break the news?

"All right, look. Christopher, Nay's stayin' with me till we figure this shit out. Chelsea, call your sister. She misses you."

"But...what do I say?"

"Figure it out. If you're grown up enough to screw her fiancé, I shouldn't have to spell it out for you." When I threw up my hands, I caught a glimpse of my bloody palms. "Crap. Where can I wash up?"

Chelsea jutted a thumb over her shoulder. "Down the end of the hall. Second door on the left."

Neither spoke a word while I washed my hands. Good thing, too, because I'd had just about enough of their bullshit for one day.

On my way up the stairs, I left Chelsea with one final word of wisdom. "Women who bring home dogs end up with fleas. Remember that."

CHAPTER TEN

"If you talk to the animals, they will talk to you,
and you will know each other.
If you do not talk to them, you will not know them,
and what you don't know you will fear.
What one fears, one destroys."
- Chief Dan George

9:15 p.m.

The last trip to Lynn Woods proved unsuccessful. Perhaps the commotion with the Great Horned Owl spooked Chayton. Tonight, Mayhem and Poe traveled alone, the darkened path lit only by moonlight, the glow bountiful with a hint of mystery. An ideal backdrop for the upcoming *repertoire*.

Mayhem stopped outside the hatch to the underground bunker. The sod fastened to the top kept it well-hidden. He motioned to Poe, who leaped off his shoulder and circled above his head as he raised the lid, holding it open while Poe nose-dived through the hole in the earth, his magnificent black wings gliding past the inside ladder.

Such an amazing bird. He possessed more skills than any other member of his murder, though he would never insult the others by telling them so.

Mayhem climbed down the rungs, and Poe resettled on his perch—aka Mayhem's shoulder. In the distance, a woman begged for her life. Shame she must die, but the world needed to feel every tear, every atrocity, every obliterated dream.

As he crept through the tunnel, he hushed to Poe, "For now, let's see how this plays out. We'll announce our presence when the time is right."

Even though Mayhem had retired from this line of work—for now—he had no intention of stopping Chayton's reign of terror. Everything about his message rang true, vivid, and clear. Years ago, Mayhem headed down the same road, with an identical message, but nowhere near as creative.

Under his breath, he sniggered.

At the end of the tunnel, he hung a right toward the arena. Spidery vines veiled the dirt walls, lantern sconces smoldering a luminescent glow across the rich earth. For twenty years, a rich landscape surrounded this structure, designed and handcrafted by Mayhem and a hired crew of six. None of whom survived to tell the tale. As Benjamin Franklin euphemized, "Three can keep a secret if two are dead."

A collage of angels, cherubs, and clouds against a pale-blue sky artistically decorated the high, curved ceiling of the dome-shaped arena. Gold columns reinforced a raised circle in the center of the concrete floor. Three steps led to an altar, where Chayton's latest victim lay, bound by brass-buckled leather straps.

"Please stop," the woman cried out. "Why tattoo me? I don't get it. Help me understand." The buzzing of the tattoo gun almost made Mayhem miss her change in demeanor—calm now, her tears dried in an instant. "If you let me go, I promise I won't tell anyone. You can trust me."

The ploy didn't fool Mayhem. Over the years, many folks had tried the same tactic. It did not work then, either. But perhaps, Chayton would surprise him.

The young executioner showed no reaction.

Atta boy. The work remained his top priority. No human life was worth sacrificing this message.

She thrust against the restraints. "Let me go, you freak!"

Name-calling would not improve her chances of survival. Why was that truth so difficult to understand? Mayhem waited for the young executioner to unleash his wrath.

With one smooth motion, Chayton swung his mighty sword, the woman's severed head dropping into a weaved basket on the floor. He grabbed a fistful of ash-blonde hair and raised the skull high above his head—arm locked at the elbow—the wilting face tilted toward the ornate ceiling. Replacing the sword with a razor-sharp hunting knife allowed him to scalp the crown. The severed head thudded against the concrete. When he offered the scalp to the heavens, blood gushed down his bicep, droplets trickling across his hairless chest, crimson puddling by his bare feet.

Mayhem clapped—slow, loud, each beat accentuated—as he stepped out from the shadows, revealing himself to Chayton. He held the young man's gaze as he strode toward him, Poe still surfing his shoulder, his feathers tickling Mayhem's neck. "Hold on to what is good...even if it's a handful of earth." They exchanged a meaningful nod, all the while Mayhem moving closer, his gaze locked on his protégé. "Hold on to what you believe...even if it's a tree that stands by itself." He pressed his fedora to his chest. "Hold on to what you must do...even if it's a long way from here." Setting the hat back on his head, he then rested a gloved hand on Chayton's muscular shoulder. "Hold on to your life..."

The bloody scalp lowered with his hand. "Even if it's easier to let go."

"Hold on to my hand…"

"Even if someday I'll be gone away from you."

Mayhem grinned. "Truth."

Chin held high, Chayton's dark eyes never wavered. "Understood."

Poe leaped off Mayhem's shoulder and flapped toward the elegant dome ceiling. In wide circles around the arena, he rode the thermals.

Mayhem beamed. "Is he not the most magnificent being you've ever seen?" When Chayton didn't respond, he shot him a cutting glare.

The young executioner returned a quick nod.

"I suppose his timing could use some work." Long and low, Mayhem whistled, but only because they were inside. One does not whistle at night without serious consequences. "Come now, buddy. We've pestered Chayton enough for one evening."

Poe landed on his shoulder, and Mayhem tipped his fedora. "Stay safe. Stay focused. Your message is an important one for us all." He straightened the Montblanc logo, center-piecing his warm red-gold cufflinks with a delightful ebony circular band. Kimi surprised him with the pair on their twentieth wedding anniversary, quite a few years before ALS stole her mobility. Seemed like a lifetime ago.

He cleared the tears building in his throat. "Now, if you'll excuse us, we need to check in on a feisty little feline." With Poe's talons latched to the shoulder of his overcoat, he strode toward the opening of the tunnel. Before entering, he stopped and turned back to Chayton. "Where might one find the gray wolf these days?"

The name struck a chord with his protégé, and his eyes popped wide. "You don't. The gray wolf finds you."

"I see. Well, enjoy the rest of your evening. Oh, and please clean up before you leave. Blood will blemish the concrete if left unattended."

CHAPTER ELEVEN

9:30 p.m.

After leaving the House of Secrets and Lies, I drove around a while to clear my head. For one thing, I still could barely wrap my mind around what just happened. For two, no matter how hard I tried to reason away my conversation with Mayhem, something in his eyes still haunted me. Sincerity? Could a mass murderer really change his ways? From the various cases I'd worked and cold cases I'd studied, I found it a little hard to believe.

Most true serial killers fell into one of two categories—psychopath or sociopath—with a few rare exceptions. The difference being nature versus nurture. Some say a small amygdala allowed violent offenders the ability to murder without remorse. Others claim a low heartrate, damaged frontal lobe, or a deficiency in the prefrontal cortex held the key.

Some put the blame on a growing child's environment. Meaning, emotional, physical, or sexual abuse often played a role, and sometimes it's the combination of all three. And then other neuroscientists believed the deadly cocktail of various biological components blended with environmental conditions, resulting in a psychopathic monster who slaughtered humans and animals without remorse.

Most true psychopaths didn't possess the ability to show empathy, concern, love, or even hatred, even though some were inherently angry. Instead, they mimicked emotions in order to blend into the fabric of society.

Sociopathy, on the other hand, was more a learned behavior that evolved over time, which caused the killer's unstable mind to fracture. Hence why they usually chose victims that matched their abuser's physical description. Whereas with psychopaths, any potential victim could satisfy their murderous thirst. Male, female, child, adult, fat, thin, old, or young didn't make a damn bit of difference. If someone's in the right place at the wrong time, their life could end in an instant.

Let that sink in.

Problem was, Mr. Mayhem didn't fit into either category. Yet, during his reign of terror he'd killed dozens, maybe even hundreds, of innocent people. How could he just stop? Or had he simply changed his ritual of leaving one Dunhill International cigarette butt stamped out at the crime scene as a signature?

I pulled into my driveway and killed the engine. The moment I swung open the driver's door, a little girl's scream thrust me on to the asphalt of the driveway.

I jogged around the side of my A-frame to the backyard, and called into the darkness, "Mags, is that you?"

A muffled, unintelligible whisper echoed in return.

"Maggie?" I crept closer to the wood line, shrouded in blackness, my breath shallowing with each step. "Whattaya doin' in there, honey? Look, if you wanna stay the night, it's cool with me. But we need to call Austyn, so she doesn't freak out." As much as I loved the movie, *The Hand That Rocks the Cradle*, the last thing I needed tonight was Levaughn's sister goin' all Rebecca De Mornay on my ass. Besides, this one time Nadine might be right. My crib wasn't exactly the safest place in the world. Especially now, with Mayhem lurking around.

Glowing red eyes peeked out from behind a tree trunk, and I jumped back, ghostly fingers strangling my airway. What the hell was that?

"Help me, Shawnee!" Another scream. This time frantic, as though a wolf or coyote had her cornered.

Shuffling backward a few paces, I spoke low, placating, zings pinging in my gut. "Nice doggie."

Oh my God. What if there's a whole pack? The direction of Maggie's voice indicated she'd climbed a tree to escape. But where? I sprinted to my jeep and swiped the spare can of mace from under the driver's seat.

One can never be too cautious when it comes to personal safety.

Lightning fast, I sprinted back into the yard, my boots clomping across the grass. "Maggie, honey, where are you?"

No response.

That didn't mean much. At the tender age of nine, I probably wouldn't answer, either, till I knew for sure it was safe. "Stay where you are, honey. I'm comin' to get you." With deep, controlled breaths, I aimed the mace toward the wood line, my elbow locked at the joint, and slid my finger to the trigger. "Back off," I hollered, my voice firm and harsh. "Git! I mean it. Git!"

Flaming red eyes faded into a deluge of blackness, the area exuding a profound stillness. Even the tree limbs didn't dare shake. The slivered moon cowered behind the canopy of maple and oak leaves, its lackluster smolder providing little-to-no light. A raw stench of decay crawled into my sinuses, saturating my very being with a maniacal evil.

Something still wasn't right. Why wouldn't Maggie show herself?

With the mace still leveled in front of me, I trampled over sticks and rocks, my gaze combing the darkened woods. "Talk to me, Mags. I can't find you in the dark." I fumbled to swipe the cell phone from my back pocket. Crap. The battery was on E. I thumbed the flashlight app, but it refused to open.

Traveling farther away, Maggie's wispy voice rode the sultry night air. "Love you, Shawnee, forever and a day."

"Wait—come back!"

Behind me, the deck doors slid across the tracks, and I took off, bursting through the tree line in seconds flat. In the yellow cast of the porch light stood Nadine, her raven hair tied in a high ponytail, my terrycloth robe belted around her thin waist. Not for nothin' but a bathrobe was not on my items to share list. After all these years, she should know that.

She firmed a hand on her hip. "Are you talkin' to yourself again?"

"Again? Who the hell do you think you're talkin' to?" For now, I bit back the anger. One more crack, though, and the gloves were comin' off. I let my gaze wander toward the darkened tree line, the heart sinking in my chest. "Maggie's out there somewhere."

"Impossible." Nadine's waxed eyebrows V'd, and she stared at me like I had lobsters crawling out both ears. "Are you drunk?"

"What kinda question is that? I just got home from work." Okay, so I lied. Shoot me. In my defense, I needed time to construct the best way to tell her about her kid sister and her fiancé.

"At this hour?"

I slapped my forehead. "Oh, my effin' head." Who's the brainiac that suggested she move in with me? The flurry of questions never ended. "Not that it's any of your business, but I took a drive after work to clear my head. That all right with you?"

"Judging by the way you're talkin' to yourself, I don't think it worked." Her aqua eyes squinted at the mace. "What's that in your hand?"

"Nothin'." I tucked the canister behind my back. "Did you need somethin'? Or did you just feel like jumpin' all over my shit for no reason?"

When she rolled her eyes, it proved once again that we lived in two different worlds. "For your information," she said, and I braced for a lecture, "I'm the one doin' you the favor. I didn't need to come out here in my robe to tell you someone's on the phone. But that's what friends do. They go out of their way to help each other. Not that you'd know anythin' about that."

After the night I'd had, she had some nerve. Granted, she might not've known what I had to deal with in the House of Secrets and Lies, but still. "First of all, Miss High and Mighty, that's my robe you're wearing. And second, you're living in my house." I threw my hands over my head, mace and all. "For chrissakes, Nay, I'm not even in the door yet."

"Fine!" She whirled toward the sliders, her long hair pinwheeling behind her.

"Hey—" I jabbed a chin in the direction of the door. "Who's on the phone?"

"Can't tell you."

With a hand on the railing, I firmed my stance. "Can't or won't?"

"Neither." Quick shrug. "I promised."

The heels of my motorcycle boots sank into the moist soil at the bottom of the deck stairs, its crystals slurping the humidity out of the muggy night air. "Nay, I'm frickin' fried. It's been a long ass day. Can't you just take a message?"

"I will do no such thing. That little girl's over-the-moon excited to talk with you." With an open hand, she slapped her gaping mouth. A moment later, her eyes darkened to navy. "Now look what you made me do."

"Wait, wait, wait. Back up. Are you talkin' about Maggie?"

She shook a stiff finger at me. "You better act surprised when you answer."

"You sure it's Mags?"

"Do any other nine year olds call the landline?"

Good point. But how could Maggie be on the phone when two seconds ago she'd screamed for me from the woods? Even if she called the house from her cell, I would've at least heard her voice. Wouldn't I?

I darted up the deck stairs, then stopped on the landing. Another feather. This time, Mayhem wedged the quill under the base of the porch light. Unless Mayhem wasn't the one sending them. Who else could it be, though?

To test my theory, I jabbed a chin at the feather. "What's that about?"

Nadine's expression crinkled like a Shar Pei puppy, only nowhere near as cute. "Why're you askin' me?"

"So, you didn't stick it there," I said, more of a statement than a question.

"What? Why would I do that?"

During my conversation with Mayhem, he'd made it a point to mention Jack Delsin aka The Creator. Admired his handiwork, my ass. Mayhem probably helped him kill those people. But then, why even bring him up? I would've never made the connection otherwise. And why leave me feathers? None of this made sense.

Eyes in a squint, I didn't dare remove the quill from the porch light. "Any guesses as to what type of bird this is from?"

"I dunno." Nadine scratched her eyebrow. "A crow, maybe?"

Icy tingles excoriated my spine as though Poe was dragging his razor-sharp talons down my back. Damn scroll. Whatever possessed me to open it?

"Since when do you care about birds?"

I clamped a hand on my hip. "You mean to tell me, you don't find a feather stuck to the porch light the least bit strange?"

"Not really. The wind probably blew it." As if no danger existed in the world, she dragged the louver blinds aside, holding them open for me. "C'mon, Maggie's waiting."

I hustled up the stairs, slipped through the sliders, and snatched the cordless phone off the breakfast bar. "Hello?" Backtracking, I peered through the glass door. The feather taunted me, just sitting there like that. What did Mayhem want from me?

On the other end of the line, a little girl giggled. "Hi, Shawnee. It's me."

"Mags?" *What the—?* "Didn't you hear me callin' you?" Ever since I picked up that damn scroll, it's like I'd stepped into an alternate universe, a bizarre one at that. Why would I read a message from Mayhem, never mind meet him? The second Poe glided into the parking lot, I should've bolted inside the station house.

Could crows have fluffy white feathers at the base of their quills?

"You called me?" Confusion laced Maggie's tone.

"'Course I did. I looked for you, too, but couldn't find you. Didn't you hear me?" That must've been Maggie in the back-yard. I didn't know any other children. More importantly, none knew me. Or could this moment—right here, right now—be the precise second my mind finally fractured from reality?

Trying to make sense of all this, I said, "Where are you right now?"

"Home."

"Like, home in New Hampshire?" After Austyn adopted Maggie, she bought a cute bungalow in Gilford, near Weirs Beach. The move increased the miles between us—the quick thirty-minute drive grew to over two hours—but Nay and I still visited as often as we could.

"I'm in my room." She belly-laughed. "JoJo just jumped on my bed. Wanna say hi?"

"I will in a minute." I was still trying to wrap my head around how this was even possible. "Where's Austyn?"

"Downstairs. Why?"

"Lemme holler at her for a sec."

"I miss you, Shawnee. Can I come stay with you? Summer camp doesn't start for another two weeks. Hey—" her pitch rose — "maybe JoJo can come, too. *Pretty please…*"

"'Course you can come. Not sure how Berkley and Katie McGuire will deal with a puppy in their house, though. Besides, do you really wanna leave Austyn by herself? If you take JoJo, she might get lonely with no one around."

"That wouldn't be very nice of me, huh? I don't want her to be sad."

One problem solved.

A gentle *tap, tap, tap* on the sliders nearly rocketed the heart from my chest.

With the phone still pressed to my ear, my sight shifting between Nadine and the deck, I crept toward the doors. Slow. Cautious. Every creak accented, every wisp of air enhanced. Blackness consumed the outside. Only my reflection stared back at me. I reached for the light switch but pulled back. Part of me didn't want to find out who, or what, lurked in the shadows.

What if Mayhem sent another one of his psychos-for-hire?

Above all else, the most important thing was to ensure Nay's safety. If anything happened to her on my watch, especially after a serial killer had already punished her for my indiscretions once, I'd never forgive myself. So, I pawned Maggie off while I checked it out.

"Hey," I said, all happy-like, "wanna talk to Auntie Nadine for a sec?"

"Sure."

I covered the mouthpiece. "Nay, she wants to say hi."

Sprawled on the couch, she lowered her paperback. "But I just spoke with her."

"What can I say? She loves you."

"Aww…"

That was almost too easy.

Gesturing for me to pass her the handset, she shook her hand. I passed her the phone.

"Hey, Maggie." Her pitch rose ten octaves. "I bought a new mystery the other day. Almost forgot to tell you. It's called Shadows Beyond the Grave. Really spooky. What're you reading?"

Nadine might be a pain in the ass, but she's also an amazing human being. That I couldn't deny. When Maggie stayed with us last year, Nay shared her love of reading. Even though my mind wandered the minute I cracked open a book, literature's important contribution to a young child's life didn't escape me.

With Nay and Maggie occupied, I backtracked to the sliders.

Nails scratched the smoky glass.

My ribcage compressed, my abs straining against the act of flipping on the outside light.

A streak of fur barreled down the stairs.

Even from a quick glimpse, I could tell that thing stood taller than me. What kind of animal ran on hind legs? My mind raced. Did black bears roam the wooded areas of Saugus? In all my time living here, I'd never read about any man-versus-bear encounters. Conservation officers hung at the same bars as RPD cops, and rumors ran rampant there. If black bears were bold enough to scratch at someone's door, wouldn't I have at least heard about it by now?

I'll end this right now. I hustled to the breakfast bar, snatched my laptop, and logged in.

A quick Google search confirmed that black bears hadn't travelled this far east. In the western part of Massachusetts, as well as the Berkshires, authorities reported sightings around Route four-ninety-five, but Saugus was still a long way away from "the zone."

On the surface, this seemed like good news, but if black bears weren't in the area, then what was that on my deck?

CHAPTER TWELVE

"There is a special magic and holiness about women.
They are the bringers of life to the people,
and the teachers of the children."
- Sweet Medicine (Cheyenne)

10:45 p.m.

K imi would not be pleased that he hadn't spoken with Chayton about Ms. Daniels, even though he highly doubted that Chayton would target her. His protégé would never dare to go off-script. The ramifications were too great. Rather, the way he'd chosen his victims, as well as the means he used to end their lives, revealed a clarifying intent, his ultimate purpose. Hence why Mayhem inquired about the gray wolf.

Until he was able to locate Mr. Wolf, however, Ms. Daniels would need to stay alert.

Leaning over the bed, he kissed his loving wife's cheek. The fragrant aroma of honeysuckle toyed with his emotions. No woman ever smelled as sweet, no man ever as helpless to fight it.

Within a few moments, Kimi's eyelids fluttered open.

"I apologize, darling." He palmed the side of her face. "I didn't mean to wake you."

Her gaze shifted between the computer and Mayhem. Even without words, she had no trouble communicating. A master of the unspoken language, Poe recognized what she longed for and flew to perch on the flat-screened monitor.

"Whatever is on your mind, sweetheart, let's discuss it in the morning." He caressed her silky cheek with the back of his curled fingers. "You know the ALS wins if you don't get enough sleep. Everything else can wait."

She squeezed her eyes closed in frustration. Tiny lines indented the skin beside her long, dark lashes. Crow's feet, if you will.

How could he censor his wife when he'd given each of his victims the right to speak freely? Their final words, in most cases. Although, if memory serves, he had come across a chosen few who showed remarkable verve in the precious few hours they had left in this world; they also showed an unparalleled zest for life. Mayhem had released those kindred spirits. By presence alone, they contributed to this wondrous land. He never once regretted the decision. Some people were meant to do great things. Chayton was a prime example of this. Through his wrath, countless others could soon rest.

"As you wish, my love." He hoisted his wife into his arms and carried her to the leather executive chair, where he slid the electrode cap over her dark, silky hair. With a flip of the switch, the monitor blazed on, the glow irradiating antiseptic wipes, rubbing alcohol, and unused syringes on the mahogany desktop.

"Whenever you're ready, my darling…"

With intense focus, Kimi typed letters across the flat-screen, the BCI technology—Brain-Computer Interface—doing all the heavy lifting. "Cat safe?"

"I'm afraid it's not as simple as that."

"Protect her."

From behind his loving wife, he snaked his arms around the chair, enveloping her in a warm embrace. "Working on it, my love, but some things are out of our control."

"Warn her."

Straightening, a heaviness weighed down his stomach. "I tried. Ms. Daniels refused to listen. Remember? I even arranged lunch with her best friend, at your insistence."

"Do more."

With a deep exhale, he tried to explain his position. "I will not risk your safety to save Ms. Daniels. If that is not an answer you will accept, then I'm afraid we've arrived at a crossroad."

Kimi's gaze shifted between his face and the monitor. As though Poe could read her thoughts, or he'd interpreted the slight shift in her demeanor—brilliant bird—his unflinching stare followed her focus, with quick side-glares tossed in Mayhem's direction.

How could he allow Ms. Daniels' problems to affect this family? Perhaps a moment of peace would change his wife's mind. "Poe looks like he's hankering for something sweet. I better go cube the melon."

The moment those words left his lips, Poe's widened gaze shot toward him as if to say, "Really?" No one had to ask him twice.

A grin stretched Mayhem's cheeks as he leaned down to give his wife a peck on the forehead. "I'll be back in a jiffy, sweetheart."

He scuttled into the kitchen and snatched a cantaloupe from the wooden bowl, along with a handful of seedless grapes and a Macintosh apple. On the butcher block, he skinned and de-seeded the melon. Sliced it into bite-sized pieces, then popped a cube into his mouth. Honeyed juices trickled down his throat. Delightful.

Soaring past the row of cabinets, Poe's beak fell open as if to say, "Did you just eat my treat?"

When he glided down to the granite island, Mayhem slipped an apple slice through his parted lips. "You don't mind if we share, do you?"

Head cocked, Poe tossed him a look as though the word "share" was in a foreign language.

"Shall I save the rest for Edgar and Allan, then?" Reverse psychology worked wonders for motivation.

Poe marched closer and nuzzled his head against Mayhem's arm.

"Sucking up, I see. Adorable." He held out a cube of cantaloupe, and his loyal companion gobbled down the over-sized bite. "You are so precious, even if your acting skills leave a lot to be desired." He scooped the fruit into a wooden bowl, rinsed, and dried his hands. "Come now. You may have your treat in the bedroom with Mom."

With Poe perched on his shoulder, he strolled toward the master suite. Once he entered the bedroom, he held a warm smile as he set the bowl of fruit on Kimi's desk. "I need to make a quick call. Will you two be all right for a moment? I shouldn't be long."

Across the flat-screen typed, "Call 4 Cat?"

"In a manner of speaking, yes."

"Who?"

Every bone in his body warned him not to answer, but he'd promised to never lie to her. Especially after the disease had progressed to this level. "The gray wolf has the answers we seek. I need to find him." He flashed a flat hand. "Please don't say it. I am fully aware of how you feel about him."

When Kimi refocused on the screen, two words appeared. "Unpredictable. Dangerous."

"Indeed, he is. But you are not leaving me much of a choice." He kissed her cheek. "I'll be back to get you settled."

Juices dripped down Poe's chest feathers when he threw his head back, devouring the fruit in a not so graceful way.

"Please don't gorge." Mayhem wagged his head. "Not only is it unbecoming, it is atrocious to watch."

Leakage out both sides of his beak dripped on the desktop as he raised his gaze to Kimi—a pitiful look designed to get Mom on his side. Classic Poe. Unfortunately for him, Kimi did not fall for the charade.

Mayhem sighed. "Good manners is not a lot to ask for, buddy." He leaned down to his beautiful wife. "Isn't that right, sweetheart?"

All she had to do was toss one glance, and Poe slurped the remaining juices into his beak.

"Good boy," he crooned, stroking Poe's head. "Now, I should probably make that phone call before it gets too late."

On the monitor came, "Wait."

Mayhem froze, his vision locked on the blinking cursor. "Would you rather I not proceed? It's not too late to stop."

"I know where he is."

He startled. "Whom, my darling?"

"Wolf."

For a moment, he set aside how his wife unearthed this information. If he had to guess, Yaz was the most likely culprit. Instead, he countered with, "All right. I'll bite. Where is the gray wolf?"

"Breakheart Hill."

"Really? Ooh sounds like fun." Prickling tingles spread across his scalp, and he glimpsed his eighteen-karat gold Patek Philippe watch, world time depicted around a stunning sapphire-crystal globe, topped with a fluted crown and alligator wristband, that he'd bought in Paris. "Better get my dance shoes ready, then." He forced a grin, his fingers lacing through the ends of Kimi's hair.

"Bed plz."

"As you wish, my love. Far be it from me to stand in the way of a woman and her beauty sleep."

When he moved to the side of the leather desk chair, ready to lift his beautiful wife into his arms, Kimi's complete focus returned to the monitor. The computer screen showed, "B Careful."

"Always, my darling. You needn't worry yourself with my safety." With an arm behind Kimi's back, another under her bent knees, he carried her to one of the many hospital beds he'd purchased for various properties. Apart from the log home in Unalaska, Alaska, the brownstone in Boston's Back Bay was Kimi's favorite place. The building was also conveniently located near the Museum of Fine Arts, where he worked most mornings as a curator.

Bent over his beloved wife, he dragged the handcrafted wool blanket—a Native design that boasted a dragonfly dead-center, which symbolized water and in turn, life—to her chin. With a gentle kiss on her soft lips, tears wet his eyes. This incredible woman warred with her disease on a daily basis, yet never did she let the ALS break her spirit. If Ms. Daniels wasn't so bull-headed, she could learn a lot from Kimi.

Perhaps another meeting was in order. Only this time, the crafty cat would need to believe it's her idea. But first, he had a gray wolf to hunt.

CHAPTER THIRTEEN

Friday
9:15 a.m.

A radio call crackled over the speaker in Levaughn's Crown Victoria P71 Police Interceptor. Swimmers found a decapitated human head on the shoreline of Revere Beach, near the Point of Pines, a private year-round community. He flipped on the lights and siren, banged a U-turn, and raced toward the crime scene. The wind from the open window rattled papers around the front seat, and he slapped his hand over the case notes before they sailed out of the opened murder book.

Levaughn zipped up the window. The air conditioning was on the fritz again. What else was new? The interior temperature increased to almost eighty-five degrees, sweat trickling down his sideburns.

As he loosened his tie, not that it did much good, he crossed on to Revere Beach Boulevard and followed the sea wall to the end, to the quiet community of the Point of Pines. Squad cars blocked off the end of Bateman Avenue, whipping blue lights somersaulting across the sand dunes. According to his information, the head lay on the other side.

Levaughn slid the shifter into park, killed the ignition.

The second the soles of his dress shoes hit the asphalt, Officer Langley jogged toward the Crown Vic. With labored breath, he bent over, hands cupped on his knees. "Glad you're here, boss." Gulping the air, he hooked an arm at Levaughn. "C'mon, the head's this way. Residents are in a panic over this."

That wasn't unusual in and of itself. Most people went their whole lives without ever having the misfortune of viewing a homicide victim. Especially one left at a place reserved for pleasure. "Any witnesses?"

"Not that I know of, but Detective Mancini's still taking statements."

Levaughn grabbed his arm, stopping him cold. "Mancini's here?"

"Yeah. He said he's part of the joint task force. I thought you knew."

Grinding his teeth, he attempted to slow the fury coursing through his system before it consumed him. If Odin continued to overstep, he'd need to do something about it, like send him back to Quantico where he belonged. Yesterday, his meeting with Chavez ran longer than expected, so he hadn't had a chance to speak with Lieutenant Holt about this so-called joint venture. The run-in with Special Agent Barrett forced him to work from the road for the rest of the day, running down one dead lead after another.

As far as he was concerned, this homicide was his case. Besides, with the lack of information being shared between departments, no one would even know a joint task force worked these serial murders. What he should do is head to New Hampshire to sort this out once and for all.

Though he couldn't pinpoint the exact source of his malaise —best guess would be Odin's presence at RPD—he pushed his personal feelings aside and concentrated on the case. "Is the Medical Examiner on scene yet?"

"Yep. Just arrived."

"Excellent." He swept an arm in the direction of the crime scene tape, an army of onlookers elbowing and shoving, the crowd on the verge of breaking out into a full-blown riot. "Lead the way."

"Comin' through." Levaughn squirmed through the mass of looky-loos, all trying to get a better view of the severed head.

Langley stopped on top of the dunes and jutted a thumb over his shoulder at the water. "It's right over this crest. Can't miss it."

"Thanks. Tell Mancini I wanna see the witness statements before he lets anyone leave the scene. Understood?"

"Yes, sir."

Levaughn climbed down the other side of the dune, beach sand filling his Italian-leather loafers, its crystals imbedding in the weave of both socks. Some days, it didn't pay to have a sense of style.

Once by the water's edge, he fished a twenty-dollar bill out of his wallet and passed it to the uniformed officer guarding the crime scene. "Go fetch us some coffee, will ya?" He jabbed a chin at Chavez, and then Odin. "Want anything?" When neither responded—in their defense, they might not've heard him over the waves crashing on the shoreline—he returned his attention to the patrol officer whose name escaped him at the moment. Already it'd been one of those mornings. "Grab a dozen donuts while you're at it. I skipped breakfast."

With Shawnee acting so distant lately, his morning routine was out of whack. Normally, he hit the gym by five a.m., but he couldn't concentrate on working out when his woman refused to return his calls. He probably should've still scarfed down a banana, a few crackers, a handful of raisins, and applesauce—the recommended twenty-five grams of carbs—but he didn't.

The officer jogged as far as the sand dune when Levaughn called out, "Get yourself something, too. My treat."

His stomach growled. If this scumbag would quit the killing spree, maybe life could return to normal. Unless something else was bothering Shawnee. What'd he say to piss her off this time?

Heaving a heavy sigh, he yanked up his pantlegs and squatted opposite the Medical Examiner. To his right, Odin knelt on the sand.

For now, he ignored him. "Whatta we got, Doc?"

"Good morning, Detective." A toothy smile spread across Chavez's face. "You look scrumptious today. Love the nutmeg blazer with the coral dress shirt. It really shows off your muscular physique." He eyeballed Levaughn head to toe. "Oooh, that tie is to die for. Let me guess, Macy's?"

Normally, he played along with Chavez's interpretation of the stereotypical gay man because the conversation made Odin squirm. This wasn't one of those days. "I don't remember. Can we please concentrate on the vic?"

"All business today, I see." He parted the body-less victim's lips. "As you know, odontology is not my chosen field of expertise, but even with a cursory examination of her teeth, I would estimate her age at somewhere around mid-thirties. I will say, however, that I'm concerned the rest of her may have floated out to sea. Which, as you also know, will drastically reduce our chances of making an ID."

Identifying a corpse through dental records wasn't as easy as it appeared on TV. Cop shows didn't help the public's view of forensic evidence. Quite the opposite, in fact. The CSI Effect—the phenomenon which caused juries to vote not guilty due to their warped view of investigative procedures—remained alive and well in courtrooms across the country.

For a change, Odin remained silent. Good.

"So—" against his will, Levaughn's nostrils flared— "Special Agent Barrett, you ready to gimme the rundown of the suspect's psychological profile? I thought I'd have a copy of your report on my desk by now."

Without hesitation, Odin rattled off the particulars as if he knew Levaughn would ask. "Dismemberment dates back to the twelve-hundreds when society viewed beheading and torture as social norms and even considered the festivity in the highest regard. During that period, the public viewed decapitation as the most prestigious form of death, believe it or not."

"Okay," said Levaughn, rather than "make your point." Trying to erase the sardonic edge to his tone drained him of energy, a subtle *pulse, pulse, pulse* drumming right behind the eyes. "But that's no longer the case today, so let's fast forward to this century if you don't mind."

"Sure." Odin cleared his throat. "Dismemberment of any kind illustrates an extreme notion of abhorrence toward the victim by psychologically dismissing their existence, disregarding them as having any value. The UNSUB who elects to dismember their victim is trying to erase their existence, thereby refusing them on a conscious level. Furthermore, the act of disarticulating a body is sexually gratifying and psychologically necessary."

"Says who, you?"

Chavez blurted out, "Ooh, snap! He's got you there, blondie."

"Case in point," Odin continued as though he hadn't heard the Medical Examiner, "Edmund Kemper decapitated his victims and buried their heads in his home garden, their faces gazing up at his mother's bedroom window because he said his mother looked down on everyone. The positioning of the heads was a literal interpretation of his thought process at the time he committed the crimes."

"Interesting." Not really. "But unlike Kemper, our bad guy doesn't keep the heads as trophies."

"True. He covets their scalps. Easier to transport, easier to conceal. However, a parallel can still be made between the two killers. An UNSUB who elects to dismember is driven by the lust and power they hold over the victim. These patterns in serial murder indicate a classification of a power-control killer."

Levaughn parted his lips to ask for clarification, but Odin beat him to it.

"A power-control serial killer receives sexual gratification in committing the murder but also takes the act one step further. Detestation as domination is equated to a psychological competition."

Levaughn's brow furrowed. "Who's he competing with, the police?"

"No. The victim. The underlying psychological warfare associated with dismemberment isn't finalized until mutilation is complete. When you think about it, it's a fascinating dynamic."

Chavez agreed, and Levaughn sneered. "Have you two lost your friggin' minds? These victims are human beings, for chrissakes, with families who love them, and you two—" his erect finger poked the air in front of each face— "find it fascinating that some scumbag chopped their heads off?" He thrusts his hand toward the severed head. "Look at this poor woman. What's left of her anyway."

Raking his nails through his short-cropped curls, he soldiered away from the crime scene. Something occurred to him, and he whirled back around. "If these homicides are sexual in nature, then why aren't all the vics the same sex? So far, he's killed, what, two women and two men?"

"Correct." Unfazed, Odin flipped open his notepad. "We found the remains of Mary Rowlandson and William Bradford in New Hampshire before you came on board, with the discovery of Patrick Couturier."

"Tell me, Agent Barrett—" he invaded Odin's personal space — "if you're right, then how does your profile explain the change in victimology?"

"Special Agent," Odin corrected, and Levaughn controlled a satisfied smirk from giving him away. "The UNSUB who dismembers tends to be very hands-on. Meaning, they'll often use their hands to torture the victims before the murder phase. Tattooing could be this UNSUB's chosen form of torture. A power-control killer also tends to use a manual weapon to get up close and personal. In this case, a sword."

Did he answer the question?

As though Odin was reciting his profile from memory, he barely took a breath between sentences. "It's also highly plausible that dismemberment began as a way to conceal the crime. The psychological connotation associated with the UNSUB who dismembers their victim is psychologically aware of their wrongdoing. A power-control serial killer will be more apt to evade all possible detection as a suspect. He may even agree to take a polygraph as an added means to corroborate his innocence, thereby reducing the plausibility of being culpable for the murders. If psychopathic in nature, he could potentially pass the test, too."

"Fabulous." This time, Levaughn let the sarcasm fly. "So, what you're sayin' is, we better find rock-solid evidence because we'll never get him to confess."

"Exactly. Dismemberment is one of the most dehumanizing acts one person can do to another. Due to the level of psychological competence and power to dominate a potential victim, dismemberment provides an opening for self-magnification and omnipotence. Which, more often than not, reaffirms the UNSUB's own sense of worth. Dismemberment, decapitation, in particular, provides psychological closure for the UNSUB."

From his peripheral vision, Levaughn caught Langley charging straight at him, military boots tromping through the sand. As he neared, he framed his mouth with his hands. "We found the rest of her. She's at the point."

Levaughn's breath stalled. "Slow down. I'm assuming by 'she' you mean the victim. Are the remains in the water?"

"No, the sand. High tide must've washed the head down the beach."

"Wow. Okay." He set both hands on Langley's shoulders and leaned in, staring him square in the eye to send a clear signal for him to pay attention. "Radio Mancini to lock down the scene. No one touches any evidence till I get there. Understood?" He kept his tone even, controlled. "Cordon off the area. We can't have onlookers trampling through the crime scene."

"Yes, sir."

He hushed out the corner of his mouth, "Almost done here, Doc?"

"I can wrap it up. Anything more I need I can do at the morgue."

"Great." He returned focus to Langley. "Tell Mancini I'm on my way." When Langley turned to leave, Levaughn snagged his arm. "Any word on how far away the Crime Scene Unit is?"

"Not that I know of, but I can find out."

"Great. Make the call. Once Doctor Chavez removes the head, this area needs to be processed. We can't assume the tide's responsible for separating body parts."

His gaze flitted around the private beach, his stomach growling for caffeine. Where's the patrol officer who took his twenty?

CHAPTER FOURTEEN

"It's your road, and yours alone. Others may walk with you,
but no one can walk it for you."
- Rumi

10 p.m.

Outside Breakheart Reservation, Mayhem stashed the Caddy on a side street and trekked through the park entrance. Too many squad cars patrolled the reservation after dusk for him to park in the lot. If an officer spotted his vehicle, he might be tempted to ask questions, lots of questions, questions better left unanswered.

A few strides past the wooden sign and he stopped, waiting for air support to arrive. Within two minutes, Poe, Edgar, and Allan soared toward him in perfect V-formation, but they squawked at decibels much louder than he preferred. One by one, they landed inches away from his Salvatore Ferragamos, stylish Oxford shoes in calfskin leather, with delightfully-crafted capped toes.

All three crows paced, their talons imprinting the soil.

"Is there something I should be aware of?"

Poe flew up to his shoulder, and Mayhem kissed the top of his bowing head.

"All right. For now, I will refrain from prying into crow business. All I ask is for you to please cease all future communications, apart from body language, until we leave the premises. Do any of you have a problem with my request?"

Two beaks tipped upward toward Mayhem, Poe's face inches from his cheek—eager stares yearning for direction.

"Thank you." He swept his arm toward the dirt trail. "Shall we proceed, then?"

Taking the lead, Poe leaped off his shoulder. Edgar and Allan flapped behind their brother. Mayhem trekked through thick, wooded terrain, the beam of his flashlight bouncing to his cautious stride, his restless mind wandering to places unknown.

Glorious beings, crows. Nature was indeed one of the Creator's greatest accomplishments. It's a shame more people didn't cherish what the outdoors had to offer. Kids today spent hours in front of video games when their parents should send them outside for fresh air.

When Cheyenne was a girl, he and Kimi taught her to respect the laws of nature, as well as wildlife in general. In turn, she passed that knowledge on to Jude. Even at his tender age, their grandson exceeded his and Kimi's expectations. Such a gentle, kind soul.

In the distance, drumming drew his full attention. Hot ash flickered into the night sky, beyond the next hill. Dead in his tracks, he stopped. Poe circled back around and landed on his outstretched forearm. With a non-verbal jab of the chin, Mayhem instructed Edgar and Allan to check it out.

While he waited for their return, he mussed Poe's chest feathers. "Please be careful tonight. You know what could happen if the gray wolf spots you or your brothers."

Poe hopped up to Mayhem's bicep, and then to his shoulder,

where he rubbed his feathery cheek against the side of Mayhem's face.

"If it weren't for Mom, I would never suggest we move forward." He kept his voice low. "The gray wolf is too unpredictable these days. But unfortunately, your mother's left us no choice in the matter." He fluffed the back of Poe's neck. "After tonight, I will need you to keep a close eye on our feline friend. I'm afraid the evil she's up against may lie outside her prowess. Would you mind terribly?"

Rattle, rattle. Rattle, rattle.

The distinct call had two different meanings, depending on context—the first was short for, "I love you"; the second meant, "I've got your six." The latter of which applied tonight.

"Ah, thank you."

Poe peeked around Mayhem's ponytail. Gliding toward them, Edgar and Allan flew wing to wing, landing moments later on a low-hanging branch.

"Is it safe to continue?"

With his magnificent wings spread wide, Edgar bounced up and down on the perch. Clearly, he'd spent too much time mimicking Poe's antics. Allan was far less dramatic. With a simple bow of the head, he confirmed safe passage.

"Thank you, boys. Then let's proceed. Oh, one caveat before we go. If at any time you feel your well-being is in jeopardy, be it physical, emotional, or psychological peril, please do not wait for my instruction. Leave immediately. Also, should you spot an unfamiliar crow, do not approach. I repeat, do not approach."

Even though his beloved companions did not understand the English language, per se, he'd still gotten his point across. Many people did not give crows enough credit, or the respect they so richly deserved.

Prompting them to follow, he signaled in the direction of the smoke, and all three members of his murder leaped into the darkened sky. He trudged uphill and down the other side. Ahead of him, a clearing showed three nude men, prancing on all fours around a campfire. On the ground by their fur boots, lay the skins of wolves, foxes, and bears, complete with heads and paws. The gray wolf sat off to the side, next to the decomposing remains of an infant—a mother's child they had robbed from the grave.

Despicable display.

The gray wolf had aged since their last meeting, which did not end particularly well for either party. Hence, Kimi's earlier reluctance when he mentioned tracking him down. What choice did he have? According to his intel, the gray wolf had a hand in the impending attack against Ms. Daniels. But before he made his presence known, he needed to determine who had hired him, and why. Without more information, a treaty would prove worthless at this point.

Staring at the ceremony of Witchy Ways, his head wagged in disgust. Dearest Cat, you have no idea what you've gotten yourself involved with.

CHAPTER FIFTEEN

Saturday
8:45 a.m.

At the station, I stuck my key in the lock of the Cyber Crimes Division. But before I even made it to my desk, Detective North strutted into the computer lab with a larger-than-normal ego.

Oh, here we go. "What do you want, Chuck?"

"Charles. You know I go by Charles."

I stifled a snicker. "Right. My bad."

He dropped a file on my desk. *Thud.* The damn thing was so thick it almost cracked the wood. "Trace the IP address of everyone on the suspect list, and then send me a report of your findings." He tapped the face of his watch. "One hour."

I curled my upper lip. "I don't answer to you, Chuck."

Like a two year old, he stomped his feet. "It's Charles!"

"Whatever." I sat in my leather chair and logged into my computer. "Go away. I'm busy."

"But LT said you'd give me a hand on my purse-snatching case."

With a one-sided shrug, I plucked a sticky note off the flat-screen. Levaughn's handwriting. The Medical Examiner IDd the latest victim as Amanda Orme, the last person to see Patrick Couturier alive.

"Till Lieutenant Holt orders me to do it, I ain't doin' shit for you." Fingers tapping the keyboard, I hacked Amanda's Face-book account. "Now, if you don't mind…"

My obvious hint to leave didn't faze him. Goes to show what a pain in the ass he could be, sort of like falling asleep with a wad of gum, and then waking with your cheek cemented to the pillow. Same thing, different animal. Actually, I'd prefer the gum scenario. Chuck's nasally tone splintered my skull. Toss in his freckled face and receding hairline, and he's lucky I didn't puke all over his gay pointy dress shoes.

Just when I couldn't stand another second of his incessant whining, Levaughn poked his head in the doorway. "Hey, you." His sultry voice sent tingles to all the right spots. With Nadine staying with me, I was practically a virgin again.

I leaned forward to avoid direct contact with Chuck's jelly belly. "Whassup?"

"Wanna take a ride?"

Chuck said, "She can't. She's helping me on an important case."

I rose so fast, Chuck jumped back a good two feet. "Abso-lutely. Where're we goin'?"

"New Hampshire."

"To see Maggie?"

"Hey—" Chuck grabbed my upper arm, and I almost decked him. "You're not going anywhere till you trace those IP addresses."

I leaned in real close. Had to work doubly hard to ignore the nauseating stench of garlic breath, though. "You've got two seconds to remove your hand."

He pulled back his narrow shoulders as though he'd actually grown a spine. "Or what?"

"Don't test me, Chucky boy." My spittle flew in his face. "Tell ya what, leave your filthy mitts on me. It'll give me an excuse to kick your ever-lovin' ass all over this room."

Levaughn clamped a hand on his shoulder. "Release her. Now."

And so, he complied.

"C'mon." When Levaughn weaved his hand with mine, he acted as if Chuck wasn't even in the room anymore. "We'll call the lieutenant from the car."

Detective North didn't say one word as we left the computer lab. Ha! That'd teach him to screw with me.

I didn't speak, either, till we hit the parking lot. Outside the Crown Vic, Levaughn held open the passenger door. Before I climbed inside, I cleared up any misunderstanding my silence might've had. "I can take care of myself, y'know."

"I know."

"Okay, cool. Didn't want you to think I needed saving back there." I set one foot inside the car, then stopped. "Are we really goin' to New Hampshire?"

"Yeah. I told you, I need your help."

"With what, exactly?"

"Y'know how you've been itchin' for a new tattoo?"

Mute, I nodded yes. There must be more to this story. No way would he drive two-plus-hours so I could get new ink, on a workday no less. What'd he really want?

"Truth?"

I firmed a hand on my hip. "No. Lie to me. I love that shit."

"I need you to go undercover at a tattoo shop."

"Lemme guess, Patrick Couturier's place? I forget the name."

"The Other Guy's Tattoo Shop, and yeah." His weight shifted as he leaned on the opened doorframe. "Didn't you get my note about Amanda Orme?"

"Yup. She's dead. And?" That came out way more callous than intended. "I mean—"

"She worked for Couturier."

"No shit? Wow. Okay. Whaddaya need me to do?"

He grinned like Berkley on the day he swallowed my one and only goldfish. Long story. "Get in the car before North goes cryin' to the lieutenant."

And so, I lowered to the passenger seat. Levaughn closed the door, hurried around the front bumper, and slid into the driver's seat. The engine roared.

Peeling out the lot, he thumbed the speaker button on the steering wheel, said, "Call Lieutenant Holt's cell phone."

Over the hands-free system, the phone rang three times before the voicemail picked up.

"LT, if you're looking for Shawnee, she's with me. I need her to clone a suspect's phone in the Headless Horseman case, but we need to be close enough for her to do it. Call the cell if you need us."

I tugged on his suitcoat. "Headless Horseman? What's that about?"

He took the ramp for Interstate 95 North. "You've never heard the story of Sleepy Hollow?"

"Sleepy, what?"

"Sorry." His cupped hand patted my knee. "Sometimes I forget how different our upbringings were."

If he only knew the validity of that statement.

Levaughn slid on the gold-plated shades with dark-green lenses that I bought him. Looked sexy as hell, too. Okay, so maybe "bought" might be a bit of a stretch. Last year, I borrowed the thousand-dollar sunglasses—without the intention of ever returning them—from this rich prick who used his wife as a punching bag. Unbeknownst to me, that rich prick turned out to be the son of the most powerful family in the area. Whoops.

All right, so maybe I kinda knew who he was when I climbed through the window of his Victorian contemporary. Big deal. That didn't discount the fact that he treated his wife like shit. Poor woman. Thanks to Mr. Mayhem, the Medical Examiner bagged and tagged her body, along with countless others.

"The legend of the Headless Horseman begins in Sleepy Hollow, New York, during the Revolutionary War," explained Levaughn, rattling me from my thoughts. "Traditional folklore says the Horseman was an artilleryman who died during the Battle of White Plains in seventeen-seventy-six when an American cannonball decapitated him. His shattered skull laid in pieces on the battlefield while his comrades carried his body away. Later, his men buried him in the cemetery of the Old Dutch Church of Sleepy Hollow. And now, every Halloween night, his malevolent spirit rises from the grave in search of his lost head."

He wiggled his fingers at me. *"Mwahahaha."*

I forced a chuckle. "Ha-ha. Ya got me." Hey, no judgements. Women faked shit all the time for men. Did they really think we hung on every word? "Remind me how we got on this subject?"

"Because some journalist with far too much time on his hands dubbed the scumbag we're chasing as the Headless Horseman."

"And you think what, exactly, that Couturier's business partner could be our guy? What's this jerkoff's name, anyway?"

"Devin Norton. All the vics were tattooed before death, so the theory fits."

Tucking one leg under the other, I swiveled to face him. "But what if he's some hack? Tattoos can't be erased, y'know."

Levaughn flashed me his pearly whites before swerving into the fast lane. "I knew you'd say that. See the file on the back-seat? I took the liberty of downloading part of Norton's portfolio. Scumbag or no, I think you'll agree he's a talented artist."

I squirmed through the seats to grab the file, and Levaughn

slapped my ass. When my gaze shot toward him, he laughed. "Sorry, couldn't resist."

Two could play this game. I backed through the opening, letting my fingertips graze the bulge in his crotch. "Whoops. Hand slipped." I winked. "I really should be more careful."

With the case file on my lap, I flipped through colored prints of tattoos. Admittedly, the first photo of a tribal wolf was wicked cool. Still, I reserved the right to veto Levaughn's idea. What if wolves were all this dude could draw?

Flip. A dreamcatcher in the clutches of an eagle's talons, like he was about to scatter a child's nightmares across the open water. Sick design.

Flip. Close-up of an owl, with lifelike eyes, each feather expertly drawn. Maybe a free tatt wasn't such a bad idea.

Flip. My stomach hit the car mat. On the page, a crow stared back at me, his black-eyed stare tearing open my chest, eviscerating all hope of salvation. Kinda like Mayhem's buddy, Poe.

I slammed the cover closed.

"Something wrong?"

"Huh?" My gaze fell to the case file, and my knee bobbed to the racing beat of my heart. "Nah. It's all good."

"So, you'll do it? You can get any tatt you want."

I snarled. "No shit. It's my body."

"No, I know. That's not what I meant. All I'm sayin' is, the department will cover the expenses, regardless of size or price." He licked his full lips. "There's one other thing I should probably mention." His Adam's apple rose and fell—a surefire sign that whatever he was working up the nerve to tell me couldn't be good. "You'll need to wear a wire."

I backhanded his bicep. "Are you outta your fuckin' mind? If the dude spots a wire, I'm a dead woman." Facing front, I crossed my arms on my chest. "Nope. Find another way. I'm not wearin' any wire."

"But, babe—"

In one long continuous motion, I shook my head no. "Forget it. There's nothin' you can say to change my mind."

"Shawnee, look at me. Please."

Staring straight ahead, I refused eye contact. "I can hear you just fine, thank you very much."

"Lemme ask you this, then. What happens if Norton incriminates himself? Do you really want your past brought into a courtroom? Because without recorded evidence to back you up, it's your word against his."

I kicked the dash. "Dammit! Fine, I'll wear the stupid wire."

Needless to say, the ride went downhill from there. At this rate, I wasn't gettin' laid anytime soon.

CHAPTER SIXTEEN

11:45 a.m.

Two hours later, give or take, Levaughn pulled into the parking lot at Weirs Beach—within walking distance of The Other Guy's Tattoo Shop—and twisted the key in the ignition, killing the engine. "Ready for this?" He glimpsed his watch. "Your appointment's in fifteen minutes."

I blinked owlishly. "You set up an appointment for me? When?"

"Uh..." His gaze sidled. "Yesterday."

"Yesterday? But I only just agreed, what, couple hours ago?" Smoothing my lips, I grimaced. "You played me, Detective."

Quailing back against the door, he flashed his palms in surrender. "No. Babe, I'd never betray you. C'mon, don't be like that." He pawed at my clothes, trying to fold me into his chest, but I shoved him away.

"Save it. We're running outta time."

Like the flip of a switch, he morphed into all-business. From the glove compartment, he snagged this massive listening device that looked like it stemmed from the nineteen-eighties, along with tape that'd probably take half my body hairs with it when removed. "Take your tank top off."

I arched one eyebrow. "Excuse me?"

"Lose the shirt so I can tape you up. C'mon."

"Bra, too, Detective? Maybe I should just strip down to nothin' and really give beachgoers a show. Tell ya what, gimme the wire and I'll tape the thing on in the bathroom after I decide where I want my new tatt. Sound like a plan?"

"Babe, I'm kidding. Lighten up." Belly-laughing, tears wet his eyes as he passed me a fountain pen. "The transmitter's built in. All you need to do is click the top."

"I knew that." With a quick sarcastic smirk, I swiped the pen and stashed it inside my sock, hidden by the cuff of my motor-cycle boot, before exiting the car. "I was just calling your bluff."

The sad puppy dog eyes nearly melted my cool exterior, so I dialed back the snark and crossed my arms on the opened window. "How will I know you can hear me?"

"I tested the mic. It's working, don't worry. Remember to click the top."

"Hope you know how much I hate this." I turned and jogged away from the car.

Levaughn hollered out the driver's window, "Good luck!"

I cringed. Why not announce it to everyone that I'm working undercover? I tossed a half-salute his way before climbing the hill toward The Other Guy's Tattoo Shop. When I crested the top, I slowed. This dude was hanging around the picnic table below the shop's black-and-gold sign. Long dreadlocks hit his waist. V'd body, tall, muscular, and dark.

Mm-mmm. Maybe this undercover gig wasn't so bad after all.

As I neared, I flipped my hair over one shoulder for some unknown reason. "Hey, you Devin?" *Please say yes.*

The dude refused eye contact. "No."

Did women make him nervous? Ooh, this day was really

looking up. It's not that I didn't love Levaughn. I did. But that didn't mean I had to act like a nun. Even vegans glanced at the meat menu once in a while.

"I'm Taylor," he said. "Devin's inside."

"Thanks." *Well, so much for having a little fun while I'm here. Just my luck.*

I swung open the door, and a wave of antiseptic struck me in the face. The long and narrow empty room had a sectional couch that begged me to fall backward on it. After the crap with Mayhem and then breaking up the secret love affair for Nadine, I almost complied, too. Maybe I should stay. No one could bother me in New Hampshire. Besides, if Devin Norton was half as smokin' as Taylor, I could pick worse places to lay low.

"Hello?" Buzzing from tattoo guns drowned out my voice. I peeked over a half-wall in the waiting room. A tattoo booth sat empty, except for a reclining chair. The continuing black walls and gold border looked sick as hell. This might not be such a bad assignment. And—who knows? —maybe I'll catch a killer at the same time. Win-win.

A metal bell on the front door jingled, and I whirled toward the noise.

The blistering summer sun cascaded around Taylor's silhouette, his broad shoulders filling the doorway. "Did you find Devin?"

"No." My shoulders rose toward my ears. "You sure he's here?"

"He's here." He smiled. What a set of chompers, too.

Yum. I wonder if he likes to nibble on white women.

A Bob Marley lookalike swaggered into the lobby. "Sorry to keep you waiting. Are you Shawnee?"

Oh, man, he was even hotter than Taylor, with that deep voice. Yowzah. Bet he sang a mean Barry White. On the sly, I wiped a spot of drool off my lower lip. What was it with this place? The It-factor must be a prerequisite for hire. Not that anyone would hear me complain.

"So...are you Shawnee?" he asked a second time.

"Yes!" Admittedly, that sounded a tad overeager. Playing it cool, I wrangled my hormones under control...barely. "I mean, sure am."

He extended his hand, and I wiped my sweaty palm on my jeans as I swung to shake it.

"I'm Devin. Nice to meet you. So, do you know what you want?"

For a moment, my jaw slacked. "Uh..."

He chuckled. "Your husband said something about a black cat, I think."

"Husband? I'm not married." Shit. Did Levaughn construct a whole backstory for me? Would've been nice to fill me in. Ah, well, too late now. "He's more of a friend with benefits if you catch my drift." I winked.

Rule number one when enticing men to serve a purpose: let them believe they had a shot at the honeypot. They're a lot more amenable that way. Just sayin'.

"Gotcha." He returned the wink. "So, was your—" he flashed air quotes— "*friend* right about the cat?"

"Actually, I was thinkin' more along the lines of a weeping angel. I saw one a while back and loved the design. I'm just not sure where to put it." Or where to stick the damn pen-wire for optimal reception, but I kept that last part to myself.

"Step into my office." He swung his arm toward a spacious room to the left of the waiting area, where photos of Bob Marley lined the walls. *Star Wars* figurines stood on a lone bookshelf, with a black suit and tie clinging to the edge. An Anonymous mask—representing the notorious hacker group—peered under a black fedora, similar to the one Mayhem wears.

A demonic tongue licked up my spine. Was Norton a member of Anonymous? He also displayed a Freemason's hat, so belonging to a second secret society wouldn't be all that farfetched. Maybe Levaughn was right about this guy.

Devin dragged a chair next to his desk, where he brought up pages of weeping angel designs. Hesitant, my boots scuffed across the black-and-white-tiled floor. When I lowered to the seat, an elbow away from the main suspect in the Headless Horseman case, my nerves pinged like raindrops on a metal roof.

But then, the perfect image on his computer screen diverted my attention away from the fact that he could chop my head off if he discovered the transmitter. "That's the exact photo I saw. How'd you know?"

"Thought it might be. It's my design." With the tap of a keystroke, the printer spat out my future tattoo. "This would look cool on the side of the calf, upper arm, back of the shoulder, anywhere, really."

"Already got a few where you mentioned. Would it fit here?" I showed him my inner forearm.

"With the edges of the wings wrapping around to the front? Yeah, that'd look sick."

"Awesome. Let's do it." Now I needed to turn on the transmitter somehow. "Gotta bathroom I can use?"

He pointed toward the waiting area. "All the way to the end and take a left. Last door on your left. I need a few minutes to create the stencil anyway."

"Cool. Thanks."

I strolled past the tattoo booth I'd peered into earlier. In black latex gloves, Taylor was prepping some chick's back for new ink. Okay, so if that's his room, then where'd Patrick Couturier work? After I hung a left, I boogied down the hall to a cramped bathroom that a bunch of men took care of, evident by a lone roll of toilet paper on top of the holder, rather than in it. An empty cardboard roll hung where paper towels should be.

At least they put the toilet seat down. That's sayin' somethin'.

With one boot leveraged on the wall, I slipped the pen out of my sock and clicked the tip. Where to put it? I wasn't exactly the pen-wearing, pocket-protector type. If I reappeared with a fountain pen hanging from my neckline, there's no way he wouldn't notice it.

How close to his face did the mic need to be? One might think since I ran the Cyber Crimes Division at RPD that I'd be familiar with this type of stuff, but I concentrated on cyber-criminals, which made up twenty-five-percent of all local and regional crime. The drug unit used wires, not me.

On the same side as my upcoming new ink, I slipped the pen into my front jeans pocket, near the outer seam, then dragged the hem of my tank top over the mic. As long as I could sit with the pen facing him, there shouldn't be any technical issues. Keyword being "shouldn't." Time would tell if I was right.

On my way back down the hall, I poked my head into a doorway on my left. Empty Jack Daniel's bottles hung from a wooden frame, with wiring that led to flame-like lightbulbs.

Some plain Jane chick snuck up behind me. "Can I help you?"

"Cool chandelier. Whose room is this?"

"Pat's." Her head bowed in condolence. "Someone killed him."

I acted shocked. "He was murdered? Wow. Did the cops find out who did it?"

"Not yet."

I pressed her for answers. If she admitted to arguments between the two business partners, it might be enough to get Devin to confess. "Did Pat have any enemies that you know of, or someone who might benefit from his death?"

With a cold stare, she studied my expression like a cop.

Then, as if I'd crossed a line, she closed the door. "Devin's waiting. He told me to come get you."

"Okay, cool. Thanks." Friggin' great. So much for that lead. Maybe I'd have better luck schmoozing Norton. Either that or he'd kick me out of the shop in the middle of my tattoo, a broken angel with one wing scarring me for life.

Man, that would suck. How'd I let Levaughn talk me into this?

CHAPTER SEVENTEEN

"Maybe the wolf is in love with the moon,
and each month it cries for a love it can never touch."
- Anonymous

12:45 p.m.

Before Mayhem left the Museum of Fine Arts for the day, he added a few final touches to the "Collecting Stories: Native American Art" exhibit. As a new exhibition, and an important history lesson for young and old alike, this collection focused on the formative years of the eighteen-eighties, explored the range of perspectives, motivations, and voices of early American Indians. It showed outstanding craftmanship in the early Diné wearing blanket, the Eastern Woodlands moccasins, and the Plains roach, more commonly referred to as a headpiece.

This headpiece proved a master craftsman had used an intricate weave of deer and porcupine hair, with its rich red color, dyed leather, and vegetal cord made from seagrass. The moccasins sported moose-skin leather, woven, dyed porcupine quills, bast fiber thread made from the phloem or vascular tissue of a plant, silk ribbon, dyed moose-hair tufts, tinned sheet iron cones, and a napped plain weave wool backing.

Truly stunning.

Inspired by authentic Indian life, many East Coast collectors traveled to the Great Plains and Southwest during the eighteen-hundreds, encountering indigenous artists who created objects for use within their communities, as well as for tourists. As both works of art and souvenirs, these objects became less visible in the galleries during the early twentieth century, and like other encyclopedic art institutions, the Museum of Fine Arts lent or donated most of its holdings to ethnographic and archeological museums.

"Collecting Stories" confronted this moment in its institutional history and sought new ways to interpret these under-studied objects. Which included voices of indigenous artists of the past and present.

Kimi would adore this exhibit. Before the ALS stole her mobility, she spent hours in the museum, admiring works of art. A photograph couldn't quite capture the power and beauty of real life, but it would do in a pinch.

When he snapped the photo, his heart bled. Had the sins of his past caused his wife's illness? Karma had a way of righting injustices. Mess with her, not. What he never expected was for his beloved family to pay the price.

He strode out the back entrance, emerging in the parking lot moments later. Poe was pacing back and forth across the roof of the Caddy.

"Is there something I should know, buddy?"

Squawking non-stop, Poe flapped his impressive wings—angry and fierce—the wind he created blowing strands of Mayhem's salt-and-pepper ponytail that he'd tucked in front of one shoulder.

"Please calm down." He mussed Poe's chest feathers with a hooked finger. "I hate to see you so dismayed."

When Poe quieted, Mayhem stroked the back of his head. "That's my good boy." He cooed. "Now, is Kimi all right?"

Poe didn't budge. If something happened to his mother—orphaned as a fledgling, Kimi was the only mother Poe ever knew—he would sound an unmistakable alarm. He also would not have come alone.

"Are the authorities getting too close to Chayton?"

No movement or change in demeanor.

"Has the gray wolf made a move?"

A machine gun blast thundered in Poe's throat, wings flapping chaotically.

"All right, shhh…" He waited for his loyal partner to settle down. "Do we know where Ms. Daniels is?"

An intense stare told him all he needed to know. Even though Mayhem did not possess the ability to communicate telepathically, body language broke the barriers between human and animal worlds. If folks took the time to mingle with wildlife, they'd be amazed at the wondrous gift God afforded us. It's a shame more people were not cognizant of that fact.

"We best find out, then. Round up Edgar and let's head to Saugus. Tell Allan to keep an eye on Mom, please. If the gray wolf sensed our presence at the reservation, he might feel the need to retaliate. That we cannot allow."

Poe leaped off the roof. A reverberating *ca-caw* coiled in his wake. Magnificent creature. What he wouldn't give to experience a crow's freedom and agility. It must be truly spectacular indeed. Mayhem slipped behind the wheel of his Caddy and sped out the lot a bit faster than usual, but he and Poe had to find Ms. Daniels.

Within twenty minutes he was cruising down Lyndsey Lane. Mayhem pulled curbside across from Ms. Daniels' quaint A-frame, with the roof angled so low the shingles practically kissed the grass. A metallic green Camry sat alone in the driveway.

Cat mustn't have left work yet. Since dead men did not announce their resurrection to the police, he planned to leave her a message at home. The old adage, "Work smart, not hard" applied to many things in life. Today, it promised to bend his feline friend's free will. The power of suggestion was the psychological process by which one person guided the thoughts, feelings, or behaviors of another, and the practice worked remarkably well.

Wearing black latex gloves, he reached between the plush bucket seats and withdrew a handcrafted cedar box from the middle compartment. In which he kept a sole pristine feather that he had rubbed down with cedar oil. As Poe and Edgar landed on the hood, he twirled twine around the quill and looped in his business card. He folded the package in a swath of genuine buffalo leather, tucked the ends inside the roll, and tied a twine bow to anchor the contents together.

Out the car, he swung his legs to the pavement. Feather in hand, he stood and nudged closed the driver's door, careful not to arouse suspicion.

"Wait here, please," he told the boys. "I shan't be long."

Climbing the steps to Ms. Daniels' front door, he constructed an excuse in case her roommate interrupted him. With no signs of movement indoors, he stood the feather in the mailbox, quill pointed down.

Ms. Daniels should understand what he expected of her.

CHAPTER EIGHTEEN

2:00 p.m.

Three-quarters of the way through my tattoo, and I was no closer to getting Devin Norton to confess than I was when I arrived. Actually, he didn't seem like that bad of a guy. No doubt Levaughn wasn't thrilled with my performance so far. I tried to gear the conversation toward the murder.

"So," I raised my voice over the buzzing, "your assistant told me someone murdered your business partner. Any idea who killed him?"

Devin shut down the tattoo gun. With a stone-cold expression, his cool hazel eyes narrowed on me. "Why would I know anything about it?"

"Whoa, down boy. I'm just makin' conversation. Relax."

I swear that dude growled at me. When he parted his lips, ZZ Ward's *Put the Gun Down*—my new ringtone—broke into his response, and saved my sorry ass.

With my left hand, my right forearm still extended on the arm rest, I fished my cell phone out of my back pocket and checked the caller ID. "Crap. Gotta take this."

Bowing his head, Devin restarted the tattoo gun and returned focus to the tattoo.

I held the phone to my ear. "Hey, Nay. What's up?"

"Uh...ya know the feather that's on the back-porch light?"

"Yeah. What about it?"

"Well, I found another one in the mailbox today. Only this one was wrapped in leather with some sort of card attached."

I sucked in a sharp intake of air. "Is it an all-white business card with nothing but one line of black raised lettering across the front?"

"Yeah. How'd you know? It looks like some sort of website address, but it doesn't have a dot com, dot net, or dot org at the end." The way she paused mid-conversation meant the words that followed would probably piss me off. "What's onion mean?"

For computer users who knew what they were doin', like *moi*, Onionland, as it's known, offered an exciting playground filled with information not available elsewhere. For hackers, it's the only way to surf the web. Period. 'Course, I'd never tell Nadine about my time spent on the Dark Net. She wouldn't understand that even places like the *New York Times* had an Onion site for whistleblowers. In her mind, the deep web—not "dark web" as it's wrongly referred—was solely for nefarious activities.

My mind raced for a response that would satisfy her curiosity, but I couldn't get over the balls on Mayhem. He went to my house in the middle of the day while Nadine was home alone. "Are you all right?"

"I'm fine. Why?"

Mayhem wasn't stupid. Far from it. A TOR site—an acronym for The Onion Router— offered web servers anonymity in the form of "hidden services." TOR hid the network's locations while still offering various kinds of services, such as web posting or instant messaging. By using TOR's "rendezvous points," other TOR users could connect to these hidden services without ever knowing the others network's identity. With an Onion site, Mayhem guaranteed anonymity while safeguarding his IP address.

Even though a hidden service needed to advertise its existence within the TOR network before clients could contact them, the service randomly chose relays, built circuits to said site, and asked them to act as an "introduction point" by revealing their public key. Their specific IP address remained anonymous.

By using a full TOR circuit, no one could associate these sites to an introduction point within the hidden server's IP address. Hence, why Mr. Mayhem never offered me a secret key like some sites used. His location was already secure. The other advantage of a full TOR circuit and the most logical reason why he'd chosen this path was that it also promised potential clients that they'd reached Mayhem through private messaging, and not some other psycho killer by mistake.

Without taking a breath, Nadine continued to fire off questions. "Who sent this? Why is someone sending you feathers? What do they mean? Are you in some sort of trouble again?" She gasped. "Don't even tell me you've been catting again."

There's that word again. She knew damn well how much I hated that expression. Bo Adams, my mentor and the best cat burglar in the business before his death, taught me to take pride in my work, to own the title of cat burglar. And so, I did. But lately, with Nadine and Levaughn watching my every move, I hadn't pulled a job since I'd stumbled across Mayhem draining a dying woman of blood.

Good times...not.

Once Nadine shut up long enough for me to get a word in, I said, "You done?"

Silence encompassed the line.

"Great. Take a pic and send it to me, will ya?"

"Can't you just come home?" Whimpering, her voice lowered to a whisper. "I'm scared, Shawnee. You never tell me anything."

"That's not true," I lied. "Nothin's goin' on. I swear. Send me the pic. Please?"

"What's that buzzing noise? Where are you?"

"It's nothin'. Don't worry about it." My BFF did not approve of tattoos. Perish the thought. In Ms. Librarian's words, women shouldn't scar their bodies with ink. At times, how we stayed friends all these years remained a mystery. This was one of those moments. "Can't you just send me the damn pic without the third-degree?"

After a never-ending pause that lasted close to two years, seemed like it anyway, she said, "Fine."

The line went dead.

Did she hang up on me? Way to make me feel like crap. She always pushed and pushed, never let me have two goddamn seconds to think through a response before spitting out a lie that would satisfy her. And she wondered why I kept secrets.

My cell phone signaled a text message. When I thumbed the button to enlarge the image, a photograph of a jet-black feather, white tufts at the base, filled the screen.

Devin glanced at my cell. "Y'know eagle feathers are illegal, right?"

"Wait. What?"

"It's none of my business." He re-lowered the tattoo gun to my arm. "Forget I said anything."

I pretended to scratch my leg, but what I was really doing was shutting off the transmitter. Once Levaughn couldn't listen in anymore, I stuck my cell phone in Devin's face, never considering the fact that the sudden disruption might cause him to give my angel a weird hump somewhere. "How positive are you that this is an eagle feather?"

"Hundred percent." No hesitation at all. "An adult bald

eagle, from the looks of it. Juveniles and young adults are more brown than black."

My eyes widened in disbelief. "Well aren't you just a fountain of information. Is the feather still illegal if I didn't harm the bird? For shits and giggles, let's say I found it in my backyard."

"Doesn't matter. The Migratory Bird Treaty Act lists bald eagles as a protected species. You're not allowed to possess any part of them, including their feathers."

Wow. Didn't see that comin'. Some might mistake Bob Marley's twin for just another black dude in dreads. And they'd be oh, so, wrong.

I prodded, "How do ya know all this?"

"Easy." He shrugged both shoulders. "I'm half Cherokee."

Mind blown.

Oh. My. God. Was Mayhem Cherokee, too? Could they know each other? If I could figure out why Mayhem kept sending me eagle feathers, maybe I could unscramble his cryptic speech at the diner. The first thing that sprang to mind was the Bloody Eagle, which was Jack Delsin's preferred murder method.

What're the chances of two serial killers—both Native American, I might add—who symbolically used the eagle? The odds must be astronomical. No way was this a coincidence.

While trying to remain respectful of his ethnicity, I dug for answers. "Tell me, what's an eagle feather represent to the Cherokee Nation?"

He set the tattoo gun on the tool chest behind him and swiped his gloved fingers through Vaseline. While massaging the jelly into my skin, he explained, "The colors of the tail feathers are divided into two parts, light and dark. These two colors come from the same feather, yet they represent opposites...darkness and light, male and female, substance and shadow, summer and winter, peace and war, life and death. Dualism within the eagle itself maintains balance in the circle of life."

Gulp. "Life and death?"

Obviously, he hadn't caught my shaken words, because he responded as though I hadn't said anything at all. "The eagle feather is a symbol of love, friendship, honor, bravery, and mystical powers."

In the past, Mayhem proved he had some clairvoyance, but mystical powers? That's a stretch and a half.

"Ever attend a Pow-Wow?" he said. "The headdresses are amazing, and most are made of eagle feathers. The cool part is, each feather represents a specific honor or incident of bravery. The more feathers in the headdress, the more the warrior is honored by his tribe." He took a hit off his bottled water. "The eagle feather can also be compared to wedding bands."

Against my will, my upper lip twitched. "Seriously?" Somewhere along the line, we'd ventured into Crazy Town, but I kept that to myself. If this dude could help me understand Mayhem's motivation, then I'd sit through just about any story he told.

Plus, y'know, he hadn't finished my tatt yet. It's a bad idea to piss off your artist halfway through the design. Been there, done that, got a mangled tattoo to prove it. Thankfully, only the men I slept with could see the one-winged butterfly, and they wouldn't dare complain. Blue balls surpassed curiosity.

"Totally serious. If a native man gives his bride an eagle feather, it's a symbol of their lifelong union. Did you know that no two feathers are identical? They're as different as fingerprints or snowflakes. The only exception is twin feathers, found on each wing of an eagle. In the past, American Indians were often seen riding off to war, or to hunt, with a single feather tied to their horse while their women slept at home with the matching feather tied to their bedposts."

Sorry I asked. His explanation left me more confused than ever. Did Mayhem want to kill me or marry me?

* * *

9:30 p.m.

After my covert assignment at The Other Guy's Tattoo Shop, we visited Austyn and Maggie. The moment I strolled through the front door, Maggie dove into my arms like she hadn't seen me in years. Not true. Nadine and I drove up three weeks ago, but it must've felt more like a year to Maggie.

Against the wall next to the doorframe leaned an overstuffed knapsack, with clothes bursting out the top. Levaughn must've already coordinated Maggie's trip with his sister. News to me. I had no idea she'd be riding back with us. With Mayhem lurking around, her safety was one more concern added to a growing list.

Hours later, after our visit, Levaughn pulled into the RPD parking lot, and the long day dragged on my shoulders. Still, I held a tight smile while I bundled Maggie and her enormous overnight bag into my jeep. Behind the wheel, I waved goodbye to Levaughn, prompting him to leave. Once his taillights faded into the darkness, I snatched my laptop off the backseat.

Maggie asked, "Aren't we going home?

"Yup. One sec, honey. I need to check somethin' for work real quick. It'll just take a sec." Using TOR, I logged into Mr. Mayhem's message board.

Dearest Cat,

Keep the eagle feather with you at all times. Are you familiar with the Story of Two Wolves?

An old Cherokee chief was teaching his grandson about life...

"A fight is going on inside me," he said to the boy. "It is a terrible fight, and it is between two wolves. One is evil—he is anger, envy, sorrow, regret, greed, arrogance, self-pity, guilt, resentment, inferiority, lies, false pride, superiority, self-doubt, and ego.

The other is good—he is joy, peace, love, hope, serenity, humility, kindness, benevolence, empathy, generosity, truth, compassion, and faith. This same fight is going on inside you, and inside every other person, too."

The grandson thought about it for a minute and asked, "Which wolf will win?"

The wise chief replied, "The one you feed."

It's imperative that we meet. Someone's feeding the wrong wolf.

Hugs & Kisses,
Mr. M

Cherokee? Like my tattoo artist? Maybe Levaughn was right about that dude. Were Mayhem and Norton working together?

CHAPTER NINETEEN

*"Ever had a memory that speaks out your eye
and rolls down your cheek?"*
- Unknown Author

9:30 p.m.

With Kimi enveloped in his arms, her back pressed against his chest, he stepped into the jetted tub. Cradling her in his arms, he lowered with her to the built-in seat, where her deteriorating muscles might find pain relief. This special time also helped him cope. Money could not buy good health. Or, in their case, time away from the disease. Life threw curveballs that no one ever suspected. Without faith and a deep-rooted appreciation for the wonderous gift of existence, speedbumps had the ability to destroy a happy home.

The unmerciful ache in his soul intensified with each tender stroke of his wife's arm. In the silence of the en-suite bathroom, he breathed her in. Tears filmed both his eyes. With clouded vision, he swallowed the sadness as it swelled in his chest. From the day of her diagnosis—the worse moment in his family's history, and the beginning of his destruction—he'd only faltered once in front of Kimi. That was the day he came to terms with losing her, be it from the ALS or the alternative method that she forced him to approve.

How do you kill the one person you would die to protect?

In the master bedroom, a special alert sounded from his cell phone. Which meant only one thing—someone posted an encrypted note to his website's message board.

"Guess who that is, my love." He kissed the back of Kimi's head, aromatic honeysuckle mushrooming across his face. "As usual, your plan worked perfectly. Let's hope she's smart enough to heed the warning."

Without the BCI technology, Kimi had no means to respond.

"How rude of me. I apologize, sweetheart. Not another word while we soak." With the hand-sprayer on low, he wet down her long, silky hair. Shampooed and conditioned her gorgeous mane, and then washed every inch of her from her neck to her toes, a fresh loofah removing dead skin cells and oils. Her beautiful face he cleaned with cold-cream-dipped fingertips, a pungent eucalyptus rising from the bathwater as he rinsed the residue with gentle palms.

With Kimi cradled in his arms, he rose. ALS had stolen most of her muscle mass. The bath towel hung off her delicate frame when he redistributed her dead weight to carry her into the bedroom, where he slipped a lace-trimmed nightgown over her head. This woman had cared for him since he was a young man. To help her now was not only an honor but a pleasure.

If only he could switch places with her. If given the chance, he would gladly absorb all her pain, all her daily struggles. But sadly, the good Lord had other plans.

He situated her in front of the computer, and she spelled out, "Read plz." Meaning, Ms. Daniels' message.

"As you wish, my darling." Still naked, he slipped on crisp, fresh jeans, the seam down the front of each leg ironed to perfection. Water trickled between his bare shoulder blades as he smoothed his hair back and tied an elastic around a low ponytail. Barefooted, he tiptoed over to the bed and snatched the cell phone from the pocket of his pin-striped suit jacket, draped over the footboard.

When he read the message, he grinned. Rather than read it aloud, he showed the note to Kimi.

Dear Mr. M,

Once bitten, twice shy. Nice try, though.

Signed,
Cautious Cat

"Well, darling, we have our answer. She clearly hasn't grasped the severity of the situation. Shame, really. It's a waiting game now, I'm afraid."

Across the computer screen, the BCI technology typed, "Tell her."

"But, honey, Ms. Daniels has made it clear that she does not want my help. I left her the feathers, did I not? What more do you want me to do?"

It took a lot of energy for Kimi to write a full sentence. "Cat needs 2 know."

"But I'm not sure she would even believe me if I told her."

She added an exclamation point to "Cat needs 2 know!"

In front of his wife, he sent a return message to Ms. Daniels.

Dearest Cautious Cat,

If we shut our eyes to dangers beyond our comprehension, we become powerless to fight. My offer still stands. Should you choose not to accept it, remember this…

When it comes your time to die, be not like those whose hearts are filled with the fear of death, so that when their time comes, they weep and pray for a little more time to live their lives over again in a different way. Sing your death song and die like a hero going home.

Hugs & Kisses,
Mr. M

CHAPTER TWENTY

10:30 p.m.

I n the loft, I tucked Maggie in my bed and then padded down the spiral staircase. At the bottom, Berkley weaved in and out of my legs, his black coat glistening. I swept him into my arms and fell back on the sofa, next to Nadine. Stroking his soft fur, I positioned my arm so my new tatt stayed facedown. The last thing I needed tonight was a lecture.

Nadine lowered her cozy mystery; doubt even one swear word soiled any page in the entire book. "That package is on the breakfast bar."

"Cool. Thanks." I set Berkley in Nadine's lap and strode toward Mayhem's latest game. Unfurling the leather, the eagle feather gleamed under the recessed lighting in the ceiling. Why would Mayhem send me this? I flipped open my laptop to see if he'd written back.

When I read his message, my mouth fell open. Die like a hero? What the hell did that mean?

From the sofa, Nadine said, "You gonna tell me who sent it, or leave me in the dark like you always do?"

Head whirling with endless scenarios, each one more dangerous than the last, I glanced over my shoulder at her. "Huh?"

"Who sent the feather?"

My gaze roamed around the living room but didn't connect with anything in particular. "Where's Katie McGuire? I haven't seen her at all since I got home."

Screeching outside the sliders whirled me around. One foot, the other, I crept toward the door, separated the louver blinds, and peered outside.

Pitch-darkness blanketed the deck.

Maggie yelled, "Help me, Shawnee!" But her voice was coming from the backyard. The only way out of the loft was to come down the spiral staircase. How'd I miss her? Not important. All that mattered was her safety.

I flicked on the porch light and whipped open the sliding door. "I'm comin', Mags!" Barreling down the stairs, I felt my back pocket for my mace. Empty. Shit. "Where are you, honey?"

From the shadows stepped the largest dog I'd ever encountered. On hind legs, he stood taller than me, with piercing yellow eyes. Spit dripped off his razor-sharp canines, a low rumble growling in his throat.

Frozen in place, our gazes locked. His intense stare held me hostage, his overpowering presence weakening my resolve.

With a raised paw—gigantic, distorted, uncharacteristically canine—he huffed gray powder in my face. Shielding my eyes, I stumbled backward. Choking, coughing, I could only make out shapes; no true definition. Grit coated my tongue, and I gagged. Bent in half, I laid both hands on bent knees and spit. Lengths of drool stretched past my chin, but I didn't care. In an attempt to clear the foul taste, I spit a second, third, and fourth time. Nothing worked. My inner cheeks, tongue, roof, and gums tingled.

Did he poison me?

By the time I was able to straighten, the dog had vanished into the woods.

I withdrew my cell phone and thumbed the flashlight app. Tracking the enormous pawprints should've led me to Maggie, but they ended mid-stride. Could dogs climb trees? Nah. Impossible.

My gaze ran the length of a tall oak tree. "You can come down now, honey."

Silence enveloped the backyard.

"Mags?"

From behind me, Nadine's high-pitched shrill shattered the stillness. "You scared me half to death, skulking around out here in the dark. What in God's name are you doing? Why'd you run outta the house like that?"

I spun back around. On the porch, Nadine held a tired Maggie by the hand. My nightshirt hung midway to Maggie's tiny shins as she rubbed a balled fist to one eye, her hair disheveled as though rousted from a deep sleep.

Was she a sleepwalker? For now, I ignored my pain-in-the-ass bestie. My heart was drumming way too fast to deal with her. Instead, I climbed the deck stairs and knelt to one knee in front of Maggie. "You okay, honey?"

She snaked her delicate arms around my neck. "I'm thirsty."

"I bet." I hoisted her into my chest as I stood, her legs entangled around my waist. "There's nothin' to be afraid of anymore," I lied. Why ruin her last shred of innocence with the realization that serial killers roamed free? "The mean doggy ran away."

Her face jerked off my shoulder. "Doggy, what doggy?"

"The one by the tree line. Didn't you see 'im?"

Nadine grabbed my upper arm and spun me around. "What're you talkin' about? We only walked outside a minute ago. Are you feelin' all right?" She reached for my forehead. Before she made contact her hand stopped mid-air, her nose crinkling in confusion. "What's all over your face?"

"Oh, umm...I dunno. Can you take her for a sec?" When I passed Maggie, my knees buckled beneath me. "Whoa." The area around me twirled like I'd stepped into the eye of a tornado, and I slapped a hand on the railing to keep from falling flat on my face.

Nadine shrieked, "Shawnee!"

I raised a half-curled palm to signal I was fine, but I didn't have the ability to form words. My head fogged. My sight blurred. My ears rang with such intensity, I could barely piece together what'd occurred between me and that evil dog. There's no way I could ever explain the bizarre encounter to Nadine.

"Go inside," I urged. "I just need a sec to catch my breath."

"Is that a tattoo on your forearm?"

"Not now, Nay. Please." I dropped my forehead into a cupped hand. "Get Maggie back in bed. I'll be right in to kiss her goodnight."

In the last week, a serial killer kept sending me eagle feathers, I failed a nine-year-old by not living up to her Wonder Woman image of me, my BFF was driving me half-insane, and tonight, a rabid dog almost blinded me.

What's next?

CHAPTER TWENTY-ONE

11:40 p.m.

Levaughn's cell vibrated the nightstand. Feeling around in the dark, he managed to find his phone, answered, "Samuels."

"It's Langley. LT told me to call. Promoters of New England's Sand Castle Festival forgot to cover their logo artwork before they left at dusk, so they returned to the beach tonight, and one of the women noticed someone suspicious hanging around the bathhouse. When she checked it out, she found a DB on the bench, with a decapitated head in its lap."

"Did she give a description?"

"Of the victim?"

It was much too late to deal with rookie questions, especially with the five-hour drive today, which proved almost worthless after the wire malfunctioned at the tattoo shop. "The suspect, Langley. You said the eyewitness saw someone hanging around the bathhouse. Did she get a good look at him?"

"Tall, thin, long black hair past the shoulders. Could be female. She wasn't close enough to say for sure."

"Female? Decapitation would be highly unusual. Female serial killers lean more toward poisoning. But I suppose nothing's out of the realm of possibility." He swung his feet to the wooden floorboards and flicked on the bedside lamp. "Don't let the witness leave the scene. I'm en route."

* * *

12:20 a.m.

Out front of the bathhouse on America's first public beach, Levaughn shoved the driver's door closed. The sand castle festivities weren't far from the bridge to Wonderland Station. How'd the eyewitness get a good look at the suspect from this distance, not to mention under cover of darkness? Unless she was part hawk, her details of the suspect were virtually impossible to prove.

So much for a solid lead.

The so-called eyewitness could wait. Rather than join Langley at the cruiser, he strode toward the remains. On the park bench sat a male headless body. The face in its lap, however, wore hot-pink lipstick. Blue eyeshadow drooped with the puffy lids. Mascara streaked lines down both sagging cheeks.

Over his shoulder, Odin said, "Transvestite? Interesting choice."

He clutched his heart. "What are you part cat?" Did Langley notify him, too?

"Sorry. Didn't mean to startle you." He took a swig of his coffee. "As I was saying, killing a transvestite adds a whole other layer. We could be looking at a hate crime. Or the killer might be confused sexually."

"What is it with you lately? Nothing about these murders have a sexual component, except your profile that feebly attempts to link decapitation to some sick fantasy." He scratched the stubble under his chin. "A hate crime? I gotta tell ya, SA Barrett, I don't buy it. To me, this looks more like revenge."

Before Odin interrupted, he flashed a flat hand. "Hear me out. To swing a sword with enough power to sever a head takes a great deal of strength, of anger. Speaking of details, the dog angle is out. The hairs we found belonged to Couturier's Great Dane."

"What about the red fibers? Have you gotten a report from the lab yet?"

"Not yet." Levaughn tilted his head to one side, trying to view the decapitation from a different angle. As he examined the make-up, he told Odin, "For now, I need you to concentrate on victimology. Somewhere these victims' lives intersect. Work, play, home. We figure out where and we'll be all that much closer to finding our guy. Also, since all the vics had the same tattooing, the sevens might be a hint to the killer's identity."

"I looked into the tattoos." He took another hit off his coffee, and Levaughn's stomach grumbled. "Seven means various things, depending on culture and religion. In numerology, a number seven is the seeker, the thinker, the searcher of truth. A seven doesn't take anything at face-value. He's always trying to understand the underlying truths. A seven knows nothing is exactly as it seems, and reality is often hidden behind illusions."

"Wow. Now that sounds like our guy. What other characteristics does a seven have?"

"Aloof, hates gossip, immune to small-minded backstabbing. Money means nothing to him. He will never choose a path based on the financial outcome. Rather, his strong sense of justice rules his actions."

Again, Levaughn scratched his beard stubble. Why didn't he take the time to shave before he left the house? The itch drove him nuts. "Uh-ha. Okay, that fits with my theory so far. What else?"

"A seven is not jovial. He has a dry, misunderstood sense of humor. Never superficial. Beautiful, shallow people bore him to no end. He's not passionate about politics. His emotions run on a much deeper level. Physically, he's lanky and tall."

Maybe the witness did catch a peek at the suspect.

He shot a quick text to Langley...

Get detailed description from witness. Time, where she stood, where suspect stood, lighting, distance, what she did before and after the encounter, including if she had a few drinks tonight. Usual drill. Then have her wait for me.

"Am I boring you?"

"Sorry." Levaughn dropped his cell phone into his jacket pocket. "We may have an eyewitness."

"Excellent. I can stay if you need to leave."

Nice try. It'd be a cold day in hell before he let Odin take the lead in one of his cases. "Nope. It's all good."

"Then shall I continue?"

Levaughn nodded as he dug out his cell to read Langley's response...

Copy that.

Odin rattled off particulars from his research into numerology. "Often times, sevens dominate fields like the military, academia, and science where logical, methodical analysis of facts are the main requirements of the job. Police detectives and laboratory researchers fit into that category, as well."

He cocked an eyebrow. "Are you sayin' we could be looking for a fellow cop?"

"Not necessarily, but we can't rule it out, either." Odin flipped open his notebook, where he'd jotted down information. "Not sure how far you want to take this seven angle but the meanings are vast. For example, also in numerology—which some refer to as the divine science of numbers—it's understood that each number carries with it a specific vibrational meaning that goes beyond a simple quantity. This vibrational frequency is also found in nature, as well as celestial beings."

Levaughn raised one eyebrow. "What's that now?"

"Think of it this way. Let's say you've been waking up at three-thirty-three a.m. for no apparent reason. One morning, after several days of this, you stop to grab a cappuccino and a scone. The total comes to three-dollars and thirty-three cents. That same afternoon, at three-thirty-three p.m., a fire alarm sounds inside the station house and you're escorted out of the building. As you wait in the parking lot, you notice the connection to this particular numeric series. If the fire drill was an actual emergency, the threes would take on a deeper meaning, as though your guardian angel was trying to warn you of the danger."

Tilting back his Dunkin' Donuts Styrofoam cup, Odin chugged his coffee. The aromatic brew tickled Levaughn's senses, his mouth watering, longing for a sip. Why hadn't he stopped on the way?

"These patterns are referred to as angel numbers," Odin continued. "Single digits are not excluded. Angel numbers work through meaningful coincidence or synchronicity, a term coined by—" he flipped back a few pages— "psychologist CG Jung, who believed our minds are connected to a universal whole that he called the Collective Unconscious. It's a fascinating study, actually."

"What the hell? I'll bite. What does seven mean in angel numerology?" Little doubt existed that he'd soon regret asking the question.

"Well, that's where things get complicated. You see, some numerologists believe the number seven is so perfect and powerful that it represents a connection to the universe. It opens the door to a realm beyond our cosmic reach, a world that holds all the answers to life's greatest mysteries. There's virtually no single culture in history that the number seven doesn't play an important role—all in a positive way. Take our calendar, for example. Weeks are broken into seven-day increments. Also, if you look at ancient scripts, Egyptian hieroglyphics, or religious texts, the number seven appears more than any other number, and in almost every case, it's a good sign."

"Hmm..." Levaughn studied the inverted seven tattoo below the hip. "So, maybe this mirrored image shows the negative side of seven. Is that possible?"

"Anything's possible when dealing with a psychopathic or sociopathic mind."

Staring at the two sevens, an empty pit widened in Levaughn's gut. From memory, he recited a bible passage. "For in six days the Lord made the heavens and the earth and the sea and all that is in them, but on the seventh day, He rested."

Odin's eyebrows rose in amazement. "Exodus 20:11. Very good. There's also Leviticus 16:29 and 23:27, the Day of Atonement in the seventh month."

"Whoa. Never considered that we're in July. Maybe the sevens are biblical references." Levaughn snatched his cell to bring up the *King James Bible*, but before he had a chance, Odin recited the scripture.

"Leviticus 16:29. And this shall be a statute forever unto you, that in the seventh month, on the tenth day of the month, ye shall afflict your souls and do no work at all, whether it be one of your own country or a stranger that so journey among you. For on that day shall the priest make an atonement for you, to cleanse you, that ye may be cleansed from all sin before the Lord."

"Show off." Levaughn grinned to show that he was kidding. "What's the date today?"

"July ninth."

"So, if you're right, then tomorrow should be the suspect's day of rest."

"Unless the UNSUB's referencing Leviticus 23:27. In which

case, tomorrow's homicide could be worse than the others. Scripture says, *also on the tenth day of this seventh month there shall be a day of atonement; it shall be a holy convocation unto you, and ye shall afflict your souls, and offer an offering made by fire unto the Lord.*"

"Crap. All we need is for him to set a decapitated corpse ablaze. Let's hope you're wrong, then."

"There's one other scripture that's worth noting, Numbers 19:11. *He who touches the dead body of anyone shall be unclean for seven days. He shall purify himself with the water on the third day and on the seventh day, then he will be clean. But if he does not purify himself on the third day and on the seventh day, he will not be clean.* This verse also applies to soldiers and/or warriors in battle. The seven days gave them time to not only purify their bodies but also their souls, like a cooling off period before they returned home to their loved ones."

"That may explain why he dumps the vics near the ocean—to purify himself after the murder." A renewed energy rising in his chest, Levaughn scribbled the biblical references in his notebook. "I need a new psychological profile that focuses on what we've discussed here. Thatta problem?"

"Not at all. I'll get started on it right away."

He patted Odin's shoulder. "Thanks."

Perhaps he wasn't such a bad guy after all. As a born and bred Baptist, he certainly knew the *Holy Bible* from cover to cover. If the suspect was, in fact, a religious fanatic, his faith might actually be his downfall.

Wouldn't that be ironic?

CHAPTER TWENTY-TWO

"Everything on Earth has a purpose,
Every disease, an herb to cure it,
And every person, a mission.
This is the Indian Theory of Existence."
- Morning Dove Salish

Early Monday morning
1:10 a.m.

After Kimi fell asleep, Mayhem left the brownstone. Chayton had asked for his help with a particularly suspicious individual. Guilty men tended to keep an eye out for potential dangers, but there were ways around that—a fact Chayton would need to learn should he choose to continue this line of work.

Outside, standing by the Caddy in his designated parking space, he called for Poe. A smart man never whistled at night, for it might draw unwanted attention. Normally he would never even bother Poe while he roosted—gathering with other crows played an important role in their society—but if Poe discovered that he'd left him behind, he would be extremely upset. His loyalty surpassed most humans'.

Within a few minutes, Poe glided by the security lights and landed on the Caddy's roof.

"Thank you for your promptness. I need to run an errand for our mutual friend, and I could use your assistance. Would you care to join me?" He stroked his feathers. "Please don't feel obligated."

With an eager stare, Poe bounced up and down, his outstretched wings gleaming a stunning bluish-black in the cascade of moonlight.

Adorable. "I'll take that as a yes." He reached into his leather blazer and withdrew a *Ziploc* baggy, where he'd packed several fresh strawberries, halved. "A quick snack to show my appreciation." He passed a piece to Poe.

The fruit disappeared in a millisecond, and he reopened his beak.

"I suppose one more couldn't hurt. But then we really should head out. I'd rather not leave Mom for too long, as I'm sure you will agree."

Juices leaked down Poe's chest feathers when he threw his head back, devouring the strawberry.

Mayhem withdrew a hanky. "We've talked about your approach before." He wiped Poe's sticky feathers clean. "If you hope to have a lady friend one day, you will need to work on your manners. Thoreau was the same way before he met your birth mother, Annabel."

Before opening the driver's door, he kissed the top of Poe's head. "Ride with me, please. I'd rather you not fly alone after dark. Another run-in with one of your wildlife enemies could turn deadly without Edgar and Allan to back you up."

On the drive to Lynn, Poe perched on Mayhem's thigh, gazing out the passenger window while Mayhem stroked his back. This was not the first time he'd ridden in the Caddy, but he much preferred his own mode of transportation. Perfectly reasonable. After all, a magnificent wingspan was truly one of the Creator's finest creations.

Arm draped over the back of the seat, Mayhem reversed into a dark corner of D'Amici's Bakery parking lot. The heavenly aroma of fresh-baked Italian Scala wafted through the open window, and he reclined his head. Closing his eyes, he took a moment to appreciate Mr. Smith's talent. Shame he had to die, but someone must pay for the carnage his family caused.

About ten minutes later, a man in a white apron exited the building. While his key was still in the lock, Mayhem crept up behind him, with Poe riding on his shoulder. "Mister Adrian Smith, I presume?"

The baker whirled around. He first glanced at Poe, then at Mayhem, then Poe again, and back to Mayhem, as if trying to make sense of the relationship. "How do you know my name? Who are you?"

"How rude of me." He jutted out a gloved hand. "Mr. Mayhem and this gorgeous creature is Poe. Pleasure to make your acquaintance. It's unfortunate that we need to meet under such nefarious circumstances."

"Look, buddy. I just finished a ten-hour shift, so if you don't mind..."

"Actually—" he stepped closer, and Poe leaned in— "I do." As he narrowed on the man's widened eyes, he slid a hunting knife from the sheath on his belt. Paused till the moonlight kissed the blade, and then grinned. "I need to pat you down for weapons. Please do not resist. I would hate for things to turn ugly at this point."

The man couldn't tear his gaze away from Poe.

"Please don't stare, Mr. Smith. It's rude, and he doesn't like it." Once Mayhem finished searching the baker, he listed his head to one side, his complete focus on the man's harried expression. "What's going through your mind right now?"

"W-what?"

"Pardon me. Perhaps I should rephrase. Are you frightened? I realize the question is a bit obvious, but I find myself genuinely curious about your innermost reaction to my presence. Will you share with me?"

"I...I..."

He snickered. "Cat got your tongue, Mr. Smith?"

"W-what do you want me to say?"

"Why, the truth of course. This is certainly not the time to lie."

Mr. Smith yelled, "Help!"

And Mayhem heaved a sigh. Why must they always ruin the moment? He spun the baker around and shoved him toward the Caddy. Poe soared ahead, landed on the roof, and tossed a deadpan glare at Mr. Smith, who was dragging his feet like a death row inmate on his way to the execution chamber. Once he got within a few feet of the passenger door, he spun—reached for the hunting knife—and Mayhem slashed open his palm, blood gushing from the wound.

"Well, now I'm afraid you must ride in the trunk." He shoved the bleeding man toward the back bumper. Waving his foot under the car, the trunk hatch rose by itself. Prior to leaving the brownstone, Mayhem had lined the truck in plastic for this very reason. Some people were so predictable at times. "Climb inside please, Mr. Smith."

Cradling his hand, blood leaking down his forearm, the young baker pleaded for his life. "Don't do this. I'm sorry, all right? I panicked. If you were in my position, you would've done the same thing."

Without a word, Mayhem shoved him inside the trunk and slammed the lid. A strong character was so hard to find these days. Shame, really. He hustled around to the driver's door.

Before he climbed inside the vehicle, he paused a moment to appreciate this wondrous universe.

"Beautiful night, isn't it, buddy? Look at all those stars." He jutted a finger at the sky. "Oh, look, the Big Dipper. One might even call it kismet, considering our goal tonight."

Ca-caw! Poe concurred.

CHAPTER TWENTY-THREE

Monday
6:45 p.m.

I was not a fan of Mondays, but I only had fifteen minutes till the end of my shift. After examining crime scene photos of Amanda Orme—her head found on one part of Revere Beach, her body on another—I searched social media for clues.

Why would the killer tattoo double-sevens on the body?

Levaughn also theorized two killers might be working in tandem, one in Massachusetts, one in New Hampshire, but the more I dug, the less convinced I became. Lieutenant Holt continued to cut several rolls of red tape. Without the two states sharing information, the killer, or killers, could walk.

That I couldn't allow. As it was, I could barely lay my head down at night after making a deal with the devil aka Mr. Mayhem. No way would another serial killer escape justice on my watch.

The complex MO—the number seven tattooed on the victim's chest, an inverted seven tattooed right below the hipline—indicated one killer to me. But if there were, in fact, two, they must have a way to communicate. Stalking social media seemed like the easiest way to prove it, but without a positive ID on the latest victim, my job turned grueling and repetitive. There's only so many political rants, video life stories, and garden photos I could take.

Before the end of my shift, my fingers tapped the keys one last time.

If Amanda Orme's Facebook posts were any indication, she seemed a little twisted in the head. Lots of murder memes. Casual jokes about serial killers. I mean, c'mon! The chick's favorite holiday was Halloween for chrissakes. Unless it was all an act. Hard to tell these days.

Fifteen minutes later, I logged off and bustled past the desk sergeant and out the main entrance.

Halfway to my jeep, a crow swooped out of a nearby tree, and I ducked. The gold band on his ankle indicated he was Mayhem's pal, Poe. I was about to tell him to beat it when the back of my tongue swelled. Gasping for air, I latched a hand around my throat. Poe flew closer, encircling my head as if waiting for me to pass out. Or worse, suffocate to death.

I stumbled toward my jeep.

Long gouges scratched the paint while I missed the hole for the key about a million times. In the window, my reflection stared back at me. I stuck out my tongue—the back near my tonsils was as black as the eagle feathers Mayhem left for me. Poe squawked, carried on and on, his caws burrowing deep into my bones. I couldn't tell if my suffering excited him or if he feared for my safety. Probably the former.

One thing was for sure. He knew something I didn't.

I managed to open the driver's door and collapse inside. Poe landed on the hood. As he stormed closer to the windshield, he cocked his head, as if taking mental snapshots of my condition to report back to Mayhem. Was he waiting for me to die? Did

Mayhem lace the feathers with venom? Maybe that's why he told me to carry one with me at all times.

Closing my eyes, I counted...one, Mississippi...two, Mississippi...three, Mississippi...By the time I got to ten, I'd barely gotten my breathing under control. When I reopened my eyes, two other crows stood wing-to-wing with Poe on the hood—six beady eyes staring through the glass. I set my left hand on the steering wheel, and it slipped off as if I had no control over it. With my hand in my lap, pins and needles spread from the wrist to the tip of my fingers. I leaned toward the side mirror and stuck out my tongue again.

Still half-black. What the hell's happening to me?

Using only my right hand, I slid my laptop off the passenger seat and logged into Mayhem's message board.

Mr. M,

Lone Ranger will be there in 15 min. Tonto better not be late.
Better the devil you know than the one you don't, I guess. I'm leaving word with Inspector Clouseau, so don't try anything stupid.

Signed,
Pink Panther

I hollered out the window at Poe and the gang. "You win! Happy? Now, get the hell off my jeep!"

When I glanced at the laptop, Mayhem had already written back. That was fast. It's almost like he knew the exact moment when I'd cave to the pressure. Was he stalking me?

Dearest Pink Panther,

Air support will escort you to the new rendezvous point. Please refrain from pestering them. It's unbecoming and rude. We'll discuss the Tonto remark in person.

Hugs & Kisses,
Mr. M

Uh-oh, he's pissed. In retrospect, the Tonto reference might not've been my best choice of words ever. With any luck, he'd forget all about it. Yeah, right. I had a better shot of stumbling across Dwayne Johnson aka The Rock sprawled across my bed, naked, with a red rose clenched between his teeth.

With a quick scan of the parking lot, I searched for Mayhem's Caddy or the gold Hummer, but couldn't find either vehicle. Leaning forward, I squinted at Poe's gold ankle band. Unlike the night I rescued Maggie from the House of Horrors, he only wore one, and nothing indicated it had a microphone or camera attached.

Then how did Mayhem know that I yelled at his freakshow?

As if Poe could read my thoughts, he glared at me through the windshield. My neck turtled between my shoulders, and I offered him an awkward grin. "Sorry." I swallowed hard. "Lead the way?"

Needless to say, nothing about this situation elicited a warm and fuzzy response, in me or them. The three crows leaped off the hood and took flight. A glance back from Poe urged me to follow. I started the engine and shifted into first gear, my knee helping me steer. Banged second, then third to keep up as the crows cawed non-stop, no doubt discussing how moronic it was for me to follow.

Admittedly, they had a point. But I had to figure out why these weird things kept happening before I landed in a hospital. Or worse, in a morgue.

The crows led me into Lynn. I hadn't been back since last

year. They headed toward the entrance to Lynn Woods, and I slammed on the brakes.

How stupid does Mayhem think I am? No way am I going back into that underground bunker, at least not willingly.

Aw, shit. This really was a trap, and I'd fallen right into it. *Nicely played, asshole.*

I jammed the shifter into reverse, but then my laptop dinged. Glancing at the message board, Mayhem had left a new note.

Dearest Cat,

I realize this locale may stir some negativity for you, but it's imperative that we speak in private. As it is, I have no business meddling in matters of this nature. The least you could do is trust that I will not harm you during your time here. I can assure you, if I wanted you dead, you would be.

Hugs & Kisses,
Mr. M

Every inch of my being warned me not to follow Poe, but I did it anyway. Albeit, reluctantly. My foot pressed the gas pedal, then the brake, then the gas, then the brake. It may sound silly to trust a serial killer—believe me, I get it—but Mayhem had this trancelike way about him that compelled me to comply, no matter how hard I tried to resist.

The murder of crows soared in circles above the entrance to an unmarked footpath, a symphony of caws echoing through the treetops. I slid the shifter into first gear, killed the engine, and yanked up the emergency brake. With any luck, I wouldn't die here.

Cradling my numb left hand, my right bracing it against my washboard abs, I hiked up a stone-treaded walkway to an area I'd never been before. Rough terrain, massive rocks, the pine-needled trail led to a stream with single file boards laid across the water, from the side where I stood to the continuation of the path.

Angry caws coiled through the canopies of oak, maple, and birch leaves, Poe screeching at levels unfit for human ears. I'd made it halfway across the rickety bridge when Mr. Mayhem stepped out from behind a hundred-foot conifer. I stopped dead.

"Thank you," he said.

"For what?"

"Why, your trust, of course."

This time, I let the eyes roll. "Listen, pal, don't mistake my presence for anythin' other than what it is—necessity."

"Pal." He chuckled. "Love your style, I really do."

I firmed a hand on my hip. "So you've said. Tell me why I'm here."

"Why are the youth of today always in such a rush?" He swept his arm in a semi-circle. "Look at the beauty that surrounds us. Take a moment to absorb Mother Earth in all her glorious wonder." Like a friggin' fruitcake, he closed his eyes and inhaled pine-scented air. "Ahh...isn't she beautiful?"

"Enough!" I stomped my boot, and the wooden boards quaked beneath me. "Why am I here, dammit?"

"It's become obvious that you are not in the right frame of mind, I'm afraid. Shame, really. I had such high hopes this time. Ah, well, I gave it the ol' college try." He tipped his fedora. "Contact me when you *are* ready to listen."

"Wait—" I hopped on to the dirt trail, inches from the serial killer who'd nearly killed me and Levaughn months earlier, my pulse soaring higher than an eagle's nest. Blood surged through my veins, scorched me from the inside out, rising in my chest, my face sheathed in sweat.

As casual as ever, Mr. Mayhem said, "Yes?"

"Look." I stuck out my semi-black tongue, the tip and rims still flesh-toned. "You owe me an explanation."

"Oh, my. That changes things. Follow me." When he turned to leave, I latched onto his leather suit jacket that probably cost more than my annual salary. Slow, almost robotic, he rotated toward me. A slight smirk emerged as his gaze lowered to my hand.

I let go.

Backing away, panic thrashed at my ears. Screw this. A victim, I was not. Besides, Mayhem didn't deserve the upper hand. If tonight was the night I died, then so be it, but I sure as hell wasn't going down without a fight. "Tell me the truth. You helped The Creator kill those people. Because if you didn't, then why else taunt me with black feathers?"

"Quid pro quo applies. I will answer one of your questions if you answer one of mine. Do we have a deal?" He extended a gloved hand, but I wasn't stupid enough to shake on it.

"Why not." I shrugged. "I've got nothin' left to lose." *Except my life.* "Let's play."

"Super. Jack Delsin—wrongly dubbed The Creator, I might add—worked alone. As I told you earlier, I knew him. A powerful man, ol' Jack. I believe it's my turn now." He rubbed his gloves together. "What is your last memory of your parents?"

I should've told him to pound sand...but I didn't. Instead, I played his stupid game.

Raking a hand through my hair, I stared up at the open sky, its dusky hue lulling me to share one of the worst moments of my life. "The night they died, I begged my mom and dad not to go out, but Ms. Andrews had already shown up to watch me. I should've cried harder. I should've pleaded with them not to leave the house. But I didn't. Ms. Andrews assured me everything would be okay. But it wasn't okay."

Tears trickled from the corner of my eye, and I wiped them away as quickly as they fell. "It will never be okay. And now, I have to live with the knowledge that while I waved goodbye to my parents, I let them walk out of my life forever."

Why was I telling him this crap? Mayhem had a way of digging through my subconscious, and I was paralyzed to fight it. I should've never played into his mind games, but I needed answers.

"Aw, I'm sorry." He pouted his lower lip. "That's a heavy burden for a child to carry. You do know their passing was out of your control. If memory serves, I believe you said they were murdered. Did you not?"

"Nice try." I pulled back my shoulders, stood straighter, taller. "It's my turn, Mr. M. Quid pro quo, remember?"

He grinned. "I do, yes."

"If you weren't involved with Jack Delsin, then why bring him up at the diner?"

"Ah, you are a sharp one. I'll need to first ask a follow-up question, if I may. My answer will depend on your truthfulness. At the precise moment of Jack's death, did you experience anything unusual? A spiritual awakening, perhaps?"

How did he know? I'd never told anyone what happened between us that day. I debated whether to lie. In the end, I admitted the truth, even though I still couldn't wrap my head around it. "When he died, his spirit passed through me. Sounds insane, I know. Believe me, it was one of the strangest moments of my life. But I'm guessing you already knew that, or you wouldn't've asked. There, I answered your question, now answer mine."

"Fair enough. Jack and my wife had history. The details of which are not important. Suffice it to say, Jack and I didn't always see eye-to-eye, but I did respect him on a spiritual level. The reason you felt what you did the day he crossed over was that he meant for you to."

Weaving his fingers together, his hands dangled in front of a tasteful yet elegant turquoise stone on his belt. "You see, there are things in this world that defy reason, defy logic. And these beings that I speak of surpass most people's capabilities to understand. That, however, does not make them any less real."

Against my will, my lip curled into a snarl. "Y'mean like ghosts?"

"*Au, contraire.* These gentlemen—and I use the term loosely —live in our world, the physical plane if you will. I am referring to evil, Ms. Daniels, pure evil, palpable evil that you are clearly unprepared to battle."

Obviously, we'd crossed into Crazy Town again. "So, demons, then."

"Once again, you refuse to listen. This was a waste of time. You're not ready to comprehend what I am telling you."

"Here we go. For shits and giggles, let's say you're right and move on. I came here for one reason and one reason only, to find out what you laced the eagle feathers with because obviously, you did somethin' to 'em. Just tell me one thing before I split. It's payback, right?"

As though I'd offended him, he jolted back. "Payback for what, if I may ask?"

"How the hell should I know? You're the serial killer, not me. Maybe you wanted revenge for your boy, Delsin. Or to elim-inate the one person who could identify you." Shit. Now was not the time to remind him that I could get his ass thrown behind bars. "Only you know why you did it."

"Dear girl—" he wagged his head in disappointment— "you have completely misinterpreted my meaning."

I raised my chin, refusing to let him double-talk me. "Enlighten me, then."

When he parted his lips, Poe swooped down and biffed me upside the head with his wing. He landed on Mayhem's shoul-der, and Mr. M dug into his jacket pocket and withdrew one perfect cherry. While he held the stem, Poe gobbled down the fruit in one bite.

Hope he chokes on it.

"Please excuse him," remarked Mayhem. "I'm afraid he still harbors a bit of resentment. You did slap him out of mid-air, after all."

Poe bent closer, glowering at me as if the incident happened yesterday.

"But that was a total accident." I threw up my hand just as another crow flew in, and my fingers tangled around his outstretched talons. He spiraled to the ground in front of Mayhem. "For fuck's sake! Someone needs to keep these crows on a leash!"

The air grew thick.

Uh-oh. If he didn't kill me—right here, right now—it'd be a miracle. The only plus here was that he'd witnessed the whole thing. Surely, he could tell the collision wasn't my fault. The crow flew into me, not the other way around. If nothing else, Mr. Mayhem was a reasonable man, right?

"Ms. Daniels," his tone turned cold, vengeful, callous, "if you insist on behaving in this vile manner, with a blatant disregard for the world around you, I will lose my patience. Neither of us wants that."

Correction: he's psychotic. I must've been outta my frickin' mind to come here.

With the dazed bird cradled in his black-leathered palm, Poe gazing down at his compadre from his shoulder perch, Mayhem nudged a cherry toward its beak. Then shot me a side-stare, as if he were the Great Shepherd and I was the asshole after his flock.

"That's my good boy," he crooned. "Shake it off, Edgar."

Backpedaling, I tried to reason with him. "I would never harm an animal, even one hellbent on making me look guilty." My anger got the best of me, and I jabbed a chin at Poe. "He probably planned the whole thing."

Mayhem paused a moment before responding in a cool tone.

"If that were true, Ms. Daniels, then even you must admire his brilliance."

"No, I don't."

"I see. What a shame. I'm afraid I've misjudged you. This meeting is adjourned." Once again, he tipped his fedora. "Stay safe, Cautious Cat."

"Fine. You win. He's brilliant. Okay?" Unbidden, the forest around me spun like a newly-wound top—faster and faster. Tree bark, moss-covered rocks, thick brush, a streak of black…tree bark, moss, brush, several wings flapping in unison…tree bark, moss, thick brush, water…

Mayhem hooked my arm before I took a header in the stream. But I didn't have the energy to push him away, my body uncooperative, my mind spent.

When I was finally able to regain my bearings, my focus narrowed, eyes slitted at the serial killer in my midst. "You did this to me."

"I assure you, Ms. Daniels, I did not."

"But the eagle feathers…"

"You are so predictable at times." Again, he wagged his head in disappointment, and I'd had just about enough of that crap. "Dear girl, the eagle feathers are for your protection, not your destruction. *He will cover you with feathers, and under his wings you will find refuge. His truth is your shield and armor.* ~ Psalms 91:4."

Now he's quoting bible passages? Rather than call him on it, I asked, "Protection from what, exactly?"

He explained that someone hired a hitman of sorts, that this killer wouldn't rest until he murdered me, that this killer was evil personified, unimaginable darkness. That after my death, he still wouldn't stop. Next, he'd kill everyone I ever cared about. And that this executioner would be my ultimate undoing. There's nothing I could do to stop him. Unless…I surrendered. Which meant, putting all my trust into the most prolific serial killer this state had ever known.

"How do I know this isn't just an elaborate trap to silence me?" What possessed me to keep reminding him that I could get him locked up? *Get it together, Daniels.*

He shot me a look as if I'd disappointed him again. "If you truly believe that, then we have nothing more to discuss."

"Listen to me. Maggie came to visit. I can't let anything happen to her or Nadine." I clawed a hand through the bottom of my hair, sap collecting under my half-bitten nails as I conceded. "Fine. Whaddaya need me to do?"

A wide smile spread across his face and churned the acids gurgling in my gut. "I'll be in touch. In the meantime, make a list of your enemies. Who wants you dead, Ms. Daniels?"

An easier question might be, who didn't?

CHAPTER TWENTY-FOUR

6:45 p.m.

At the end of the day, Levaughn conducted his own research into why a suspect might scalp his victim. Odin's explanation that a scalp was simply easier to transport than a human head seemed contrived, at best.

The first article stated that while long believed to be a traditional Native American practice, modern apologists argued that Europeans introduced the custom of taking scalps from slain or captive enemies in America.

During King Philip's War of 1675–1676 in New England, the colonies of Connecticut and Massachusetts offered bounties for the scalps of their Wampanoag enemies. Colonial authorities paid ten shillings to Indians and thirty shillings to non-Indians for every enemy scalp. The French in Canada first encouraged the scalping of whites. In 1688, they offered ten beaver pelts for every scalp brought to them.

Scalping and scalp bounties continued through the colonial wars of the eighteenth century, with a noticeable increase in colonists' willingness to scalp Native enemies.

In the American colonies, a posse of New Hampshire volunteers came across a band of encamped Native Americans and scalped ten, in the first significant appropriation by European colonists. When they returned to Boston, the group received a bounty of one-hundred pounds per scalp from colonial authorities. In addition to its value as a war trophy, a scalp was often believed to bestow the possessor with the powers of the scalped enemy.

Butchering the skin from an enemy's skull became a widespread practice across the country—America's dirty little secret that played a hidden role in every major moment in the nation's history. Settlers of the New World treated scalping as nothing more than an efficient way to take home the enemy's head.

Wow. As much as it pained Levaughn to admit, Odin's explanation might be spot-on. The suspect scalped the victims as a memento of the kill. Could it be that simple? Keeping trophies did align with serial murder, so he clicked the next article.

Which stated that not long after the *Mayflower* set sail to the New World in search of a Christian utopia, white men began coveting scalps, the first scalps claimed during the Pequot War. When Native Americans killed a trader named John Oldham, the Puritans of the Massachusetts Colony started fighting a full-on war with their neighbors. Soon, the governor promised a reward for any man who could bring home the head of a Native American. Heads, though, were large and cumbersome, and the men could only carry a few. So, instead, the Puritans filled their bags with bloody scalps.

There's the reference again. More and more it looked like Odin nailed it. He read on...

Other colonies followed suit.

By 1641, the governor of New Netherlands put out the first official bounty on any and all scalps from a Native's head. The Massachusetts Bay Colony also had their own bounty of forty pounds for the scalps of warriors and twenty pounds for women, the same bounty for children under the age of twelve years old. The governor declared open season on Native Americans. Every citizen was called upon to embrace the opportunity to pursue, capture, kill, and destroy them all.

In the early 1700s, some U.S. Rangers worked full-time as scalp collectors. They traveled into the wilderness searching for Native Americans to kill, determined to bring home a bag full of scalps and reap the rewards. One of the most successful was a man named John Lovewell, who became a minor celebrity for the vast number of scalps he brought home. At one point, he sewed a wig from the torn scalps of the men he'd killed, and then paraded through the streets of Boston wearing his prized possession.

Scalping was a profitable business.

An electrical surge shot through Levaughn, and he jolted to his feet.

In a flash, Odin hurried to his side. "Why the look? Did you find something specific that points to the UNSUB?"

Shuffling papers around his desk, Levaughn couldn't find what he was looking for. "Where's the Couturier file?"

"On my desk. Why?"

"I read somewhere that his business partner was half-Cherokee."

Odin sighed. "If this is about scalping the victims, I told you, it's most commonly practiced for convenience."

"I don't disagree, but we'd be remiss if we didn't look into his alibi. Where's his written statement?" His gaze skimmed the murder board toward the back of the room. Under Devin Norton's photo, his alibi read, "At home with kids." "Has anyone confirmed that he was, in fact, home the night Patrick Couturier was killed?"

"Yes. Around the time of the murder, Norton was on the phone with his common law wife, who was attending a baby shower."

Levaughn's lips twisted. "That's convenient."

"I know, but cell towers back up his story."

Levaughn fell back into his leather desk chair, his arms dangling off the edge. "Crap."

Hovering over his shoulder, Odin was reading the article on Levaughn's flat-screen. "Ah, yes, the dispute between soldiers and the local Cheyenne tribe during the Civil War. Heartbreaking story."

"Think it's worth looking into as a motive?"

He covered his heart with a flat hand. "In my personal opinion, war crimes aren't the answer. Nothing about the MO matches the story. If it did, the victims would be butchered, with their ears and noses cut off, as well as their genitalia. Colonel John Chivington was a real piece of work. It's disgraceful how he slaughtered the entire Cheyenne tribe, not to mention the massacre of their chief." He pointed to the screen. "Check out this quote."

"Damn any man who sympathizes with Indians," declared Chivington. "Kill and scalp all, big and little; nits make lice."

Odin added, "What the article fails to recognize is the story of a white man named John Smith whose son died with the others in the camp. When he went in to claim the remains, he witnessed bodies lying everywhere, cut to pieces, scalped and brutalized. Even the children and women, some of whom had their unborn babies ripped out of their wombs. The worst, though, was the body of a man called White Antelope, who after being scalped and defaced, had his testicles cut off and turned into a tobacco pouch—a keepsake for the soldiers who slaughtered a peaceful village."

Levaughn spun his chair to face him. "Hope you're right about this. War crimes or no, this story seems like the perfect reason for revenge. Unfortunately, the sevens tattoos and the location of the body dumps don't fit." He rose to his feet, patted Odin's shoulder. "C'mon. I've got an idea."

CHAPTER TWENTY-FIVE

8 p.m.

After Mayhem sprinkled a silky-yellow, powdery-like substance into my numb palm, the feeling returned to my left hand. I was so shocked that it worked, I couldn't form the words to ask what it was, or how this was even possible. He then told me to figure out who might want me dead. Ed Parsons, controller of my trust fund, was the first person who sprang to mind. Problem was, last I checked he was in a coma.

Since I hadn't visited the hospital in months, I cruised to Boston after I left Lynn Woods. Massachusetts General Hospital's main campus spanned nearly thirty buildings, housing inpatient and ambulatory care services, as well as research labs, administrative offices, and amenities like cafeterias, cafes, a chapel, healing garden, gift shop, even a museum.

In the parking lot, I slammed the driver's door and careened across the asphalt. Rather than deal with the front desk, I took the stairs two at a time, burst through the door, then slowed when I reached the long corridor of rooms outside the entrance to the ICU. If they'd moved Ed, I'd have no choice but to ask for the room number. Which would totally ruin the surprise.

Rest up, asshole. You're mine now.

I skulked down the hall. The door to his room was closed. With two faint warning knocks, I slipped inside.

"Hey there, kiddo." Propped up in bed, Ed acted as if nothing had transpired between us like this was an ordinary night and he hadn't confessed to Jack Delsin.

Nice act, but I didn't buy it for a second. Without a word, I dug the letter out of my wallet and tossed it on the bed. My upper cheek twitched, my eyes narrowing to thin slits. "You prick. How dare you sit there like an innocent man. You belong in prison with the rest of the felons, and as soon as I find enough evidence, I'll lock your ass away for life. Feel free to destroy that, by the way." I jabbed a chin at the lined paper, folded and refolded so many times it left worn-thin creases. "It's a copy."

Complete bullshit, but he didn't need to know that. Truth was, I'd read the letter so many times I'd almost become numb to its contents. Once Levaughn told me the confession wasn't enough for an arrest without corroborating evidence, I pretty much lost all hope of seeking justice. In the eyes of the law, Ed's attorney could argue the confession was made under duress before Delsin hung him from the rafters in his home.

Too bad he didn't kill the bastard.

"I wondered when you'd show." Ed never even glanced at the paper atop his blanket. "You don't actually believe those lies, do you?"

"'Course I believe it. Why wouldn't I?"

"Because it's a fabrication. My life was in serious jeopardy. That man forced me to write exactly what he said, verbatim. If you were in my position, you'd have done the same."

"Confess to a murder I didn't commit? Bullshit I would." I

swatted my hand at him. "Y'know what? Save your lies for the cops. I'm done."

"Shawnee, wait." His hands reached for me. "Please. I loved your parents."

I lunged on the bed, pressed a fist into each side of his pillow, and screamed in his face. "You killed them! You let them die in the street!" Inches from his ear, I punched the wall. "Next time, I won't miss. Don't you ever come near me or anyone I love ever again, or so help me God, I'll kill you with my bare hands."

He wiped my spit off his nose. Cool and calm, he said, "There's something I haven't told you."

"No shit." I crawled to the foot of his bed. "Apparently, you've been hiding all kinds of secrets from me throughout my life. Why would Delsin fabricate a story? It doesn't make any sense. What would he have to gain?"

Ed cringed but didn't answer. Instead, he went with, "While it's true your parents did not die in a fatal car wreck—at the time, Lieutenant Holt and I agreed an accident might be easier for a young child to accept, and maybe I should have told you the truth when you turned eighteen, but you were dealing with the loss of your friend, Bo, at that time. As God is my witness —" he raised his palm to the Lord— "I would never have had a part in their untimely demise. Never."

"Lemme see if I've got this straight." A gazillion different scenarios skidded through my mind. "So, you admit they were murdered, just not by you."

"Sadly—" his eyes tilted downward— "yes. That's the God's honest truth."

I flung out my hands. "Stop bringing God into all this. He obviously wasn't there that night."

"Oh, yes, He was." His eyes saddened even more. "Who do you think carried them home?"

Not sure if it was the way he told me, or if it was because I still couldn't grasp the ultimate betrayal by a man my parents and I called family, but a large part of me longed to believe his story. Other than Nadine, Ed was one of the few people in my life who loved my mom and dad. To an orphan, that meant something. It's everything, really, the last connection to a time before life splintered into a jigsaw puzzle with so many missing pieces it could never be made whole.

With hair gripped tight between my fists, elbows resting on bent knees, I stared at my boots, dangling off the side of his hospital bed. "If not you, then who?"

"Leave the past where it is. They're at peace now."

"Please tell me." When I raised my head, tears rolled off my nose. "I've never needed anythin' as much as I need this. Help me. Please...I need to know what went down that night."

"But I don't know what happened. If I did, I would tell you. I do have my suspicions, though, but that's all it is—conjecture."

"Are you blind, old man?" I grabbed clumps of my hair. "My life hasn't exactly been a cakewalk y'know. And as an adult, I'm barely hangin' on." I shook a stiff finger in his face. "You owe me the truth. Or I'll walk out that door, and you'll never see me again."

With a long exhale, Ed held praying hands in front of his lips. "All right. Point made. Shawnee—" He said my name to buy time; classic stall tactic. "How much do you remember about your trip to New Mexico to visit your maternal grandparents?"

"My grandparents?" My stomach hardened, the muscles tightening into a fist. "But they died before I was born."

"No, kiddo, they didn't. You were quite young at the time. I'm not surprised you don't remember."

A flame of familiarity warmed the emptiness inside me. "Are my grandparents still alive?"

"That I can't say."

"Can't or won't?"

"Your parents and grandparents had a falling out." Gazing downward, he rubbed the edge of the blanket between two fingers. "Your mother downright refused to talk about it, and Josiah—excuse me, your dad—respected her wishes."

Dragging information out of him was next to impossible. "What caused this falling out?"

"Please let sleeping dogs lie." Eyes closed, his head fell back against the stack of pillows. "It's not healthy to dwell in the past."

I jumped to the floor, paced back and forth beside the bed, my lungs heaving with adrenaline. "Obviously somethin' awful happened in New Mexico, or you wouldn't've asked me if I remembered the trip. So, how 'bout we skip the part where you pass out fatherly advice? It's a couple decades too late, anyway." Staring out the window, the Boston skyline shimmered with the city lights as a weight bore down on me. "Just say what you gotta say. I've dealt with enough mind games for one day."

In a quiet voice, he said, "I'm tired, kiddo."

It wasn't until that moment that I noticed the wires protruding from the collar of his pajama top, his chest hooked to an EKG machine. A steady *bleep, bleep, bleep, bleep, bleep*...if I didn't stop pressing him for answers, he might have a stroke.

I scooted closer to him and laid my hand over his. "I'm sorry. How're you feeling?"

"Pretty good. You know. I have good days and bad days."

"Hope you get to come home soon." I really did.

"Me too."

"Ed?"

"Yes, kiddo."

"Last question, and then I'll leave." My stomach fluttered as if a colony of Monarch butterflies all got spooked at once. "Can you at least tell me their names?"

"Your grandparents?"

I nodded.

"Jacy and Bly Lee."

"My middle name's Lee."

"I know." A slight smile barely arched the corners of his pale lips. "Your sweet mother honored her family by giving you her maiden name."

Wow. What else didn't I know?

CHAPTER TWENTY-SIX

11:11 p.m.

The whole drive home I spent in silence. No stereo. No cell phone. Rubbing Mom's rosary beads, hanging from the rear-view mirror, brought some solace. "How could I know so little about you and Dad?" My lips trembled. "You lived an entire life that I wasn't a part of, a life I knew nothing about."

Tears flooded my eyes and obscured the dark road ahead. I didn't care. Over the course of one day, I'd learned that my childhood stood on a bed of lies. What else hadn't my parents told me? What truths had they purposefully withheld? How could they not tell me about my grandparents?

After my parents died, the one thing I held onto, the life raft that kept me from sinking, was knowing I came from good, solid roots. But now, even that was in question. Maybe Josiah and Leah Daniels weren't even my biological Mom and Dad.

A sharp breath escaped my opened mouth. Could I be adopted?

I was so preoccupied, I almost missed my street. Slamming the brakes, I jerked the wheel to the right, cruising on to

Lyndsey Lane. By the time I pulled into my driveway, the house was in total darkness.

I darted up the front stairs, unlocked the six padlocks, and nudged open the front door with my hip. Tiptoed past Nadine, snoring on the couch, and padded up the spiral stairs to the loft. Maggie tossed and turned so many times the blankets cocooned around her tiny frame. I shook out the quilt, folded near the footboard, and let the material float across the bed.

I crawled under the covers, weaved my fingers behind my head, and stared through the skylight. Diamond-like specks of light waltzed across a velvet-black sky.

What happened in New Mexico all those years ago? What could be so awful that a daughter, my mother, never spoke of her parents again, so horrific that she told her only child they were dead? No matter how hard I tried to reason it away, the truth was, I didn't understand. How could they let me believe I had no other family? Granted, they might not've known death was coming for them, but so what. Parents had a responsibility to prepare their kids for the unthinkable. Life was too unpredictable not to have a plan B in place. By shutting out my only living relatives, they sentenced me to hell.

Tears soaked the sides of my face, my chest heaving so heavily I could barely catch my breath. I glanced over at Maggie. This poor little girl had no bloodline, either. What would her future look like?

Fuck that. She had me. Nadine, Levaughn, and Austyn also loved her. But I, and I alone, was the one person in her life who inherently grasped, deep in the gut, the terror she experienced in foster care. Like me, she's a survivor. That gave us a special, unbreakable bond.

A sad smile quivered my lips as she rolled toward me. Half-asleep, she slapped her limp arm across my chest.

To reassure her, I whispered, "I'm right here, babe. Don't worry."

When she sighed, I returned my gaze to the night sky. Maybe she's the reason I survived my messed-up childhood. Could the night I saved her be the night I saved myself?

My eyelids grew heavier and heavier as I drifted into a sweet abyss. Something massive thudded on the roof, and Maggie shook me awake. When my eyes flashed open, she was pointing at this enormous owl peering down at us through the skylight.

"*Yenaldlooshi.*" She ducked under the covers. The entire mattress shook—hard and fierce—from her trembling. Next, she raised the blanket over my head. Lying face-to-face, her hot breath hit my nose. "Don't look at him, Shawnee."

"Honey, it's just an owl."

She said "No" with such conviction and certainty, it almost made me a believer. "*Yenaldlooshi.*"

What the hell was she talkin' about? "Okay, okay. We'll stay right here till it leaves."

I wrapped my arms around her, but she couldn't relax. Whatever she believed was standing on the skylight scared the crap out of her. Her tiny frame quaked all over. Nothing I could do to calm her fears, no matter how tight I held her.

Finally, I asked, "Is *yenaldlooshi* a word you made up? It's okay if it is."

Her head rocked back and forth in an emphatic no.

"I've never heard it before. Is it English?"

In a soft voice, she said, "Athabaskan."

"Is that what you spoke at home, honey?" Why hadn't I ever asked her about her biological parents till now? With all she'd endured in foster care, especially at the hands of that scumbag Jessup, I should've known better. Because when I was her age, no one talked to me about my parents, either. Not that I blamed them. It's difficult to find the right words to say to an orphan. When the wound's fresh, it's even harder.

She added, "It's Diné."

"Diné?"

"Navajo."

"Oh, okay. So, what does *yenaldlooshi* translate to in English?"

She scooted toward me, her body pressed into mine, with both arms tucked to her chest, and I held her even tighter. If we were any closer, she'd be inside me.

Her voice muffled against my tank top. "With it, he goes on all fours."

CHAPTER TWENTY-SEVEN

"The souls of my ancestors peer out from behind
my mask of skin, and through my memories they live again."
- Tȟatȟaŋka

Midnight

At Kimi's instance, Mayhem tracked Chayton to the underground bunker in Lynn Woods. It'd been twenty-four hours since he'd delivered Mr. Smith. If Chayton waited too long, the authorities might form a search party before his remains could be positioned. If they didn't figure out the why behind these killings, then all his work would be for naught.

That, Mayhem could not allow. Nor would he, even if it meant breaking his promise not to kill again. Kimi knew nothing of Mayhem's motivation. Rather, she had a favor to ask of Chayton. Although he appreciated her intention, he wavered whether to follow through. As someone who preferred to handle things on his own, asking for assistance with the gray wolf seemed illogical, at best.

Nonetheless, he'd given his word to the woman he loved.

How could he not grant her request when it was made with the purest of intentions?

With Poe flying close behind, he weaved through the tunnels to the main chamber. On the altar lay Mr. Smith, his wrists and ankles bound by leather straps.

Revealing himself, he stepped from the shadows. "Still alive, I see." He raised an eyebrow at Chayton. "Don't you think it's time that changed, my dear boy?"

"But he says he's not related."

"He's a Smith. What more do you need?" He shook his head. "Perhaps I chose the wrong man for the job."

Chin raised, Chayton pulled back his bare shoulders. "You didn't."

"Then proceed as planned."

He aimed his mighty sword toward the heavens. "I am the staff of his power in his youth."

"And he is the rod of my old age."

"Whatever he wills happens to me."

Mayhem stepped toward the altar. "I am the silence that is incomprehensible, and the idea whose remembrance is frequent."

"I am the voice whose sound is manifold, and the word whose appearance is multiple."

Mayhem palmed the back of Mr. Smith's head. "I am the utterance of my name. For I am knowledge and ignorance. I am shame and boldness."

"I am shameless," said Chayton. "I am ashamed."

"I am strength, and I am fear." Gaze locked with his protégé, Mayhem raised his voice. "I am war and peace. And they will find me there."

"They will live. And they will not die again." In one swift movement, Chayton swung, the breeze from its force blew loose strands of hair that'd fallen out of Mayhem's ponytail.

When Mr. Smith's head thudded into a woven basket, tears

welled in Chayton's dark eyes. Mayhem set a soothing hand on the young man's bare shoulder and offered one last piece of advice. "A necessary evil, indeed. Stand proud, son. Your sacrifice will not be in vain."

Mayhem hopped over the arch of blood splattered across the concrete. "Clean up this filth, please. We'll wait for you outside the hatch."

He called for Poe, who was flying in circles about a foot beneath the ornate ceiling. Which he'd do for hours if Mayhem allowed it. For reasons outside his purview, his beloved crow companion adored the cherubs and gold trim. Even as a young fledgling Poe could not get enough bling. Hence why Kimi spent a small fortune on gold ankle bands. Plastic simply wouldn't do.

* * *

"It does not require many words to speak the truth."
- Chief Joseph

Tuesday
12:40 a.m.

Next to the moss-covered hatch in Lynn Woods, Mayhem glimpsed his watch for the third time in five minutes. This was taking much longer than he'd anticipated. Kimi was home alone, and he hadn't told Yaz that he was going out. Poe also hadn't returned to the nest before tagging along, so Edgar and Allan had no way of knowing to keep an eye out for dangers of any kind, especially intruders.

Perhaps it's safer to reschedule. But with the gray wolf in the area, uncertainty hung in the air like a blood-soaked blade, its razor-sharp ability to obliterate the very heart of his existence— his wife. With his hands clasped behind his back, he paced across the dark forest floor.

Chayton shoved the plastic-wrapped Mr. Smith out the hole in the earth. A moment later, he climbed out, his muscular chest and arms sheened in blood. Swipe marks of sweat on his forehead showed the exertion used to carry dead weight on his shoulder.

"I apologize if you misunderstood me," said Mayhem. "I will not be accompanying you to pose the body. Rather, I am requesting your assistance in a separate matter."

"Oh." Chayton's gaze lowered to Adrian Smith's remains. A moment later, his attention snapped back to Mayhem. "I'd be honored." He rustled up twigs and brush to conceal the corpse where it lay. When he finished, he brushed off his hands on his jean-clad pantlegs. "What sort of weapon will I need?"

"The ultimate, my dear boy. Faith. For with that, you are unstoppable, impenetrable."

Judging by Chayton's blank expression, he did not understand. "Who's the mark?"

"Gray Wolf."

Flashing his hands in surrender, Chayton backed away, his whole body shuddering. "Please don't ask this of me. The gray wolf? I can't fight him. No one can." When he paused, he swept strands of hair out of his eyes. "Remember what happened last time?"

"I do, yes. And yet, I find myself in a similar circumstance." He draped his arm around Chayton's shoulders and nudged him through the woods. "Our target is one of Gray Wolf's men, who goes by the name Red Buffalo."

"We need his birth name, though. Do you know it?"

"Working on it."

Chayton stopped dead. "Then how do you plan to stop him?"

"Trust me." Mayhem nudged him forward. The longer Kimi was home alone, the more dread needled his side. Nonetheless, he forged ahead. Between twin conifers—gorgeous specimens that stood over one hundred feet—he gestured toward the dirt path that led to his Caddy. "Right this way, please."

Poe couldn't resist soaring ahead, and Mayhem called out, "Stop." With that one word, his loyal crow companion circled back and landed on a low-hanging branch, his beak hung to his chest feathers.

As Mayhem strode past, he gave him a mild tongue-lashing. "We do not have the time nor the manpower to deal with any shenanigans tonight. You are cognizant of that fact, are you not?"

Silent, Poe fluttered down to Mayhem's shoulder and rode the rest of the way. As much as it pained him to reprimand Poe in front of company, he could not risk his safety. Night hunters hid in the trees. If they ran into another Great Horned Owl, Poe could be in real trouble. On the sly, he passed Poe a cherry. A treat worked wonders for morale.

Before opening the passenger door, Mayhem shook out a fresh hanky. "If you wouldn't mind cleaning up first. Blood could blemish the leather."

Nodding, Chayton dragged the fine white cotton over his face, then went to work on his hands. Neither action was very effective.

"Hm. One moment, please." Mayhem reached into the glove compartment and withdrew a package of wet wipes. He pulled a few sheets through the plastic slit, handing the wad to Chayton. "Try these."

Crouched down to the side mirror, the young executioner scrubbed off all the blood.

"Much better. Thank you." He swung his arm toward the passenger seat, and Chayton climbed inside. Mayhem darted around the front bumper and slipped behind the wheel with Poe. "Buckle up for safety, please."

With Poe nested on his thigh, he drove to Breakheart Reservation and parked down the street from the main entrance, like he'd done nights before. Once he killed the lights, he swiveled toward Chayton. "In my trunk, you will find various knives. Pick your poison, as they say."

The young man didn't move, so Mayhem clapped twice. "Chop, chop. Time is of the essence."

"But Uncle—"

He shot him a penetrating glare. "Do not force my hand, son." He opened his eyes to reveal the whites, a menacing stare that worked remarkably well. "Go. Now."

Like a good soldier, Chayton obeyed.

They reconvened at the trunk, where Chayton chose a gorgeous hunting knife, handcrafted by an old friend who, sadly, no longer walked this great earth. With a flat hand on Chayton's back, he nudged him toward the dirt trail.

Halfway up the hill, Chayton stopped again. "I can't do this. No one can fight the gray wolf." His whole body pleaded for answers. "His men could be anywhere. Why are we confronting him without Red Buffalo's birth name? Help me understand."

Mayhem turned him toward the campfire smoke billowing through the treetops. "They're right over that crest. Now, I need you to get ahold of yourself, or we might lose our only advantage."

"And what's that?"

A wide grin stretched his lips. "The art of surprise."

Mayhem rooted around in his pocket and withdrew a side-by-side container of war paint, which held special meaning to warriors. Created from clay, berries, plants, minerals, and tree bark, some believed war paint held supernatural powers—including strength and protection—derived during the application. This act made the warrior feel confident, invincible, and protected. The symbols and color of paint determined the type of powers bestowed on the wearer. An added benefit was to strike fear in the enemy.

"This will help to revitalize your soul." As he encircled the young man's eyes, a mask of war-red for strength, success, and energy, he recited the first line of an inspirational mantra. "I am the warrior who rests."

Chayton closed his eyes. "I am the warrior empowered."

"I am the warrior who rests."

"I am the warrior who breathes deeply."

Mayhem drew three lines from the hairline to the right eye. "I am the warrior who rests."

"I am the warrior who sees clearly."

He drew three lines from under the left eye to the jawline. "I am the warrior who rests."

Empowered, Chayton held his gaze. "I am the warrior who chooses wisely."

In black, which symbolized a powerful warrior had proven himself in battle, Mayhem drew one line from under Chayton's nose, down the crevice of his smooth upper lip, and continued to just below the chin-line. "I am the warrior who rests. I have learned to be in touch with my own strength. I am the warrior who rests."

"I have learned to direct my life with intuition and intent," said Chayton. "I am the warrior who rests. I have learned that resting is the key to my unlimited potential."

To complete the ceremony, he drew one black line from each corner of the lips straight down. "All things come to the warrior who rests. And all things become nothing for the warrior who waits. The promise of power is the promise always kept."

With unrivaled focus, Chayton announced, "Let the battle begin." He marched up the incline to the crest that overlooked the camp.

Poe firmed his stance on Mayhem's shoulder as they caught up to him on the crest. He peered down at the smoldering campfire. Right then, a massive crow leaped into the air, its wings spread wider than an eagle's. No humans existed here anymore. Mayhem wrangled Poe into his arms and tucked his whole body under his long coat.

Unaware, Chayton lifted his foot to climb down the hillside, and Mayhem hooked his arm. "We cannot fight what we cannot see. Our window has closed for tonight, I'm afraid."

"But what about the art of surprise?"

He slapped a gloved hand on his shoulder. "The advantage, my dear nephew, no longer belongs to us."

CHAPTER TWENTY-EIGHT

2:00 a.m.

Because the suspect dumped bodies on two main beaches, Levaughn rounded up the joint task force and positioned unmarked vehicles on the three-mile stretch of Revere Beach Boulevard, one car per mile of shoreline, and three unmarked vehicles in various places around the southernmost part of Lake Winnipesaukee in Laconia, New Hampshire, otherwise known as The Weirs, by its locals.

Hunkered down with Odin in his Crown Vic, he planned for a long night of surveillance. Two hours into their shift, and the suspect still hadn't shown. Which was a good thing for the public—no one died tonight—but not so great for the investigation as a whole.

In the passenger seat, Odin was reading the autopsy reports of the victim found at the bathhouse—IDd as John Winthrop—and a subsequent victim found two hours north, in New Hampshire—IDd as Theresa Jackson. "The UNSUB's playing games. He switched the heads on the last two victims."

"Ya mean, Winthrop wasn't a transvestite?"

"No. That was Theresa Jackson's head that we found in the bathhouse. This tells us the UNSUB views them as interchangeable. Which may explain why he crosses the gender barrier. The sex of his victim is irrelevant."

"Have we found a connection between the vics yet?"

"Other than being Caucasian and in their thirties, the victims have nothing in common. They all worked in different fields, traveled different routes, lived miles apart, and as far as I can tell, were never in the same place at the same time. The four who previously had tattoos didn't get them done at The Other Guy's Tattoo Shop, except for Amanda Orme. But since she worked there, that isn't conclusive in and of itself. The last two victims never even had tattoos or piercings prior to death."

Levaughn scratched the stubble on the back of his neck. "I feel like we're missing the obvious. Starting tomorrow, we need to focus on the first victim found in Revere. Why would the killer take the chance of crossing state lines?"

A few car lengths ahead, a man hoisted a large cocooned object out of the back of a black Cadillac Escalade, with a duffel bag slung over his right shoulder.

Levaughn leaped out the driver's door and took aim, his flashlight levelled under his service weapon. "Revere Police. Don't move."

Freaky red and black war paint covered the suspect's face, evident when his gaze connected with the flashlight beam.

Levaughn shuffled his feet closer to the suspect. "Lace your fingers on your head."

The suspect dropped what looked like a plastic-wrapped corpse and took off, the duffel bag bouncing on his back as he fled on foot.

Levaughn chased him across the bridge to Wonderland Station, veering toward the parking garage, and was gaining momentum when his shoe caught in one of the numerous potholes. His knee folded in on itself, and he crashed to the pavement. Running at full speed, arms pumping to increase momentum, the suspect vanished between swarms of parked cars.

With an opened hand, Levaughn slapped the asphalt. "Dammit!"

Ego bruised, he limped back to the Escalade, where Odin had torn open the plastic. Inside lay a decapitated male corpse. "The suspect must still have the head."

Cupping his bent knees in scraped palms, the skin burning, he breathed out a lot more than in. "Did you run the plates?"

"Reported stolen two nights ago."

"Fuck." Swirling blue lights headed in their direction, and he kicked the Escalade's back bumper. "I almost had the bastard. For chrissakes, why didn't you follow us in the car? For that matter, where the hell was backup?" Without waiting for a reply, he limped toward the Crown Vic. Next time, the scumbag won't be so lucky.

CHAPTER TWENTY-NINE

5:00 a.m.

I jolted awake in bed, the roots of my hair soaked in sweat. Beside me, Maggie was still sound asleep, the quilt rising and falling with her chest. I tiptoed out the loft and down the spiral stairs, slid my computer off the breakfast bar, and slipped out the back sliders to the deck.

Sweat needled my scalp, my temperature rising to a raging one-hundred-and-six, my cheeks and forehead scalding hot to the touch. But no matter how ill, I still needed to find a rational explanation for the psychotic dog who tried to blind me and the massive owl who Maggie claimed was an evil supernatural beast of some kind.

At the deck table, my slippery fingers slid off the keys as I logged into the deep web. Rather than press a nine year old about a creature who petrified her, I ran a search for the word *"yenaldlooshi."*

Pages of articles filled the screen. The first to pique my interest was on a site called the Paranormal Priest. I clicked the blog post just as Nadine opened the sliders.

"What are you doing out here?"

I feigned innocence. "Uh...I didn't wanna wake you."

"You look terrible. Did you sleep okay?" She pressed the back of her hand to my forehead. "My God, you're burning up. Close the computer and come inside."

"I'll be in in a sec. Lieutenant Holt needs me to research somethin' real quick." Okay, so I lied. Shoot me. It was easier than explaining what happened last night.

She peered over my shoulder, and I slammed the laptop closed. "You don't have clearance, Nay."

She bought the excuse and stormed inside. Sometimes television came in handy. Reciting lines from her favorite crime dramas worked the nuts, no better determent. I didn't have much time, though. Nadine Couture didn't possess the ability to remain silent for too long.

I lifted the screen of my laptop and read a few paragraphs.

In the Navajo community, witchcraft is viewed with the highest contempt and is a very serious crime. But the most volatile and dangerous of these witches is the *yenaldlooshi*.

A witch? That's what all the fuss is about? There must be more to it.

I read on...

Translated, yenaldlooshi means "with it, he goes on all fours" or "he that walks like an animal."

Not that I doubted Maggie, but gaining confirmation was in my DNA. I continued reading...

Also known as the Mai-Coh or Limmikin, it's more commonly known by outsiders as the skinwalker. They're witches that shapeshift into animals using magical animal skins. These people are evil to the core, hell-bent on nothing more than destroying the lives of those around them. The best way to fight a skinwalker was to announce his birth name, for this act would prevent him from ever shapeshifting again.

What the hell was the author of this article smokin'?

Shapeshifting and witchcraft...pa-lease. What's next, King Kong?

I skimmed the rest of the article, my stomach flipping and flopping from whatever flu virus I'd picked up at Mass General.

Mostly male, blah, blah, blah... They took the form of a coyote, fox, and dog, which granted stamina, enhanced senses, and the ability to traverse great distances at high speed. The bear form gave the witch great strength, endurance, formidable claws, and teeth. The cougar's hide bestowed speed, grace, and stealth, and the form of the crow and owl afforded them keen vision, sharp talons, and the ability to soar through the sky without alerting anyone to their presence. It's said that the animal form of the skinwalker was more powerful and larger than any natural beast.

Hmm...this gotta be a coincidence. These things couldn't be real. No sooner did the thought cross my mind and vomit sprayed from my mouth, soaking my keyboard in bile. The stench sent me dry-heaving over the railing. With no food in my stomach, my abs clenched, twisted, and I buckled in half. Weak, I inched my way back to the table and collapsed in the chair.

Nadine raced out to the deck, a cupped hand shielding her gaping mouth. Then, as if transforming into Florence Nightingale, she slung my arm around her neck and lifted me out of the chair. While she assisted me in to the house, Maggie held open the louver blinds. But once I laid down on the couch, my little buddy hurried over to whisper in my ear, *"Yenaldlooshi."*

I played with strands of her long locks. "Honey, don't worry. It's probably just the flu."

Eyes watering, her chin dimpled and quivered.

Nadine scooted her out of the way and held a digital thermometer in front of my closed lips. "Open." She coaxed me like a three year old, but I was too sick to resist. When I opened my mouth, she cried out, "Oh my God! What happened to your tongue?"

Bawling, Maggie dove on top of me as if I only had seconds to live. She tucked her head under my chin, and I rubbed her back in large circles as she blubbered all over my neck.

A knock at the door diverted their attention.

"Whoever it is, Nay, tell 'em I'm contagious or somethin'. I don't wanna see anybody."

Swatting at me, she darted toward the door. *Twist—pop, twist —pop, twist—pop, twist—pop, twist—pop, twist—pop.* Unlocking the padlocks sent sharp pangs through my aching skull. But that was nothing compared to the female voice who yelled, "Surprise!" when Nadine swung open the front door.

I craned my neck around the pillow under my head, and there stood my BFF and her sister embraced in a bear hug. Could this day get any worse?

Scratch that. It probably could.

Chelsea said, "Hey, Shawnee." Makeup concealed her black eye and cut nose. "Nice to see you again."

I winced. Rat bastard.

Nadine echoed, "Again?" She planted her hands on both hips. "You knew my sister was in town and didn't tell me?"

Gritting my teeth, I glowered at Chelsea as I rose to my unsteady feet. Forcing a fake smile, I said, "Surprise?" I snagged the keys off the breakfast bar, then bent down to Maggie's level. "I need to go out for a while. You gonna be okay while I'm gone?"

"But you're sick." She threw her arms around my waist, her cheek pressed against my washboard abs. "Take me with you."

Her pleading tone drained my heart of blood, but I had to do this alone. So, I peeled her off of me. "I won't be long, I promise. Hey, do me a favor and grab my netbook from the loft?"

"But—"

"I'm feeling much better, I swear. Now, scoot." While I waited for her to return, I stumbled into the bathroom. Staring in the mirror, a blend of smudged black eyeliner and mascara encircled both eyes. No lipstick. No base. No face powder. It's little wonder why Maggie was so upset. I looked like holy hell.

I clipped my hair away from my face and scrubbed off the old makeup, dried my face, and outlined my eyes in jet-black liner, combed my lashes with dark mascara, powdered my fair cheeks and nose with ivory mineral makeup, and smeared on dark-russet lipstick. With my hair undone, I brushed cherry-tipped angles toward my face, feathering my raven bangs in place. Last touch, I stashed my usual bobby pin under the back of my hair, by the nape of my sweaty neck.

Wearing a makeshift lockpick came in handy on numerous occasions.

By the time I'd finished and flicked off the bathroom light, Maggie was waiting, her thin arms clutching my netbook against her chest as if holding it hostage. She refused to hand it over till I listened—someone's spent too much time with Nadine.

"You need medicine man."

I mussed her hair. "I need a lot of things, babe, but a medicine man isn't one of 'em." I held out my shaky palm. "C'mon, I gotta go."

With reluctance, she passed me the netbook, then reached for me, her tiny hands opening and closing. Even though weakness practically paralyzed my limbs, I swept her into my arms, and she nearly choked me to death with how fiercely she clung to my neck.

"Don't die, Shawnee." Her back shook in and out. "I won't make it without you."

Gently, I tugged on her arms, but she refused to let go. "Look at me." I waited for her to face me before reassuring her that I didn't have one foot in the death bucket. "Nothing's gonna happen to me. I will always come home. Don't you trust me?"

Eyes watering, she nodded.

"Good girl." I lowered her to the floor and patted her tiny

behind; so cute in her bedazzled leggings. "Now, go help Auntie Nadine. I have a feelin' she's gonna need a hug soon." She'd need more than that if Chelsea planned to confess, but I kept that juicy tidbit to myself.

Strolling toward the door, faux confidence emanating off every steady step, I saluted the two sisters. "Ladies." Almost made a clean getaway, too, until Nadine chased me on to the front stoop.

"Where're you going? You shouldn't leave the house with a fever."

"I've got a work thing," I lied.

"But today's your day off."

"I know. I won't be long, I promise." *Seemed like I was tossing around a lot of promises lately. Let's hope I could keep 'em.*

"But you should be resting."

"Nay, go visit with your sister." I jogged down the stairs, waving over my head, trying to pretend that I didn't feel like a cast member from the Walking Dead. "I'm fine. Really, I am."

I slipped behind the wheel and turned the key. *Tick, tick, tick, tick, tick.* Rubbing the dash, I tried sweet-talkin' Ol' Bessie. *Tick, tick, tick, tick, tick.* The little bitch flat-out refused to turn over. With a closed fist, I punched the cloth ceiling. "Dammit, I can't catch a break here!"

I slid the shifter into neutral and got out. Slogged to the front bumper and heaved the jeep out of the driveway, jogged alongside the driver's side and dove for the doorframe. Before the SUV slammed into the maple tree across the street, I reached over the driver's seat, yanking up the emergency brake.

Movies made the move look easy. It wasn't. In addition to scraping my palm—which burned like a bitch, by the way—I banged my knee off the metal doorframe. Wrenching the damn wheel took what little energy I had left.

Defeated, my jeep dead in the middle of Lyndsey Lane, I rested my forehead on the steering wheel. A knock on the window snapped my head up, my mind on high alert, my heart working overtime as the sudden disruption almost catapulted me into cardiac arrest.

As I rotated my head to the left, Mr. Mayhem motioned for me to lower the window. I complied. A smirk arched his thin lips, and it took all my energy not to wipe that smug look off his face.

Outside the opened window, he tipped his fedora. "Greetings, Ms. Daniels. Need a lift?"

"From you? I'd rather walk barefoot over shards of broken glass, thanks."

"Be careful what you wish for. That could be arranged."

I was in no mood to take shit from him or anyone else today. "Did you want somethin' in particular, or do you just get off by makin' my life miserable?"

With a resounding *thud*, Poe left a plate-sized dent in the hood beneath his talons. Glaring at me, he stepped onto the windshield wiper arm. Slow. Precise. As if he'd practiced the move in a mirror to stimulate maximum alarm within his opponent. It worked, too.

My unsteady hand twisted the key in the ignition. *Tick, tick, tick, tick, tick. Tick, tick, tick, tick, tick.* For luck, I stroked Mom's rosary beads. A prayer couldn't hurt, either, but my thoughts scrambled from the serial killer hovering inches from my door. Not to mention his presence outside my home, with Nadine and Maggie inside. Who cares about Chelsea? After the crap she pulled, she could fend for herself.

Another stroke of the beads and I tried one last time to fire up Ol' Bessie.

Vroom, vroom.

Hanging an arm out the window, pretending that Mayhem couldn't crush me if he felt like it, my knee jumped with excess energy. "Either tell him to move—" I jabbed the side of my head at Poe— "or he's goin' for the ride of his life. Your call, pal."

With a short whistle, Poe flew right to his shoulder, all the while never taking that beady, black-eyed stare off me. Mayhem gripped the doorframe and leaned in. "The incident on your back deck will continue to happen if you refuse to seek help."

"What, puking? Not that it's any of your business, but I've got the flu."

He threw his head back like a friggin' fruitcake, an audible inhale as though he was absorbing the area around him. "Ah, wouldn't it be grand if things were exactly as they appeared?"

Mute, I didn't bother to respond to his whack-job question.

"The cause of your illness is something far more sinister than a virus, I'm afraid. Your life, your very existence, depends on which direction you take from here. Will you risk venturing outside your comfortable zone, or stand your ground and fight? Take the time to choose your path wisely, or your next misstep may be your last." He tipped his fedora. "A pleasure as always, Ms. Daniels."

Whatever Mayhem meant by "your next misstep may be your last," I had no clue. As I shifted into second gear, accelerated to third, my feet working the clutch and gas in perfect harmony, I replayed what Mayhem told me in Lynn Woods—*find out who wants you dead.*

During my visit with Ed, it became obvious that he was withholding a crucial piece of my life puzzle. The only way to prove his story was to break into his home. There's no way he hadn't squirreled away information that he never told me about. Hell, he never even showed me the will. For all I knew, he probably siphoned thousands from my trust fund.

Not that I gave a shit right now. Money was the least of my problems.

Within fifteen minutes, I cruised up Apple Hill to Ed's massive Colonial on a quiet cul-de-sac in Lynnfield. Each house screamed, "Look at me!" These homeowners had more dough than they knew what to do with, and Ed's house was no exception. No matter how he tried to reason the massiveness away, the fact was, a single man did not need six-thousand square feet of living space. End of story.

I parked out front and lumbered up the slate walkway to a solid-cedar front door. Years ago, he'd given me a key when he let me crash in the spare room for two nights. His generosity didn't last long, though. When Berkley kneaded the arm of his favorite chair—a cool leather glider that doubled as a back-massager—he cast down an ultimatum—either bring my cherished cat to a shelter or move out. Guess which option I chose? I left in such a hurry, I forgot to return his key.

Okay, maybe "forgot" was a bit of a stretch. Whatever.

I unlocked the front door. Cheap bastard never changed the locks. Classic Ed. He'd reuse paper towels if no one would find out. Paper plates got rinsed in the sink, not thrown in the trash. And it's not like he lived on a fixed income. That dude was rolling in dough.

Smoky gray and white swirls pirouetted across the marble floor of the foyer. An overwhelming urge forced me to kick off my motorcycle boots and slide across the tiles in my socks. Halfway across the floor, I slipped, snagging the rod-iron railing at the last second, impeding my fall.

Whoa, that was close. It'd be just my luck to crack open my skull in a house where no one expected the occupants to return anytime soon.

Inhaling a few deep breaths to slow the adrenaline coursing through my mind, body, and spirit, I surveyed the downstairs. Off the great room—otherwise known as the living room to mere mortals like me who made well under three-hundred K per year—cherry-wood double doors masked Ed's library-slash-office. I slid out the bobby pin I'd stashed in my hair and picked the lock in seconds flat. Child's play. I smiled like Chester Cheetah—Cheetos' coolest cat—with all my teeth exposed.

The double doors opened in as if entering a grand ballroom,

my arms spread as wide as they could open. The high-glossed floors made it impossible not to skate across the wood to his desk. Ed locked every drawer. Some people were incapable of trust.

The irony was not lost on me.

After I picked the lock on the bottom drawer—most kept valuables down low in a desk—files clanged together on a metal hanger. My fingertips walked across the top of each tab, searching for one marked "Daniels."

No such luck. All the files held were house bills and receipts. The dude paid hundreds to the electric company each and every month to keep the lights on. I figured he paid inflated land taxes, being Lynnfield and all, but the dollar amount blew my mind. The fee exceeded five times what I paid in Saugus. Guess it didn't pay to worship a prestigious address. Big shocker there.

I closed the drawer. How 'bout a safe? He must have one somewhere.

Scoping out the room, I stood before an enormous abstract painting of...no clue. Looked like a huge purplish blob to me. Didn't matter, anyway. No safe hid behind it, so I moved on to the next painting. This time, red and black swirled together to represent something like rage or inner turmoil. Which, actually, wasn't far off from my current mood.

The second I lifted the painting off the hooks, the room spun and spun and spun, the painting slipping from my sweaty grasp, crashing on the parquet floors. The corner of the frame splintered a crack to the canvas. *Shit!* Now I needed to stage a burglary. So much for getting in and out undetected. But first, I wasn't leaving without answers.

Let's hope Ed hadn't installed a security system since my last visit.

Dizzy, I stumbled toward the wall safe. The keypad breathed in...breathed out...my vision blurring as I dialed in Ed's birthday. Most folks used dates for their passcode so they could remember it.

The safe offered no love, the steel door sealed shut. If this were a removable safe, I could use the bounce method, where you slammed it against the floor or a corner of a table, but Ed had the safe built into the wall. The most discreet way to crack a safe was by lock manipulation. The safecracker needed patience, knowledge of locks in various forms, which I had, as well as a familiarity with the owner of the safe. Check and check.

The scientific approach, created by Harry C. Miller in nineteen-forty, required a three-step process. One, determine contact points. Two, discover the number of wheels. And three, graph the results. Since I was doing this on the fly, I had to fudge the graph with a scrap of paper and a pen.

Most combinations ranged between three and eight digits. Each number had a corresponding inner wheel. But first, I needed to discover how many inner wheels made up the pack. By determining the contact area, I could dial in the opposite direction from that point, and then let the dial rest there—a process called "parking the wheels." Much like the hands of a clock, if, say, the contact area was at two o'clock, I'd rest the dial at eight, the number opposite the contact area.

After figuring out the contact area and the number of wheels, I reset the lock by spinning the dial several times to the right and then parked the wheels at zero. As I redialed slowly to the left, I leaned my ear close to the safe, waiting for the telltale click. I notated the first click, then repeated the process, only this time parking the wheels three numbers to the left of zero. With each click, the process restarted at a different position until I'd graphed all points on the dial.

Though the graph revealed the wheels in the proper position, it wouldn't show the numbers in the correct order, which left me with six variables of the three-digit passcode. Running a finger down the list, I found my date of birth. In the off-chance Ed meant every word he said at the hospital, I dialed it in.

The door popped open.

Whaddaya know, the guy actually remembered my birthday. Maybe the concerned parent charade wasn't all an act.

I swung open the safe door. And there on the top of a stack of manila folders laid a file marked "Josiah and Leah Daniels."

I reached for the file, and the room whirled at an unprecedented speed. As my sloppy hand made contact with the file, I lost my balance, the whole office a whipping blur, and I crumpled to the floor. Papers rained down, rustling, scattering all around me. Footsteps approached, a screeching caw bellowed, and then...blackness.

CHAPTER THIRTY

"For every wound, there is a scar,
and every scar tells a story,
a story that says, I survived."
- Craig Scott

6:43 a.m.

As expected, Ms. Daniels did not last long before she lost consciousness. Which was why he and Poe had followed her to Lynnfield. Poe soared up the grand staircase to check for anyone who might impede their exit while Mayhem stepped over the oil painting in the elegant library-slash-office.

Whoever lived here appreciated the finer things in life. Kudos to them.

Slipping off his leather glove, he knelt to one knee and checked for a pulse. Ms. Daniels' heartbeat was weakening. Corpse powder would do that. Especially when created from a dead infant's remains, as despicable as that sounds.

What brought Cat here?

Scanning the room, a framed photograph on the desk

showed a child who resembled a young version of Ms. Daniels. Perhaps seven or eight years old, she was riding the shoulders of a white man in his late thirties, her delicate hands clasped under his chin. A memory of Cheyenne at that age washed over him, warming him from the inside out.

Could the man in the photograph be her father?

He glanced down at Ms. Daniels, her breath shallowing more and more with each passing moment. Before she reached the point of no return, he scooped up the contents of the file strewn across exquisite parquet flooring, polished to perfection. He tucked the file under one arm and slung Ms. Daniels' limp body over the opposite shoulder.

In the foyer, he called for Poe. "Time to go, buddy."

Poe flapped out the door behind him.

* * *

7:45 p.m.

I woke in the backseat of my jeep. A coolness swept up my body, and I glanced down at my nakedness, except for a sarong knotted between my breasts. Hair soaked, all my pores tingled as though I'd spent hours in a sauna or steam bath.

What the hell happened? I glimpsed my watch—7:45 p.m. You've gotta be frickin' kiddin' me. This morning, I was breaking into Ed's safe, and more than twelve hours later, I wake up half-naked in my vehicle? Sunset was about thirty minutes away, give or take. How'd I lose an entire day?

Slapping a hand on the passenger headrest, I pulled up to a seated position. Someone had folded my clothes and stacked them neatly on the driver's seat, my motorcycle boots below on the car mat. Barefooted, I opened the back passenger door and stepped on to the cool asphalt of Lyndsey Lane.

Mouth agape, I stood across the street from my house. How'd I get here?

It took several more minutes for me to acknowledge how amazing I felt, like I'd been rejuvenated, reborn, renewed, all signs of sickness eradicated from my system. Staring at my reflection in the side-mirror, I stuck out my tongue. No black streak. I also didn't have any makeup on. No eyeliner. No mascara. No ivory powder. My face washed clean.

How was this even possible?

I reached into the jeep to grab my clothes. The Daniels file sat on the passenger seat. My sight shifted between the house, the file, the house, the file, the house, the file. Before Nadine or Maggie peeked through the front blinds, I slid behind the steering wheel and shut the door. My hand trembled as I flipped open the manila folder.

Ed kept meticulous records. This looked like a diary of sorts, only Ed was the one telling my parents' story as if scribbling notes after my dad confided in him. Or maybe, Dad feared the worst and had asked him to memorialize the events in case something happened to him and Mom.

Tears streamed down my face as I learned of my mother's rape on the Navajo reservation in New Mexico, the subsequent birth of a son whom she'd planned to give up for adoption, and her parents'—my grandparents—reluctance to let her. Instead, they insisted on raising the child as their own.

Whoa. No wonder they had a rocky relationship.

Still, the fact remained that somewhere out there I had a brother. I scrubbed a hand over my face, took a moment to wrap my head around the news, then flipped to the next entry to find out his name. But the page numbers skipped from four to six. All these years I held onto the belief that I was an only child. Not much pointed to a rational reason why Ed kept this secret. Had he promised my father? If that's true, why hide his identity?

The file ended with the mysterious death of my grandparents —no details given as to how they died—the entry dated six months prior to the murder of Mom and Dad.

Nothing made sense anymore. Why would Ed conceal a brother from me? Did Lieutenant Holt also know he existed? After all, Ed said the carefully-constructed lie about my parents dying in a car crash was his idea. How deep did this cover-up go, and why all the secrecy?

CHAPTER THIRTY-ONE

Wednesday
11 a.m.

I'd already been at my desk for hours, combing through archives of car accidents to no avail. I also tried searching through old homicide cases, but the Daniels name wasn't listed on any of them. Big surprise there.

The toughest hurdle standing in my way was, prior to the year 2000, fatal car crash reports weren't digitized. Rather, the department copied the information onto microfiche before destroying the paper reports. Worse yet, the dude who ran the off-site records department was a whiny little twit. We'd had run-ins before. Long story.

How was I supposed to know he'd take offense to being called "needle-dick" at the Christmas party? Sometimes the truth hurts. He's lucky I didn't coldcock him for grabbing my ass. If we weren't surrounded by a bunch of cops, his night would've ended with a trip to the emergency room rather than skulking away with a bruised ego. Needless to say, he's the last person who'd do me a solid without sexual favors in return.

Vomit lurched up my throat, and I gagged. Pass.

I couldn't involve Levaughn. Between running the joint task force and trying to catch the serial killer in our midst, he had enough stress. I might be able to ask Lieutenant Holt to sign off on my request, but then he'd know I was looking into my parents' murder. For now, keeping him in the dark made sense. There's no telling what he'd do to prevent me from learning the truth.

In a nutshell, I had a zero chance of accessing the microfiche. Which meant, it'd take time to unravel this mystery. At this rate, I might never figure out what really happened on that fateful night twenty-three years ago.

"Shawnee—" Levaughn jogged over to my desk— "the suspect is a Native American male, around mid-thirties, lean but muscular build, about six feet, dark hair and eyes. I need a list of cameras in and around Revere Beach Boulevard. Looking for a black Cadillac Escalade—" he rattled off the plate number— "reported stolen two nights ago. In fact, pull the report for me, too."

In Massachusetts, traffic cams—red light and speed cameras —were still illegal. The only acceptable place was at toll booths on the highways. A few cities outside the state got caught short-timing yellow lights in an attempt to increase tickets, the dirty bastards.

"Well, good morning to you, too, Detective."

His stiff shoulders relaxed. "I'm sorry. It's been a helluva night." He rubbed my upper arm, his touch soothing my frazzled state. "How ya doin'? I've been so wrapped up in this case, we haven't had much time together outside of work."

I sloughed off a lame half-shrug. "Okay, I guess. Maggie misses you."

"I'll make time to swing by the house, I promise." His gaze darted back and forth between the computer and me, and it didn't take a genius to figure out why.

"Gimme a couple hours. I'll have that list later this afternoon. You want me to send requests for the footage, too, right?"

"If you don't mind." He flashed his pearly whites at me, knowing damn well his perfect smile made him virtually irresistible. "Really appreciate it."

"Consider it done." I set my fingers on the keyboard, then glanced up at him. "Hey, did Lieutenant Holt tell you the cell towers confirmed Norton's alibi?"

"I just heard. Doesn't matter, though. He looks nothing like our guy."

I sprang back in my chair. "You saw the suspect's face?"

"Yup. Last night. Almost caught the bastard at Wonderland Station."

Where was Mr. Mayhem last night? "How sure are you about his age?"

"Hundred percent. Well..." He paused, backpedaled. "I mean, it was dark, but I got a pretty good look at him."

"You didn't happen to see any crows nearby, did you?" What would possess me to ask that question? Between the new mystery surrounding my parents' death, a phantom brother who appeared out of nowhere, and the weird skinwalker thingy hellbent on freakin' me out, not to mention losing an entire day—my mind still blank on where I was, who dressed me, or how I ended up outside my house—I'm lucky I'd held it together this long. What I didn't need was an interrogation at this point.

"Crows?" Levaughn slid onto the corner of my desk. "Is there something you wanna tell me?"

"Me?" My voice rose so high it revealed my deceit. Before he noticed, I swatted away his comment. "Nah. Just being thorough."

"Crows are a very specific detail, Shawnee. Why do I get the feelin' you know more than you're letting on?"

My only recourse was to flat-out lie, but his warm amber eyes crushed my spirit. Staring at my computer screen, I averted my gaze in the hopes of veering the conversation back to the investigation. "Do you want a list of all privately-owned businesses on the boulevard, or can you narrow it down for me? Oh, didn't you say you chased him into Wonderland Station? MBTA has cameras, I think."

"Yeah, but I'm lookin' for the route he took to the beach. Good idea to reach out to MBTA. Do it. I'm thinking if we backtrack far enough through local surveillance and find his driving route to the beach, we may be able to pinpoint the basic vicinity of where he lives. Worth a shot, right?"

"Sure, but it'll be tough with no traffic cams."

He played with the ends of my hair. "I know, but I have faith in you."

"Flattery will get you everywhere, Detective." I winked. "Now, get the hell outta my lab and let me work."

Once he left, my breathing accelerated, my knee bouncing out of control. There's no way Mayhem wasn't involved in these murders. The only question was, who'd he get to do his dirty work?

Over the next two hours, I sent out at least thirty requests for surveillance footage. But I needed a break. Grabbing a bite couldn't hurt, either. So, I locked the computer lab and hustled through the lobby, out the front entrance, and into the parking lot. When I approached my jeep, Poe was sitting on the hood, with an eagle feather clenched in his beak. The moment he spotted me, he leaped into the air but hovered nearby till I snatched the dropped feather off the roof.

Written in black ink on the quill, it read, "You've got mail" with a smiley face.

I swiped my netbook off the backseat and logged into Mayhem's message board.

Dearest Cat,

I trust you're feeling better. You're welcome.

It's imperative now more than ever that you remain vigilant, aware of your surroundings. Your life and the lives of those you love are at great risk.

Better a thousand times careful than once dead.

Hugs & Kisses,
Mr. M

Was that a threat? I read the note several more times in an attempt to decrypt the parts he left out. A shockwave sent chills spiraling down my spine. Oh. My. God. Mayhem's the one who stripped me, washed me, redressed me in a sarong, and left me to wake in the backseat of my jeep.

Why would he do that? While I was unconscious, he could've easily ended my life. Why the hell would he save me, cure me? Every move Mayhem made had a reason behind it. But this? This made no sense.

A dull ache branched out across my skull, and I dropped my forehead into an opened hand. He's the one who took the missing page of Ed's file. Which also meant, he knew more than I did about my mother's past. Bastard! Two could play this game.

I put my plan into action by writing back…

Mr. M,

Meet me at the diner. One hour.
Remember, it's rude and unbecoming to be late.

Signed,
Confused Cat

Gotta admit, using his line felt pretty fuckin' awesome.

Staring at the blinking cursor, I waited for him to respond. When I focused on my watch, the second hand *ticked...ticked...ticked...* C'mon, take the bait.

Months ago, I'd learned he'd been blessed with the gift of prophecy. Or maybe, he just got lucky. Not sure anymore. What if he sensed I had no intention of meeting him? Man, that'd suck.

It took ten full minutes for words to appear on the screen. But by then, every nerve ending in my body had been stripped raw, vulnerability sizzling beneath my skin. Maybe that was the point, to give me time to back out.

Dearest Confused Cat,

Forget what hurt you in the past, but never forget what it taught you. It's a date.

Hugs & Kisses,
Mr. M

I dragged a fist toward me. Yes—he bought it.

With step one complete, next came the hard part. With any luck, this plan wouldn't get me killed.

CHAPTER THIRTY-TWO

"Learn to be alone, because no one will stay forever."
- Matlabi Duniya

2:25 p.m.

At his wife's side, Mayhem told her about Ms. Daniels' response to his message. "She wants to meet. You were right, my love."

Kimi's chest heaved with each hard breath. These past few days she'd had a difficult time. The stress over the gray wolf returning to the area was most likely the culprit for her malaise. Once he neutralized the problem, life could return to normal.

Concentrating on letters, Kimi typed, "Poe?"

Not surprising. Poe had a way of soothing her fears. Wildlife sensed all sorts of ailments. Praise be. "He'll be along soon, sweetheart." With the back of his hand, he caressed her silky cheek. Even with ALS, her golden complexion looked amazing. "You're even more beautiful than the day we met." He kissed her soft lips. "What did the doctor say earlier?"

Tears spilled over the rims of her gorgeous dark eyes.

"Honey?" he prompted, his fingers rubbing the side of his forehead raw.

As she mentally typed, she gasped for oxygen. The words "It's time" sent his mind reeling in five different directions.

"Time for what?" A switch clicked in his brain; he'd made the connection, his head rocking in a continuous no. "Whatever it is, we'll get through it," he said, his voice choked by emotion, his mouth running dry. "We always do."

"U promised."

He ground his jaw. "What did the doctor tell you?"

Tears streamed in straight lines over her high cheekbones.

"Honey, talk to me."

Diverting her watery gaze, she concentrated on the flat-screen. "Tube."

"Intubation?" Even though doctors warned him this day might come, the world crashed in on him, a deep ache piercing his heart, obliterating any hope of a future together. "When do they want to do the procedure?"

The coloring drained from her face and neck as she struggled to breathe, but she remained vigilant. Nothing could prevent her from following through with their master plan, a plan she forced him to agree with, a plan that promised to destroy the lifeblood of this family.

She typed one full sentence. "Let me soar with eagles."

When he bent over to read it, a separate computer window popped open. A love letter filled the screen. Every inch of his being warned him to look away, but she must have spent hours on the two-page document, concentrating on one letter at a time. This decision—her decision—was not an easy one to make.

Promise or no, how do you kill the one person you'd die to protect? She's the mother of his child. She's Jude's grand-mother. She's the light that kept him grounded and the water that quenched his thirst for vengeance. Without her, even he questioned what he might do—innate darkness misconstrued by many but understood by few.

"Read plz."

He wasn't unsympathetic to her plight. No one knew better than him how hard she'd fought in her immobile shell. Through all the hardships, all the pain, and sorrow, the love they shared never wavered. Not once. How could she ask this of him?

He didn't respond. If he hoped to remain strong, he could not read her final words. Not yet.

"Plz!"

"Darling, I have done everything you've asked of me. And now, Ms. Daniels is expecting me to show for our appointment." He kissed her long and hard, breathing her in, the sweetest of honeysuckle filling his senses, and crushing his soul. "Under the circumstances, perhaps it's best if I reschedule our meeting."

"No." Breath caught in her throat, and she coughed, wheezed. "Cat needs 2 know."

"I understand this is important to you, but hasn't Ms. Daniels taken enough of our time?"

"Tell her."

"I intend to, my love." Fire and ice warred within him, and he scrubbed a hand over his face. "Once she learns the truth, she's on her own. We've done enough. Agreed?"

"Thx. Luv U."

"I love you, too, sweetheart." A lump formed in his throat when he kissed her again. "While I'm gone, I urge you to reconsider your proposal. Please," he pleaded, his voice crackling with pain. "At least tell Cheyenne. Without knowing why, your passing will haunt her the rest of her days. Ms. Daniels is the perfect example of that. We've both seen how great loss has affected her. Have we not?"

Kimi's teary gaze fell to her lap.

"Thank you, my love." For now, his stiff shoulders relaxed a bit. Before she changed her mind, he darted toward the doorway. "I'll round up Yaz to come stay with you, in case you need anything while I'm gone."

In the foyer, he pressed his back against the mahogany column, his head fallen in an open hand. Tears built in his chest, and he let out a soft whimper. He could barely recall a time when he didn't love that woman with all his heart. How could she ask him to set her free? He ran two fingers under his eyes, drying his tears. Then snagged his fedora off the coat rack. Rather than let her soar with the eagles, perhaps a trip to their tiny abode in Alaska would lift her spirits. Kimi loved it there. But first, he needed to finish this.

With one last glance back down the hall, he strode out the door, every part of his soul keening, wavering whether to leave.

CHAPTER THIRTY-THREE

4:00 p.m.

Levaughn prevented me from leaving the station on time. As I was driving out the lot, he pulled alongside my jeep to ask how I made out with gathering the information he requested for the Headless Horseman's case. Even though I'd sent him an email that detailed every security camera on the strip, along with a copy of each request for footage, he rambled on and on.

"Where are you off to?" he said, pressing me for my itinerary. "Wanna have an early supper?"

"Can't." I glimpsed my watch. "Hey, ya mind if we continue this later? Gotta be somewhere."

"Oh." He sounded hurt. "Sure."

"Thanks." I sped out the parking lot, the gas pedal pinned to the floorboard, my long hair floating out the window. If I didn't arrive at Mayhem's brownstone in Boston's Back Bay within ten minutes, I'd miss my chance.

Once I hit Boston, city traffic slowed to a crawl. Some snooty bitch in a Beamer with New York plates even cut me off, and I laid on the horn, yelling out the window, "Yo, princess! Daddy called. He wants his car back."

I swerved into the left-hand lane and slammed on my directional, almost breaking the plastic arm clean off. Cars whizzed by my window, the force rattling my jeep. On the dash, the green arrow blinked to the rhythm of the directional. *Ta-tick…ta-tick…ta-tick…ta-tick…ta-tick…*

My fingers drummed the steering wheel; nobody would let me take the turn. C'mon! I'm growing old here.

The congested traffic finally showed a break in the chain, and I gunned it across the street, horns blazing at me for cutting them off. Massholes. The front tires hit a massive pothole, and I flew out of my seat, my forehead colliding with the rear-view mirror, a throbbing ache spreading from temple to temple. I banged third gear, then fourth, my feet working the pedals, my jeep careening around the side of the brownstones and into the back parking lot.

Hope I'm not too late.

Halfway through the entrance, I stalled to stare through the skylight, searching for Mayhem's freaky pets while I slipped my fingers into black latex gloves. The building was oddly empty. That's strange. On my last visit crows lined the roof of his unit.

Huh. Maybe I'd timed it right after all. Cool. Finally, something went as planned.

I coasted right below the fire escape, where I parked and got out but left the engine running. Climbed onto the hood, and then the roof. Raised to my tippy toes, my arms stretched high above my head, I managed to snag the metal ladder by my fingertips. As a precautionary measure, the manufacturer designed these escape routes so the bottom rung hovered ten feet above the ground to deter burglars. Some good that did. 'Course, not every criminal possessed mad skills and perseverance like *moi*.

After I positioned the ladder in place, I hopped to the hood, then the asphalt, and boogied back behind the wheel. In case Mayhem came home early, I drove out of the parking lot and stashed the jeep on a side street, around the corner from the brownstone.

Arms pumping to increase my momentum, I sprinted toward the fire escape and dove for the ladder. Caught the bottom rung with my fingertips and pulled my chin over the metal bar. I reached for the next rung, and the next, straining to hook the lowest tread with my foot.

Ahh, that's better. Hand over hand, I climbed up to the bathroom window. Which, conveniently, was already open. This must be my lucky day. Things didn't normally go this smooth.

Uh-oh. What if Mayhem expected me to come here?

In hindsight, I probably should've listened to that tiny voice inside my head, warning me this could be a trap, but I didn't. I couldn't. An overwhelming need to learn the truth propelled me to crawl through the opened window.

Sweet vanilla potpourri fragranced the room as I crept through the bathroom, craning my neck around the doorframe to scope out the hall. An eerie stillness veiled the house. Morose. Dejected. Forsaken. Its feelings unlike anything I'd ever encountered. One nagging sensation kept pestering me, though. Almost like I wasn't alone, like someone—or something—was watching my every move. Darting glances to my left, right, and behind me didn't help. Uneasiness intensified in the living room, my senses heightened, my calf muscles hardening more and more with each step.

Shake it off, Daniels. You're imagining things.

With gloved hands, I rummaged through the desk drawers. Found no correspondence that pertained to me or my family. I lifted all the couch cushions. Found one quarter, two dimes, and a flattened cherry, the stem broken in half. Most people stashed valuables in the kitchen, but I doubt Mayhem would leave the missing page of Ed's file in plain sight. He was way too cunning for that. No, he'd hidden the paper in a more secure location, a place where he could safeguard it day and night.

I changed direction, prowling back down the hall to the master suite. Mrs. M was a reasonable woman. If I pled my case, maybe she'd help. She'd done it before. Either that or she'd kick me out and notify her husband. Man, that'd suck. Mayhem wouldn't take kindly to me invading his home. But what the hell did he expect me to do? He stole the missing page!

Fair is fair. He meddled in my business, I meddled in his.

I announced my presence as I strolled through the doorway of the bedroom so I wouldn't startle her. "Hey, Misses M, it's Shaw—" Frozen mid-stride, my jaw slacked, my heart thudding to a stop.

Blood bathed the walls and stucco ceiling in crisscrossing arcs of crimson, a sickly-sweet metallic stench polluting the air. More blood leaked down the Apple insignia on the back of the computer screen, the leather chair tipped over on its side. Vomit lurched up my throat, and I gagged, my boots shuffling back into the doorway, head down, my frantic gaze scanning the carpet to make sure I hadn't left bloody footprints. It wasn't until a hellish gurgling noise diverted my attention that the full picture manifested, the savageness that took place here.

Beyond the bed, Mayhem's wife sprawled on her back, vacant eyes staring at the ceiling, blood spurting from a severed neck, her face and chest bathed in violence.

I ran to her, skidding on to my knees, my gloved hands covering the neck wound, silently praying I could slow the bleeding. "Stay with me, Misses M. I'm gonna get help."

Her bloodshot eyes tilted toward me.

"Don't worry." One hand still covered her neck while I rooted around in my back pocket for my cell. "I won't leave you." My thumb hit nine-two, and I disconnected. Nine-one-two, and I disconnected. While I fumbled with the keypad she drew in a final pained breath—eyelids fluttered twice—a deep guttural rumble rattling in her throat.

I tossed the phone on the floor. "No, no, no, no, no." With one hand over the other, I compressed her chest again and again. "C'mon, dammit!" I tilted her head back, pinched her nose, and set my lips against hers, blowing out as hard as I could in attempt to push air into her dying lungs.

When I returned to chest compressions, I cried out, "Breathe!" Tears blurred my sight. "Please breathe!"

Blood oozed from the gash on her throat—her heart had stopped beating. Dragging my sleeve across my bloody mouth, I grabbed my phone and scrambled away from her, crawling backward like a crab, my boots sliding me across the blood-stained carpet. I don't know how long I sat there; felt like hours, staring at her, trying to make sense of the violence.

By the time I rose to my feet, my whole body had gone numb, my mind trying to process what had happened, replaying every second, my gaze roaming the bedroom in search of answers. Outside the double windows, lines of crows perched on the sill. Mournful screeches eviscerated all hope of escaping the brownstone alive.

"I...it wasn't me." Gaze shifting between the crows and Misses M, I begged them to understand, my voice rising in pitch and volume. "Ya gotta believe me. I tried to save her."

Locked in a taciturn battle of wills, I froze, my boots rooted to the bloody carpet. The crows' keening intensified, and I shielded my ears.

"I didn't do this. I swear I didn't!"

Dead-center in the mob, sunlight glinted off Poe's gold ankle band, his sight zeroing in on me. Then he pecked the glass. Slow. Melodic. Each beat emphasized. An I-will-kill-you look shrouded his unmistakable beady, black-eyed glare.

Thud...thud...thud.

One by one, the others joined in. *Thud...tap, tap. Thud...tap, tap. Thud...tap, tap.*

Each peck raised more hairs on my forearms as more and more crows added to the chaos.

Thud, thud...tap, tap, tap. Thud, thud...tap, tap, tap, tap. Thud, thud...tap, tap, tap, tap, tap.

Oh. My. God. They're trying to shatter the glass. Through my mind fled mental snapshots of crows jackhammering my eyeballs, smashing my teeth, erasing all traces of my identity. Against my will, I couldn't stop blinking, my nerves frazzled, spent.

I caught a slight shift in Poe's eyes, a split-second glance to the left, and I whirled around. Next to the computer screen laid a red folder. Could that be the missing page? I slapped a hand on the file, and Poe spread his ginormous wings like a cape, shrilling with a mind-numbing fury. This psycho bird couldn't wait to sink his talons into my flesh.

No time to breeze through the folder's contents. Glass panes could only hold for so long. I stuffed the file into the waistband of my jeans and hauled ass, my boots barely touching the hardwood as I careened down the hall, down the stairs to the front of the brownstone, my rubber soles squealing around the end of the banister.

Since Poe and the rest of Mayhem's psychotic murder pecked the window out back, it only made sense to head in the opposite direction. Every two seconds, though, I glanced over my shoulder to ensure none of the crows had made it inside yet. Charging for the front door, focusing more on the crows than where I was going, the tip of my boot wedged under something heavy, something that stopped me cold, and I sailed through the air, smashing headlong into a solid mahogany column.

Dazed, my mind saturated in adrenaline, my body mangled on the floor, I cradled my forehead in bloody gloves. From the corner of my eye, I peeked back to figure out what had tripped me, praying to all that's holy that it wasn't an evil dog with spit dripping off razor-sharp canines. Or worse, a pet wolf.

Feet away from me lay a second woman. Dead. Blood saturated her back and the waistband of her jeans, her disheveled hair covering the side of her face, a growing scarlet pool consuming the wooden tiles beneath her. I crawled to my feet. Slipped. Crawled again. Slipped. I slapped my hand on the Cherrywood chair rail, gripped it like a vice, and dragged myself to my feet.

Unsteadiness weakened both legs.

Gaping at the carnage, my heart slammed against my ribcage, my breathing shallowing more and more. Why would Mayhem slaughter his entire family?

Time was running out.

Any minute that window could shatter. So, I hopped from tile to tile, as if playing a deadly game of tic-tac-toe, and swung open the front door. The hot July sun struck my lungs, and I gasped for air. Sliding down the railing saved me a few seconds, but I still needed to make it to the side street before Poe and his crew noticed my absence.

At the corner of the brownstone, I peered around the side of the building. The crows had half the window shattered and were working on removing the last few remaining glass shards. But from this angle, I couldn't tell if Poe was still on the sill. If I had any chance of survival, a face-to-beak stand-off must be avoided at all costs.

I sprinted across the parking lot entrance, my sight locked on the crows, and then slowed, jogging down the side street to my jeep.

It looked like someone had smashed the driver's window with a baseball bat, glass scattered across the seat and the car mat. The weapon was probably more like a sharp, black beak. Why not puncture the tires? I didn't have the energy nor the mindset to unravel a sick and twisted crow's thought process, so

I slid the folder out of my waistband and swept the glass off my seat.

When I peeled away from the curb, burnt rubber wafted through the broken window, the ends of my hair collecting glass fragments from the frame. Most of the ride home blurred. Until I crossed into Saugus, which sent a clear signal to my thundering heartbeat to decrease to a quick *pitter-patter, pitter-patter, pitter-patter*.

The red folder mocked me from the passenger seat. *"Shawnee, double-dare you to open me."* Okay, maybe it didn't actually call my name, but it may as well have.

A few car lengths down from my house I pulled curbside and killed the engine, snatched the file off the passenger seat and flipped open the cover. Squinting at the cursive handwriting inside, wrinkles creased between my eyes. I skimmed the first page. What the hell was this?

CHAPTER THIRTY-FOUR

"Master the art of knowing when to be aggressive,
and when to stay patient."
- The Wolf

4:30 p.m.

W hen Ms. Daniels did not show at the diner—missing their appointment was not a smart move; now he'd make her wait to learn the truth—Mayhem drove to Lynn Woods to check on Chayton. Kimi would ask about him the moment he walked through the door. With the gray wolf skulking around the area, she feared for everyone's safety. Bless her heart. Kimi never let her own wellbeing take precedent. Which made her decision to cross into the spiritual realm all the more baffling.

How could she ask him to do the unthinkable? Surely with a little time, once she had mulled over what her loss would do to the family, she'd postpone her plans. What he witnessed earlier was simply a knee-jerk reaction to the news of intubation. If he were in her position, he might consider the same option.

Although, mindsets tended to change with the realization of leaving a loving spouse, daughter, and grandson behind. Kimi would soon come to her senses.

He strode toward the dirt trail, a tiny nibble of doubt chewing at his side. What if her family was not enough incentive? What if she thought of herself as a burden?

A deafening chorus of caws exploded through the treetops and stopped Mayhem dead in his tracks. In the distance, Edgar and Allan soared toward him, screeching at decibels that might arouse unwanted attention.

When they glided down to the walking path, he bent down to their level. "You two know better than to cause a ruckus while on assignment." Straightening, he scanned the sky, his gloved fingers sweeping back and forth under his chin, a pit widening inside him. "Where's Poe?"

Magnificent wings flapped with fury, incessant machine-gun blasts vibrating in their throats—a clear signal that something terrible had happened.

His chest constricted, his mind whirling with questions, but all he could manage was, "What's wrong?"

Edgar sounded an ear-piercing alarm call. Within seconds, Allan joined in. Complete bedlam erupted—mayhem, if you will —as the uproar intensified.

Ca-caw, caw, caw. Brrrrr...brrrr... Ca-caw, caw, caw. Brrrr... brrrr... Ca-caw, caw, caw. Ca-caw, caw, caw. Brrrr...brrrr... Ca-caw, caw, caw. Ca-caw, caw, caw. Ca-caw, caw, caw. Brrrr...brrrr... Ca-caw, caw, caw. Ca-caw, caw, caw.

The last time he'd witnessed anything close to this display was when Kimi found Thoreau, lifeless on the grass below the nest. Small-minded folks might believe crows did not possess the ability to feel things as deeply as humans, and they'd be oh, so mistaken. Thoreau's sudden death sent shockwaves through the community. Crows from miles around gathered in the treetops around the house, all mourning the gut-wrenching loss, as well as processing how and why he passed.

To soothe Edgar and Allan, Mayhem stroked their chest feathers. "Please calm down. I hate to see you so dismayed." Once they quieted enough to listen, he silently rephrased the following question four or five times. A lump swelled in his throat when he asked, "Did something happen to your brother?"

Edgar and Allan did not respond.

Raising praying hands in front of his lips, he released a breath he hadn't realized he was holding. "Thank the Lord." He exhaled a second time. "Has the gray wolf shown his hand?"

The question did not upset Edgar nor Allan. As if to help him decode their language, they leaned forward, a penetrating stare burrowing into the very core of his soul.

"Is..." He wrung his hands. "Is Mom safe?"

Mournful yelps screeched out their beaks as they leaped into the air and took flight, wings flapping, soaring in circles, the forest exploding in chaos. Mayhem spun, hurtling toward the Caddy, Edgar and Allan's wind tunnel walloping his face. At the door, he laid a flat hand on his gut—paused to absorb the tsunami of pain, his breath shortening, his chest caving—and he collapsed on the driver's seat.

The entire ride home blurred.

Once he sped into his designated parking space, the tires squealing in protest, he killed the engine and leaped out the driver's door, his gaze searching the back of the brownstone for Poe. But he wasn't with the others; he couldn't spot his gold ankle band among the masses of black feathers. Mayhem careened around the side of the building to the front door and bounded up the stairs, vaulting three at a time.

Someone left the front door ajar.

From his ankle sheath, he slid out a hunting knife. Cautiously, he elbowed open the door. On the parquet floor lay Yaz, her lifeless body sheened in blood. Now Edgar and Allan's reaction made sense. Fala Yazza Locklear—known fondly as Yaz—grew up with Cheyenne. She'd been a valued member of this family since she could walk.

Kneeling, he slid off his leather glove and swept the bloody hair away from her face. He pressed two fingers to the side of her neck, under her jawline. No heartbeat. He pressed his fingers to the inside of her wrist. No pulse.

He turned his gaze toward the heavens. Who would want to harm such a sweet young mother? Yaz's passing would devastate Kimi. From the second level, it's possible that she never heard a thing, that she slept through the savage attack. Her troubled mind needed rest; she needed peace. Above all else, she needed to hear the right words from him; he must break this news as gently and as lovingly as possible, or she might use Yaz's death—the loss of her home health aide—to rationalize her earlier decision.

A fiery rage smoldered inside him when he rose. The gray wolf underestimated Mayhem's bloodlust for the last time. Whether he had to chase him day and night, he would not rest until he enacted sweet revenge. No one harmed this family and lived to tell the tale. No one.

He strode into the living room. Nothing seemed out of place. Hm. Robbery was not the motivating factor. Yaz hadn't interrupted a burglar in the act. His grip tightened around the handle of the hunting knife as he moved toward the master suite. Slow. Cautious. Aware. Each step silenced, in case the perpetrator was still in the brownstone.

Halfway down the hall, a bloody handprint marred the paint on the wall. Muscles flexed under his skin as he quickened his pace, ramping up, jogging toward the bedroom, his breath trapped somewhere in his chest.

When he stepped through the doorway, an invisible strike to the gut buckled him in half, and he fell to his knees, his hands clawing at his stomach. "Dear God, no," he cried out, the chords in his neck straining in anguish. "No!" He crawled over to his precious wife and slid his arms under her fragile spine, pulling her dead weight onto his lap, her battered body clutched to his heart, rocking her, her head fallen cockeyed as he crumpled the back of her nightgown in tight fists, her limp arms dragging across the bloodstained carpet.

With one hand cradling the back of her head, he pressed her bloody cheek against his, grief drilling into the quick of his core. Tears rained down, thinning the bloodstains on her cheeks.

He pressed his quivering lips to hers. "Please don't leave me, sweetheart." Breath hitched his shaken words. "I'll gladly accept my fate...I'll pay for the sins I've committed against humanity... but please...please spare this amazing woman. She's never harmed a living soul in her life."

Pleading for a reprieve, a do-over, an overwhelming yearning to rewind life's clock consumed him. If he had granted Kimi's request, he could have spared her suffering. With a slight pinprick, she would have drifted into an eternal slumber, rather than the brutality committed against her, hours after he left the house.

Hyperventilating, his lungs heaving, dizzy, he leaned in again, pressing his trembling lips against hers, murmuring, "You will outsoar every eagle, my love."

Poe hopped up on Kimi's bent legs. With an intense stare at Mayhem, he dropped a string of rosary beads.

"What's this?" He weaved his blood-soaked fingers through the string, the cross dangling against his inner wrist. The truth punched him in the face, and his watery eyes flashed wide. "Did you steal these from Ms. Daniels' rear-view mirror?"

A volcanic blast ignited within him. "Are you telling me the gray wolf isn't responsible for this? Ms. Daniels murdered your mother?" Blinding rage rose from the deep recesses of his psyche, his teeth clenching, scalding heat flushing his neck and face, every part of his body shaking, and he roared. "She... murdered...my...wife?"

Eyelids closing, Poe's beak lowered, raised.

Exhaling through his nostrils, he tried to slow the surge of adrenaline from swallowing him whole. "You did the right thing by allowing her to escape." With his sight tunneling on the rosary beads, he spoke calm, controlled. "Let's give her a little breathing room, make her feel nice and safe while we honor your mother." He cocked his head toward Poe. "When we return, the game will change. New rules, same players. Only this time around, Ms. Daniels will endure a hailstorm of wrath like no other has ever experienced."

Poe caped his magnificent wings wide. *Ca-caw!*

CHAPTER THIRTY-FIVE

4:30 p.m.

A spiral of varying emotions tornadoed through my system, my gaze flitting back and forth the across the letter in the folder.

Dear Kimi,

I hope one day you can find it in your heart to forgive me for not saying goodbye. Leaving the reservation wasn't an easy decision. I'm sure my parents told you that I married a white man. He loves me, fills my spirit with laughter and unconditional devotion, and never lets me down. What more can one ask for?

Don't blame yourself for running away that night. No one could have stopped them. If you visit my parents, please keep an eye out for Kajika. Never forget his father's blood runs through his veins.

No matter the miles between us, you will always be my soul sister.

Much love,
Leah

Either Kimi was Mayhem's wife, or he'd stolen this letter from Ed. Without a corresponding envelope, I had no way to tell. Even though my mother had a good reason to flee her homeland, her words only conjured up more questions. Was Kajika my half-brother? What kind of name was that?

As I reached for my netbook, the empty rear-view mirror captured my full attention. No rosary beads. My gaze lowered to light gray bird shit on the dash, dripping down the front of my stereo. Oh my God—Poe! He's setting me up for Mrs. M's murder. I grabbed bunches of hair, almost tearing the strands from my scalp. There's not a chance in hell that Mayhem won't believe his story. That psycho bird had proof of me being at the brownstone!

My gaze shot out the passenger window, back to the driver's side, around to the back windshield, my head swiveling like a pinwheel at a carnival. I bundled the red folder and netbook in my arms and catapulted out the door, barreled across the street and hurtled up the stairs. Nadine locked the friggin' deadbolts! Patting my pockets, I couldn't find my keys.

With a closed fist I pounded on the door, kicking the bottom to get her attention. "Let me in—hurry!"

It felt like two years, standing on that stoop, my harried stare checking left, right, and behind me. Nadine never came to the door, so I lunged off the top stair, almost broke my damn ankle when my foot collided with a rock and bolted across the street to my jeep. Keys dangled near the steering column. I snatched them out of the ignition and charged back to the house, unlocked the deadbolts, and stampeded into the living room.

"Nadine!" I darted in and out of every room downstairs. "Maggie!" I double-stepped it up the spiral stairs, Berkley leaping off the top landing, Katie McGuire wedged against the wall to let me pass.

No one was in the loft.

Where'd everybody go? Nadine's car was in her usual spot in

the driveway. How far could she and Maggie walk? Where would they even go at this hour? It's a little late to take a stroll around the neighborhood.

My quickened breath kept pace with my heartbeat as I jogged down the stairs, blood thrashing at my ears, a steady hum dulling the world around me. Did Mayhem beat me home?

The blanket was neatly folded on the back of the sofa, where Berkley and Katie McGuire kneaded a fresh resting spot as though this was an ordinary day. No toppled over furniture, no broken dishes, no cabinet doors or drawers left ajar. Nothing indicated a struggle had taken place. The house gave me no reason to worry about their safety, yet I couldn't shake this niggling suspicion that something horrible happened to them.

If I didn't hear from Nadine within five minutes, my only alternative was to call Levaughn and report her and Maggie as missing persons. With Mayhem convinced that I murdered his wife, thanks to Poe, I couldn't take the chance of him seeking revenge.

How might that conversation play out? I'd need to confess to all the strange yet unexplained occurrences...the evil dog who tried to blind me, Mayhem sending me eagle feathers for protection from a Navajo skinwalker who stalked me, tormented me, and thirsted for my blood...the massive owl peering through my skylight in an attempt at mind control, not to mention the murder of Mrs. M, whose body I found after breaking into her home, and somehow, losing an entire day while Mayhem cured me of an illness I couldn't legitimize.

If Levaughn was still listening by that point, I'd then need to find a way to explain why and how a crow was setting me up to take the fall for a crime I didn't commit.

Who would believe *that* story? Even I could hardly wrap my head around it. There's no way Levaughn—a rational, level-headed detective—wouldn't ship me off to the psych ward, lock me in a padded cell for god-only-knows how long.

The phone rang, and I whirled around, my nerves sizzling like water droplets in hot oil.

Hesitant, I raised the cordless handset. "Hello?"

"Oh, good, you're home," said Nadine, and I released a deep breath, my forehead cradled in an open palm. "I forgot to leave you a note before we left. Chelsea took me and Maggie out for dinner. Wanna meet us?"

"No thanks." Looks like dear, sweet Chelsea was still working up the courage to confess to screwing her sister's fiancé, and I couldn't stand to be around her till she did. "I'll just see you guys when you get back."

"Want me to bring you home a doggy bag? We're at Monte's," she teased, "your favorite pizza joint."

Staying as far away from me as possible was probably their safest option. "On second thought," I said with a cheerful tone, "maybe you guys should make a night of it. Why don't you and Mags crash at Chelsea's place tonight?"

"Ooh, how fun!" Her pitch raised five octaves, and I yanked the handset away from my ear, so I didn't go deaf. No one should be subjected to a tone that high. She probably woke dogs for ten miles.

"Wanna come?" Even via phone, I could tell she was bouncing on her toes. "Oh. Em. Gee. It'll be just like the old days."

All this excitement splintered my skull, but I had to play along. "I'd love to, really I would, but Lieutenant Holt asked me to review hours and hours of footage from surveillance cameras —nothing dangerous; don't worry—so I've got a date with my laptop. My night's ruined." To back up the lie, I mumbled, "Sucks" like I was all bummed out. "Try not to have too much fun without me."

"Aw, stinkersville. You sure you can't sneak away for a little while?"

I blurted, "Positive" too fast. "I mean, yeah. Guess I'll just have to catch the next one." *Unless, of course, she finds out who's been sucking Christopher's dick.*

"Alright, I guess. See ya later, alligator."

I droned, "In a while, crocodile."

Cradling the handset, I banged my forehead against the wall, my mouth souring from deceit. I just conned my best friend into not coming home. Could I sink any lower?

* * *

7:30 p.m.

After pacing the house, chewing my fingertips down to nubs of raw meat, checking and rechecking the locks on each and every door and window about a bazillion times, my jaw clenched so tight that thunderbolts of pain tunneled through my eardrums, I finally snatched the red folder and netbook off the breakfast bar and sat cross-legged on the couch. Reclining my head in between Berkley and Katie McGuire, their purrs vibrated my cheeks, but that didn't slow the massive surge of blood coursing through my veins, heating me from the inside out.

I tried focusing on the file, a list of names drawing me in...

Mary Rowlandson
William Bradford
Patrick Couturier
Amanda Orme
Theresa Jackson
John Winthrop
Adrian Smith

A hit list? I knew it! Mayhem could play innocent all he wants. Serial killers never just stop; they can't shake the ingrained thirst for bloodlust. Mayhem's the Headless Horse-man? Or did he work with a partner?

Why kill these particular people? Mayhem scrawled their

names for a reason. What connected them? It also couldn't be a coincidence that he'd jotted down seven names. Not eight, not nine. Seven.

I searched the social media of each victim. From what I could tell, Patrick Couturier and Amanda Orme were the only two on the list that knew each other. The others had no connection. William Bradford and John Winthrop didn't even have a Facebook or Twitter account, their online footprint almost nonexistent. Both played sports in college. John Winthrop made the newspaper in college for his outstanding batting average in baseball, and William Bradford was being scouted for a minor football league before a torn ACL injury ended his career.

Mary Rowlandson portrayed a happy homeworker lifestyle online, her children the center of her world. Lisa Jackson was single, her timeline filled with endless photos of her five cats. And Adrian Smith worked as a baker. Sucky hours, but other than that, nothing unusual stood out. If the specific individuals' lives didn't intersect, then how had they crossed paths with Mayhem?

My grandparents' names still haunted me. Why give me the middle name of Lee if Mom wasn't proud of her heritage? What was her heritage? Last names evolved as a way to sort people into groups, by occupation, origin, clan affiliation, patronage, parentage, adoption, even physical attributes, like hair or eye color. I brought up an ancestry website and typed "Lee" into the search box, but the last name had so many clan affiliations it was almost to pinpoint my family's origin.

My fingers rose to my parted lips, my skin tingling, eyes widening in disbelief. What if I searched the names on the hit list? If their lives didn't intersect, maybe their surnames did.

One by one, I typed the names into the search box.

"Rowlandson" dated back to eighteen-eighty-one, when most worked as farmers in the United Kingdom.

"Bradford" was a habitational name from any of the many

places, large and small, particularly in West Yorkshire, which in the old days, rose to prosperity as a wool town.

"Couturier" doubled as an occupational name for either a tailor or a smallholder, from an agent derivative of Old French couture "small plot."

"Orme" was Northern English, from the Old Norse personal name Ormr, originally a byname meaning snake, serpent, or dragon. It also had a French connotation.

"Jackson" was English, Scottish, and northern Irish, a patronymic from Jack. As an American surname, Jackson absorbed other patronymics beginning with "J" in various European languages.

"Winthrop" was an English habitational name from places in Lincolnshire and Nottinghamshire called Winthorpe. The former stemmed from the Old English personal name or byname Wine, meaning "friend" plus the Old Norse þorp, meaning "settlement."

The meanings of "Smith" were also English in origin. An occupational name for a worker in metal, from Middle English, which was probably a derivative of the Old English word "smitan," which meant "to strike, hammer." Metal-working was one of the earliest occupations that required specialist skills, and its importance ensured that this term and its equivalents were the most widespread of all occupational surnames in Europe.

All the names had one thing in common—Europe. What's Mayhem's beef with Europeans?

I darted into the kitchen and snatched the cordless handset off the wall. With Mayhem involved in the Headless Horseman murders, the best form of protection was to show Levaughn what I'd found. Especially now, after Poe set me up for Mrs. M's murder. Besides, at least now I had a concrete story that didn't sound like I'd been smokin' crack.

While I separated the blinds on the front window, ensuring

the Caddy wasn't parked on Lyndsey Lane, I thumbed the keypad.

The phone rang three times before he answered, "I was just thinking about you, gorgeous."

As sweet as those words were, I had more important issues to discuss, life and death problems. "I found a connection between the victims. You home?"

"No, I'm near the beach, collecting footage from the last few businesses. Can you tell me over the phone?"

"Umm…" Shit. If I couldn't get the hell outta Dodge, then I needed a way to lure my armed boyfriend here. Mace would only protect me for so long. "It's complicated. I need to show you. Is there any way you can swing by my place?" I added a bit more incentive. "Nadine and Maggie are gone for the night."

"Sure, gimme 'bout an hour. I'll grab a pizza on the way. Need anything else?"

How 'bout a few hand-grenades to fight the vicious serial killer who's on my ass, the *Holy Bible* to ward off evil spirits—what was the best way to fight a skinwalker?—and a fifth of Schnapps to numb my troubled mind?

I parted the blinds again, skimming the road for headlights, my unblinking eyes shifting up and down the darkened street. "Nope. All good, thanks." An annoying tic of my upper cheek twitched faster. "Hurry."

If Mayhem beat Levaughn here, I was as good as dead. Something heavy thudded on the porch, and I whirled around, the blinds snapping back into place. What was that?

CHAPTER THIRTY-SIX

"Above all, protect your inner light.
There are those that seek to take it from you."
- Sara Sacora

8:40 p.m.

Although Yaz deserved better than this, Mayhem dug her a grave at the base of a glorious old tree in the state park where she often brought her young daughter in the stroller. After a quick moment of silence, his fedora held over his heart, he raced home. Scrubbed the foyer from top to bottom, the five-gallon bucket crimsoning more and more with each twist of the sponge. He poured the filthy water down the kitchen sink and refilled with a hearty dose of bleach.

Upstairs, he tried to concentrate on washing the blood off the walls, carpet, flooring, and ceilings rather than on his wife's battered body, his insides twisting, his eyeballs sinking into the sockets, the irony aroma slashing open his chest.

An hour later, he stripped off all his clothes and slipped his bare feet into leather moccasins. Respecting a traditional burial rite ensured safe passage for his beloved wife to cross into the spiritual realm. Nothing else mattered.

Under Poe's watchful eye, Kimi's blessed vessel lay in the jetted bathtub while Mayhem smudged the house with sage, rather than set the unit ablaze. Old school custom recommended destroying the home if the deceased died inside, to prevent their ghost from lingering there. Destruction of the building allowed the soul to travel to the spirit world, unencumbered. But a fire in Boston's Back Bay would draw too much attention.

Nostrils flaring, he punched the wall, and Poe jerked off the edge of the bathtub, eyeballing him up and down as though he didn't approve.

"I apologize. You're right. Our main priority must be to provide a peaceful transition for Mom." His tone deepened, a vein shoving through the skin on his forehead. "We'll deal with Ms. Daniels soon enough."

He drew in calm, steady breaths when he slipped into that bathtub behind his loving wife. With the water on low, he snaked his arms around her waist, her blood-soaked hair feathering streaks across his bare chest. Whimpers escaped his parted lips as he gripped the hand-sprayer, angling the waterfall toward Kimi, his free hand shielding her eyes, his knees bracing her upright.

Blood swirled with the bathwater.

He lathered in a dollop of shampoo, her long, sudsy hair splashing arcs of scarlet across the tiled wall. With the tips of his fingers, he massaged cold cream on to her blood-drained face and pallid neck, tiny circular motions to scrub off crusted blood, careful to skip over the open wounds. A cool rinse washed off all of the residue.

Holding his precious wife by the wrist, her back slumped against his chest, he rubbed a soapy washcloth along her right arm, the curve of her elbow, her sculptured hand, and in between each delicate finger. He did the same on her left side, pausing briefly at her diamond-and-ruby wedding band, the memory of that glorious day threatening his resolve.

Closing his eyes, he pressed his lips to the back of her head, breathing her in. The sweetness of honeysuckle no longer existed. Ms. Daniels stole that too. His watery gaze fled to Poe. In a slumped stance, his beak hung to his chest feathers.

"Why did Mom insist we return to Boston?" he hushed, his tone hollowing. "If we had stayed in upstate New York, she might still be alive."

Poe threw his back and screeched, the mournful cry shredding the knots in Mayhem's stomach. He reached for him and then recoiled. Poe needed to absorb this devastation in his own way, in his own time.

With his foot, he flipped the lever. The bloody water slurped into the drain as he rose, his beloved wife cradled in his arms. Dripping wet, his long hair draped down his spine, he carried Kimi into the master bedroom, her lifeless body riddled with stab wounds. The full moon—big and bright—cascaded through the stained-glass window, spilling colors over the bedspread. Kimi loved the eagle depicted in the glass; she'd stared at it for hours at a time. What he never counted on was her joining them so soon.

How did he let this happen?

Poe flew to Kimi's pillow. Head down, his neck sunk. Inconsolable, his mournful wails plucked Mayhem's heartstrings. Why hadn't he seen the pent-up rage inside Ms. Daniels? If he had known, he would never have agreed to help her.

Mayhem slipped a black Tom Ford cocktail dress over Kimi's wet hair and straightened the sweetheart neckline, tulle overlay, and lamb-leather trim into place. This was the same dress she wore the night they celebrated the birth of their grandson.

He sat behind her on the bed and braided her hair. Once

perfect, he veiled her in a shroud and added dry ice. Covering her face signaled her to join the dance of the ghosts.

Within four days they must arrive at her burial site before her spirit completed its earthly journey. If he buried her nearby, the gray wolf and his men might be tempted to pilfer her grave of valuables, as well as strip off her dead flesh to use in their maniacal rituals. Necrophilia was also not beyond their disgraceful praxis.

He had the perfect spot in mind, one that would grant her final wish. The drive, however, would take much too long. A private plane could decrease travel time to twenty-one hours if it did not stop to refuel. No private planes had that luxury, so that simply would not do. The most practical solution was to drive to Colorado and rent a biplane for the last leg of the trip. Which meant the pilot would need to be dealt with afterward, but he had no other choice. Kimi's journey to the spiritual realm took precedent. No one else mattered.

Before he left on his trip, he scrawled a note to Chayton—specifics for his *coup de grâce*, the blow of mercy, one final killing to end the suffering—and handed it to Poe. "Deliver this, please. And keep an eye on Ms. Daniels. We cannot allow her to escape before my return."

CHAPTER THIRTY-SEVEN

8:40 p.m.

W hile waiting for Levaughn to arrive, I climbed into my rattan basket chair, its weaved walls sheltering me from the world. Berkley hopped in my lap, and I ran a palm down his silky black coat. "How ya doin', buddy? I feel like we haven't chatted in days."

His purr filled the room, slowing the thrum of my pulse to a manageable pace. Katie McGuire's head popped up from the sofa, and she thinned her eyes, glaring at me as if I was playing favorites.

I blew her a kiss, but she ignored me. Might as well have flipped me off, the way she preened her belly as though I wasn't in the room, her scratchy tongue snagging on fluffy, white fur. The "M" on her forehead looked more like a "W" from this angle, but I didn't dare tell her. As it was, my name was on enough animals' shit-lists.

A loud crash thundered on the deck, freezing my hand midway to Berkley's tail. Heavy footfalls above my head likened to a horse that had galloped on to the roof, its hooves clomping across the shingles. Cold sweats broke across my back. My palms grew clammy, Berkley's hair sticking to my fingers. Back and forth the thing paced above the living room and kitchen, and I followed the sound with my eyes.

A bloodcurdling scream shook the window panes. Then complete silence. Dead silent. Almost too quiet, like it was gearing up to attack.

The pounding on the back sliders jerked me to my feet, my body board-stiff, the glass weakening from the force. Back arched, Berkley mewled, his golden eyes pinned to the louver blinds as they breathed…in and out. Katie McGuire dove off the couch and raced up the spiral stairs to hide under my bed while the rest of us got murdered.

Slow, quiet, I crept toward the sliders, my whole body warning me to stop. "Who's there?" My raspy voice cracked, pitched. "Whaddaya want?"

Nails scratched down the glass. Deliberate. Ominous. Threatening.

I flipped on the porch light, and my temperature shot to two hundred degrees. A tall figure cowered back into the shadows, its human-like face blurry, flaming red eyes piercing the darkness with a sinister stare. I couldn't move, couldn't look away. This beast drew me in, beckoning me closer, my free will teetering on the edge of compliance.

"Open the door" echoed inside my head, and I reached for the slider's wooden handle.

"Yessss…" The breathy voice wispy, demonic. "Let…me…in…"

The red eyes never strayed, never flinched. My posture fell limp, head lolled to one side, my left hand dangling at my thigh, my right frozen inches from the glass.

A *rat-a-tat-tat* at the front door snapped me awake. I rotated halfway toward the knock, but an overwhelming yearning lassoed me to the sliders.

"Let…me…in…"

The breathy voice held me hostage, and I flipped open the lock.

A slight smirk emerged through the darkness, thin lips arched below flaming eyes. This beast towered over the six-foot doorframe. Whatever it was, it wasn't human, its presence unnatural, beguiling, its blackened aura an all-consuming evil.

Rat-a-tat-tat. Rat-a-tat-tat.

"Pizza delivery for the most beautiful woman in the world." Levaughn's sultry voice carried through the front door. "Babe? No sleeping on the job." The long pause of silence sent my gaze volleying between the two exits, and I shifted my weight from leg to leg. "Shawnee, you in there?"

ZZ Ward's *Put the Gun Down* blasted from my cell phone and thrust me out of the haze. I reset the lock on the sliders, killed the porch light, and bolted for the front door. Twisted open all the deadbolts and dove into Levaughn's arms, my vice-grip tightening around his neck, head on his shoulder, a fierce shudder rattling my ribcage.

"My God." He squeezed me with one arm, stewed tomatoes, mozzarella, and pepperoni rising from the pizza box in his other hand. "You alright?"

"Err…uh…" How would I explain an otherworldly creature? "Who, me?" Granted, not my best response ever, but it's the best I could come up with at the time. "Yeah." I released him, my hands straightening the bottom of my gray leopard print sweatshirt, worn edges curled from where I'd shortened it to mid-abs. "I'm fine." Seemed like I was saying that a lot lately. "Why?"

His cop eyes studied me for twenty years, trying to decipher what I didn't say. "I knocked, like, five times."

"Oh." Clearing my scratchy throat, I slid my fingers up the back of my sweaty scalp. "You did?"

"Yeah." His lips pursed. "You sure you're okay? You look, I dunno, tired." In male lingo, "tired" equaled "like shit."

"Gee, thanks."

His shoulders deflated. "I didn't mean it like that."

"Whatever." I waved him inside. "You comin' in or what?"

"Absolutely." In his mind, all was forgiven. Men were so easy at times. "Where are the paper plates? They didn't give me any."

As he sauntered into the kitchen, I scanned the street for the Caddy, the gold Hummer, or the freakshow from my porch. Behind me, cabinet doors opened, closed, opened, closed. *Slam, slam, slam.* Then the drawers. *Slide, bang. Slide, bang. Slide, bang.*

"I'm starving," he announced as if it wasn't obvious. "How 'bout you?"

"Yeah," I lied, "I could eat." Puking would be a more accurate description, but I played it cool. The pistol on Levaughn's hip could defend us if Mayhem showed, or if the beast returned.

Would bullets even stop a skinwalker?

I hip-checked him out of the way and swung open the half-cabinet above the stove. "Nay reorganized the kitchen again. Oy." Why I asked her to move in escaped me at the moment. "Yup. Here we go."

I slapped the package on the breakfast bar, and Levaughn wasted no time. He slid two slices to his plate, strings of mozzarella still attached to the pizza box.

With a mouthful of pizza, sauce dribbled down his chin. "Aren't you havin' any?"

"Oh. Right. 'Course." My stomach flipped and flopped, the acids swashing like webbed feet in a kiddy pool.

Swallowing the massive bite, Levaughn's eyes narrowed in on me again. "Don't take this the wrong way, but you seem a little on-edge."

A little? Ha! That'd be like saying Jaws was just a misunderstood fish. "What?" I flung up my hands, slapping my thighs on the way down. "I'm sitting here eating pizza like you are."

"Shawnee, you haven't taken one bite." With a hesitating nod, he ran his tongue across his bottom lip, like he questioned my sanity.

Sadly, he wasn't wrong. "I'm serious. It's all good." A sharp pang struck my empty stomach, and my fake smile morphed into a wince. "How was your day?" My tone was so upbeat it could've garnered an Oscar. "Didn't you say somethin' about an eyewitness?"

"Yeah. Me. Remember? That's why I wanted the camera footage. You sure you're—"

Sick of the ol' song 'n dance routine, I cut him off. "Right. 'Course I remember. I'm not that brain-dead." Yet.

I rolled up a slice and stuffed half of it into my mouth. Grinning at Levaughn, I attempted to swallow before chewing, and a piece stuck halfway down my throat. I swiped a bottled water off the counter and sucked it down, praying to all that's holy that it'd push the pizza down far enough, so my already-suspicious man didn't wind up giving me the Heimlich. But if he kept drilling me with questions, sooner or later this pizza would be coming back up—the one certainty in my life.

Was Maggie right about the *yenaldlooshi*? Even after coming face-to-face with a skinwalker, the notion that a Navajo witch could transform into an animal still made no sense. How was it even possible? And why did it set its sights on me?

On my stool, I nonchalantly rotated toward the sliding doors. Pitch blackness engulfed the deck. As I slapped a hand on the breakfast bar to swivel back around, burning red eyes caught in my peripheral vision, and I did a double-take. But only my reflection stared back at me.

"Monte's has the best pizza in the state, bar-none." Totally unaware of the evil lurking around my house, Levaughn snapped his fingers. "Aw, man. I shoulda picked us up a bottle of wine."

I flashed him a quick, fake smile, my pulse skyrocketing to

two-hundred beats per minute. What if an encounter with a skinwalker forced my mother to run away from her childhood home? Ed told me she'd been raped, but he never mentioned the circumstances surrounding it. What if a whole pack of these beasts gangraped her? In her letter, she used the word "them" not "him." My hand clawed at my neck, my airway constricting. What if they took turns while others held her down? Mom never gave specifics, other than her friend Kimi was with her that night.

I couldn't catch my breath, the area around me spinning faster and faster. Could these hellish creatures reproduce? Levaughn said something unintelligible, but I was trapped inside my head, consumed by the terror my mother had experienced all those years ago. How old was she when this happened? A coldness penetrated my bones, twisting my joints. Had I even been born yet? My diaphragm fisted shut. Was Josiah Daniels my real father or did I come from pure evil?

Levaughn said, "Babe?"

Could I be the product of rape, of unmerciful violence?

"Hey—" He shook me by the shoulders, jerking me out of an endless pit of uncertainty, a tangled web of deceit, betrayal. "Where'd you go?"

My mind snapped back into place. "Huh?"

"I know you said you're okay, but—" He swatted away his comment, probably afraid he'd rile me. "What'd you wanna show me?"

My eyebrows squished together. "Show you?"

"On the phone, you said you found a connection between the vics?"

"Oh. Right. That. Yeah." I abandoned my half-eaten slice on the plate and slid my netbook across the breakfast bar.

Levaughn's hand moved toward the red folder, but I slapped it away and stashed the file on top of the refrigerator. "Sorry," I said, turning back around. "Ed gave me info about my mom and dad."

He startled. "Ed? You went to see him after what he did?"

"Didn't I tell you?" I said all innocent-like, knowing damn well I hadn't. "He didn't kill anyone. Delsin set him up."

"Jack Delsin?" He clawed a hand through his short-cropped hair. "The serial killer?"

"Yeah." Both shoulders rose to my ears. "That's what he said."

"Oh...kay..." He used that condescending tone again, and my upper lip twitched in defiance. "Then who did?"

"Dunno, but I intend to find out." Before this conversation led to a full confession on my part, I veered back to the investigation by typing the first name into the ancestry website.

"Check this out." I angled the screen so Levaughn could view the page. "See where it says Rowlandson is an English surname? The same holds true for all the victims. Well, Couturier is French, and Orme is either English or French, depending on..." I let the sentence trail off because, well, I forgot what distinguished one from the other. "Not important. Anyway, they're all European. So, maybe the specific person doesn't matter. Maybe he targeted them 'cause of their ancestral roots."

Admittedly, this argument sounded better in my head.

When I was just about to retract my theory—blame it on sleep deprivation or whatever—Levaughn blinked at the screen, his eyes growing larger and larger. "I knew it!" He slapped his knee. "Odin tried to tell me the only reason the suspect scalped the victims was out of necessity—easier to carry a scalp than the whole head—but I had a hunch the stories I'd read had something to do with these murders."

"Stories, what stories?"

"The only thing that doesn't align is the double sevens."

I slapped the breakfast bar, hard, a sting tingling across my palm. "What stories?"

"I researched the history of scalping the enemy." He explained how the practice first started and how it became a lucrative business for some, and then he shared the story of an entire Cheyenne tribe wiped out by European soldiers, including details about the atrocities committed against them. Details I could've lived without knowing.

"Whoa. Fuckin' barbarians." A split-second later, my insides vibrated, a bright light surging through my system. "Lemme try somethin' real quick." I googled Native Americans versus Europeans, and numerous articles filled the screen. "Whoa." I clicked one of the links, my gaze scanning the article. "Ever hear of the Trail of Tears?"

"Vaguely. Sounds familiar."

"Says here it's a series of forced relocations. Native Americans were driven off their ancestral land by the government, an act that violated American ideals, laws, American treaties, and also the humanity, rights, and dignity of the Cherokee Nation."

I read ahead. "Wait—not only Cherokee but Creek, Seminole, Chickasaw, Choctaw, Ponca, and Ho-Chunk/Winnebago nations, as well. Scratch that. All Native Americans suffered when the US government passed the Indian Removal Act. It says American settlers had been pressuring the federal government to remove Indians—" I side-glanced at Levaughn— "that's their description, not mine."

Skimming the article, I searched for where I'd left off, but it took me a minute to find my place. "Oh, actually, American Indian is an acceptable term."

I scanned down a few lines. "Okay, here we go. The government forced American Indians outta the Southeast. Many settlers encroached on Indian lands, while others wanted more land made available to European settlers. Although the effort was vehemently opposed by some, President Andrew Jackson was able to gain Congressional passage of the Indian Removal

Act of eighteen-thirty, which authorized the government to extinguish Indian title to lands in the Southeast."

Staring at the screen, I tugged at my ear, my fingers spinning the diamond stud. "Unbelievable. The government approved this?"

Totally engrossed in the article, Levaughn didn't answer my question right away, his complete attention on that screen. "Wow. Both Presidents Jackson and Martin Van Buren were involved. The Indian Removal Act of eighteen-thirty gave the President powers to exchange land with Native tribes and provided infrastructure improvements on existing lands, but didn't allow the President to force tribes to move west without a mutual agreed-upon treaty."

His expression blanched, his head shaking back and forth. "They did it anyway. Even after the Supreme Court ruled in the Cherokee Nation's favor. This can't be right."

"Well, it is. And you—" I pointed right in his face— "wonder why I don't blindly trust authority like the rest of the minions."

"Babe, this happened a long time ago."

"And that makes it okay?" My stare turned icy cold, heat barreling up my chest. "Eight thousand American Indians died on that trail! These assholes made them walk twelve-hundred miles—barefoot!—through unbearable weather conditions! And that's not all." I jumped off my stool, slamming one index finger against the other, my voice booming. "If we count all the tribes, millions lost their lives to that Removal Act—millions!"

"Babe—" Hands held in surrender, he took a step toward me. "You gotta calm down."

"Calm down? Look at this shit!" I raced back to the netbook and clicked article after article, my ingrained heritage rising up, the blood of my ancestors pulsing through me. "Mothers buried their children in shallow graves on the side of the road. Husbands buried wives, sisters buried brothers. Think the soldiers cared? No. They wouldn't even give them a moment to grieve or honor them in any way."

Tears bloomed in my eyes, the missing puzzle piece of my life clicking into place, a sacred bond that linked me with my mom and all my distant relatives. "This was genocide."

I rubbed my eyes with the back of my hand, my black eyeliner probably halfway down my cheeks. "Do you blame the suspect for hating Europeans? They're not the only ones to blame, either. The entire white race is culpable."

Levaughn arched one eyebrow. "Isn't that a little like the pot callin' the kettle black?"

"Yes! That's my point." The moisture in my throat dried to sand, and I banged a fist against the breakfast bar, my paper plate skipping across the butcher block, onto the floor. Crumbs, sauce, and crust scattered everywhere. "Christopher Columbus didn't discover a fuckin' thing! He stole America from the Indians who walked this land for hundreds of years!"

In a soothing voice, he said, "So, then, you think it's okay that the Headless Horseman decapitated seven innocent men and women for the sins of their ancestors?"

"Obviously, I'm not sayin' that. But you of all people should relate." I crossed my arms and tossed a sarcastic smirk his way. "Just sayin'."

"Really." He quailed back in his seat, his tone deepening as if daring me to mention his race. "Why's that?"

Shit. How could I put this so I wouldn't insult him? This conversation danced dangerously close to an all-out war.

"Look," I conceded. "The Jews cried out against the Holocaust, and the world showed compassion. We were horrified at what occurred there, and we still honor the ones who managed to escape. But American Indians were also held in concentration camps. Thousands died there. Who cries for them? We don't bow our heads in a moment of silence for the unspeakable acts committed against their people. Hell, in school, no one even teaches the correct history. Instead, they fill our heads with the *Mayflower* and Plymouth Rock bullshit."

He parted his full lips, but I beat him to it. "And do you know why? Because it's America's dirty little secret. It makes us look bad, so no one dares to say it out loud. Yet, rich white assholes enslaved African Americans for years, and we learned all about slavery in the history books. Didn't we?"

I didn't give him a chance to respond. "But American Indians were also kept as slaves. Ever hear about it? No!" My blood pressure rose again. "It's like we, as a nation, have totally disregarded the true settlers of this country."

I threw up my hands, tears rising in my throat. "For chrissakes, it's the only race that's measured by blood quantum. Why don't they deserve the same respect as everyone else?"

In retrospect, I probably should've hopped off this particular soapbox a lot sooner, but I couldn't come to grips with the savagery committed against my mother's people—my ancestors. "Tribes communed with nature. The land provided clean drinking water, food from crops, good hunting. They never longed for riches, just a peaceful existence. And they took care of their own. If one starved, they all starved. If one had a harvest or caught fish, the whole tribe benefited. They lived as God intended."

Salt burned my eyes, my mother's all-consuming spirit speaking through me as if she'd swept me back in time to witness the horror firsthand, and I experienced my ancestors' gut-wrenching sadness, their torment, and pain. "The pilgrims couldn't understand the Indians' minimalist lifestyle. What we don't understand, we fear. We sit in judgement. We destroy."

He leaned toward me and set a gentle hand on my knee, his warm amber eyes saddening, pleading. "Shawnee—"

"They even gave the so-called settlers furs as a token of peace. Did they appreciate it? 'Course not." I ground my jaw, choking back my emotions. "The greedy bastards had already caught gold fever, selling the furs in Europe for big bucks, the almighty dollar blinding them to the simple and honest ways of indigenous people." Hanging my head, tears rolled off my nose. "American Indians even welcomed their new neighbors. Talk about a rude awakening."

Silence enveloped the room.

Eyes in a squint, Levaughn studied me, his stare unnerving, dispirited, searching, as though he tried to reason why this subject had such a profound effect on me.

My knee bounced in anticipation.

"Your theory has legs," he finally said. "Except for one crucial element." He ran his finger down the computer screen, stopping at the exact route taken by the Cherokee Nation during the forced relocation. "The Trail of Tears didn't pass through New England."

"But…" Staring at the screen, I rested my cheek against a closed fist, my elbow doing all the work to hold me upright. "I know I'm right." I chewed my bottom lip. "Aren't I?"

In deep circles, he rubbed my back. "I'm not saying you're wrong, but instead of focusing on the motive, I think the best use of our time is to search the surveillance footage."

What if Mayhem stepped into the view of the camera? What if his Cadillac CTS rolled into the frame, and Levaughn traced the plates? The two haunting questions rolled over and over in my mind, my scattered thoughts trying to decipher my best course of action. Should I confess, and take my chances that he'd believe me, that I didn't murder Mrs. M? Or flat-out lie?

CHAPTER THIRTY-EIGHT

Thursday
2:05 a.m.

For hours we scrolled through mind-numbing footage of vehicles pulling in and out of area businesses. I'd rather have my eyeballs pierced than sit through another second of this, but I played it cool. For now.

"There—" Levaughn jutted a stiff finger at the screen. "Whatever you do, don't lose that black Escalade."

Nice and slow, I rolled the footage forward, but the Escalade drove off-screen.

"One sec." I switched to another camera, and then fast-forwarded to approximately the same date and time. "There's the tail end of it." Punching the keys, I switched to the camera outside Kelly's Roast Beef, and the Escalade rolled by. Shifting between camera angles allowed me to track the vehicle to Oak Island Street.

I sat back. "Well, that's it. We're outta footage. Now what?"

"C'mon." Levaughn hopped off the stool and bustled toward the door.

I chased after him. "Where're we goin'? The Headless Horseman dumped the Escalade days ago. Isn't it at the impound lot?"

"Yeah, but it doesn't matter. I wanted the footage to see where he went." He opened the passenger door, and I crawled inside. Levaughn darted around the front bumper and then slipped behind the wheel. Starting the engine, he explained, "Chavez found red fibers at almost all the crime scenes. So, if we look for a vehicle with a red interior, maybe it'll lead us to his hideout. How many cars could there be in one neighborhood?"

Long shots must sound more doable at two o'clock in the morning. "A lot." I flipped open my netbook. "But maybe I can narrow it down." In the DMV database, I ran a search for all vehicles within that one city block. Only two listed the interior as red, a two-thousand-three Ford Explorer and a twenty-ten Kia Forte.

A quick Google search told me the Kia was a compact car, which wasn't an ideal choice for transporting corpses. "Okay. Take Oak Island to Arcadia. Then turn on to Argyle Street. We're looking for a two-thousand-three Ford Explorer on Ellerton Street, off Argyle."

"Which part of Ellerton?"

"Not sure if the house numbers go up or down." I waved him forward. "Just drive. We'll figure it out."

The congested neighborhood consisted of houses climbing on the backs of their neighbors, others elbowed in between. "If I was the Headless Horseman, this would be the last place I'd hide. There's no privacy. Look at this shit." My gaze roamed through the crowded area. "There are witnesses everywhere."

"Actually, it's perfect. He's hiding in plain sight." He jabbed a chin at my passenger window. "Keep searching for a vehicle with red interior. My gut tells me we're close."

He drove to the end of Ellerton Street, but we didn't find one Ford Explorer, never mind the vehicle in question.

I waved him forward again. "Cross York Street. I think Ellerton continues."

And so, he did.

While I aimed his high-powered flashlight at every driveway along the right-side of the street, he scanned the left with the spotlight mounted by his window.

"It's not lookin' good, Detective."

"Don't lose faith just yet."

Several yards down, in the cylindrical beams of light, bucket seats peeked through the passenger window of a black Ford Explorer—red cloth interior, with the corner of one seat shredded—and two flat rear tires. Either someone had let the air out, or the driver ran through broken glass.

"Found it!" I backhanded Levaughn's bicep. "Look—red interior."

"Good eye, babe. Okay, kill the light." After he coasted curbside, he dug his cell out of his jacket pocket.

"What're you doin'?

"Calling for backup."

My nostrils flared. "What if Odin responds? I'm not gettin' in another pissing match with a fed. Can't we just check it out first?"

"Shawnee…"

I flashed a flat hand, stopping him mid-sentence. "Don't even go there."

"I have to. It's my job." His jaw bone pulsed through the skin. "This scumbag killed seven people. And you're not armed."

True. I hated guns, but I never let that stop me before. My empty back pocket also illuminated the fact that I'd left my mace at home. Crap. With no good argument, I tore a page out of Nadine's book and whined. "Pretty please." I waved praying hands in his direction. "I can do this, you know I can. Unless, of course, you don't trust me."

Okay, fine, maybe I'd tossed that last comment a little low, but I had to see this case through to the end. Everything about these murders screamed Mayhem's behind the killing spree. And now thanks to Poe—a friggin' crow hellbent on revenge; the party never ends—I needed as much ammunition as I could get.

Levaughn tsked his tongue. "'Course I trust you. That's not the problem."

"Cops and their rules. You didn't seem to mind breaking SOP—" Standard Operating Procedure—"when you sent me into Delsin's house that night."

"That was different. Babe, we're talkin' about putting your life in jeopardy."

"And, what, I was safe breaking into a serial killer's crib?" I huffed. "This is stupid." I opened the door and got out. Pushed it closed without a sound and leaned back through the opened window. "Ya comin' or what?"

Massaging his temples, he looked to the cloth ceiling, yammering, "This woman will be the death of me."

"Yeah, yeah, whatever." I spun and prowled across the street, squatting behind an overgrown bush—a mere six feet from the bed of the truck.

Levaughn jogged across the street, and I darted to the side of the tiny house that some jerkoff squeezed in between two Dormered-Capes. A lit television mirrored off the glass pane above my head.

I raised to my tippy-toes, peering over the sill into a barren room with a tattered futon that doubled as a couch. An uncased pillow teetered atop a white, red, black, and yellow colored blanket, neatly folded underneath. Old hardwood showed a well-worn trail that led to a hotplate and coffee maker, near a table for two. In the center of the room, suspended from the ceiling by rope, seven bulbs illuminated glass Mason jars in a wide strip of barnboard, casting interlocking rings across the floor.

A warpainted face appeared in the window, and I let go of the sill. Huddled beneath it, my back pressed to the siding, I moved slow, careful, till I reached the truck. Then scrambled over to Levaughn, still hunched behind the bush.

With labored breath, I hushed, "He made me."

"Don't move from this spot." Gun drawn, he crossed the end of the driveway and crept across the grass of the front yard.

I followed close behind.

Next to the front door, a flag wafted in the breeze, a white background with seven red stars in the shape of the Big Dipper on one side, the colors inverted on the opposite side.

Tapping Levaughn on the shoulder, I jabbed my head at the flag. "Check it out. There's our sevens. Whaddaya think it means?" With my cell, I snapped a quick photo.

The front door busted open.

A man with a red-and-black warpainted face soldiered down the stairs, his long fingers gripped tight around the handle of a sword. "You're too late, Detective. The sacred fire's been lit. My destiny is complete."

"Drop the sword," ordered Levaughn, his voice hard, cold. "Lace your fingers on top of your head."

"Never forget the cost of this sacred land, bathed in the blood of my people." With unwavering determination he drew the blade across his throat, severing his jugular, blood spurting from the wound—conjuring in me the images of Mrs. M—and he crumpled to the ground.

"No!" I charged toward him, but Levaughn grabbed my arm, spun me around.

Leaning in, his eyes were inches from mine. "I'll handle this. Call for a bus."

Speechless, I nodded.

Levaughn kicked the sword out of reach and knelt beside the Headless Horseman while I stood frozen, helpless.

"Shawnee, call a bus!"

I fumbled to find my cell. Hit nine-one-one.

The operator said, "Nine-one-one, what is your emergency?"

The suspect gurgled, blood rattling his larynx, his lifeless eyes splayed open for eternity. Dead. This guy martyred himself, his underlying message showing a warped view of history steeped in lies, betrayal, the very country I loved blackened by truth.

Even though the Headless Horseman died, could we really call this a win for humanity?

CHAPTER THIRTY-NINE

"You see no tears falling down my face,
but if you look deep into my eyes,
you can see them flowing from my soul."
- The Wolf

Friday
3 p.m.

Crab pots lined the street of Ballyhoo Road in Alaska. Mayhem's restless fingers strummed the steering wheel as he drove past rows of stacked containers, awaiting hauls from fishermen, hungry eagles and ravens circling above. The commercial fishing town of Unalaska had the densest eagle population of anywhere in the world. Locals around Dutch Harbor fondly referred to them as pigeons due to the eight-hundred eagles that swarmed the docks to feed on the surplus of leftover catch.

A sad smile toyed with the corners of his lips. The little rascals also dive-bombed passersby and snatched cell phones right out of their hands. The quaint Post Office supplied helmets and sticks so people could defend themselves on their way to mail a letter.

Mayhem chuckled to himself. In the eagles' defense, they were only guarding their young, their nests within feet of the main entrance. Protection of family trumped all. He angled the rear-view mirror, his eyes saddening at the shroud on the backseat.

Five years before the diagnosis, after encountering nearly six-hundred eagles within a few square miles, he and Kimi built a humble abode on the outskirts of Unalaska's eighty-mile stretch of island.

Yet even here, in Mother Earth's most breathtaking state, indigenous people were uprooted from their homes with almost no warning. After the bombing of Dutch Harbor, the government evacuated eight-hundred-and-eighty Unangan residents, testing their heritage by blood quantum. Those with even one-eighth Indian blood were driven off their ancestral land, with no knowledge of where they were heading or if they'd return. The relocation forced American Indians to live in dilapidated, dangerous, and inhumane camps for the duration of the war.

Many died in captivity from malnutrition or disease.

It was a bittersweet homecoming for the Unangan in nineteen-forty-five when they returned to find their homes and churches ransacked, their family possessions stolen by servicemen or ruined by exposure to the elements. The government refused to allow the people of Attu, Biorka, Kashega, and Makushin to ever return. An engraved black monument marked this tragic historical event, the face of a tearful tribe member carved at the top as a symbol of their suffering.

Most of the world still refused to grant American Indians the respect they so richly deserved—a mindset Kimi vowed to change. Instead, early colonists built their homesteads on the blood of American Indians—an important message for the world and one dear Chayton chose to sacrifice himself to reveal.

This was such a solemn day for many reasons. Mayhem glanced again at the rear-view mirror that reflected his lifeless bride's shroud, cocooned in a tribal blanket. He'd travelled thirty-three hours to this wondrous land, with its majestic snow-capped mountains and rich, green grasslands so his beloved could soar with the eagles.

"And soar, you will, my love." Muscle tremors vibrated his forearms, and he tightened his grip on the steering wheel to hang on, his hands wringing the leather, his gaze wandering back to the holy vessel of the most amazing woman in the world.

His wet eyes blinked away the tears as he turned into the driveway of their log cabin. From the back passenger door, he slid his arms under his beloved, cradling her in his arms for the last time as he plodded into the backyard, where he lay his precious Kimi on a flat-topped rock.

With a hand over her heart, he said, "Be cautious in your journey, my love. Trust that the spirits are there to guide you." The hollowness deepened inside him. "Cheyenne, Jude, and I will miss you in this world, our temporary home, along with countless others who adore you." He rested his cheek on the tribal blanket that spanned her chest, grief drilling into him, consuming him, shredding the best part of him.

"We shall not be parted for long, my darling, for I shall soon follow."

Pinching the bridge of his nose, he tried to wrangle his emotions under control. "When you reach the happy land of our forefathers—" he sniffled, his vision clouding more and more— "may you continue to be the shining light that you were in the physical world." His lips trembled, fighting against his restraint. "I love you more than life itself."

Hanging his head, he laid a hand on his stomach, his abdominal muscles twisting in torment, the very heart of his existence in shambles on the rock.

He lumbered to the driveway and raised the trunk to gather the proper burial supplies.

When he returned to Kimi, an awe-inspiring raven landed on the shroud. As he neared, the bird lifted its beak—strong and proud—and then spread his glorious wings. Silent, the raven hopped off the shroud but only shuffled over a few inches, his talons gripping the rock. Undeterred by Mayhem's presence, he remained vigilant in his duty to lead Kimi to the afterlife, her final spiritual resting place.

When nothing profound sprang to mind—no amount of begging could repair his devastation—he uttered a heartfelt, "Thank you."

Unlike Poe, the raven showed no reaction. His eyes never wavered, his stance never wilted. And Mayhem appreciated that he took his calling seriously.

With careful consideration to Kimi's battered remains, he enveloped her from head to toe in birch bark, cinching the satchel closed with a basswood cord. While he dug her grave, the raven continued to protect her.

He bundled her in his arms and lowered her birch cocoon into the earth, with her feet facing west toward the afterlife. No sorrow was allowed now, no outward signs of grief. After a ceremonial dance, he backfilled the grave with handfuls of rich soil. Instead of a marker, he sat cross-legged on the dirt and hand-hewed the tree stump at her head.

For hours, he carved the totem, marking it with symbols of who Kimi was in life, her accomplishments, clan affiliation, and inverted spirit animals, which indicated death. A pair of hummingbirds symbolized his and Kimi's everlasting union; a raven signaled the danger had passed and good luck would soon follow. The bald eagle showed her courage and strength; it also honored her Chippewa roots. Lastly, he carved a crow for her innate wisdom, and the undying love she shared with Poe,

Edgar, Allan, and the others. Her reunion with Thoreau and Annabel would be an exciting event indeed.

As he stood before the grave, a silent mayhem hardened around his heart. Upon his return, Ms. Daniels would pay the ultimate price for betraying the one woman who vowed to protect her, all those years ago.

CHAPTER FORTY

Saturday
6 a.m.

L ieutenant Holt asked me to work for a couple hours on Detective North's purse-snatching case. The moron still hadn't solved it. Since overtime was on the table, I slogged into the computer lab with no sleep, Levaughn trailing behind me.

"I need to get back to the scene," he said. "If you finish early, call me."

"Honestly, it'll take me all of fifteen minutes to find Chuck's guy. Aren't you curious 'bout what he meant by the sacred fire?"

"'Course I am." He shrugged like it was no big deal. "Sometimes we don't get the whole picture. Nature of the beast."

"Nature of the beast? That's it, case closed?"

"Babe, we caught the bad guy. The Headless Horseman is dead. Our job isn't to sort out the twisted motivation of a serial killer."

"Well, maybe that half-assed excuse works for you, but I'll never be able to sleep without knowing why he did it or what it all meant. Chayton Kashk—" IDd through fingerprints on file

with RPD, from a ten-year-old drunk and disorderly charge—
"died for his cause. The least we could do is decrypt his final
words."

He cupped my cheek. "I love when you reveal your heart."

Pulling my face away, I yammered, "Yeah, yeah" as I logged
into my computer.

Levaughn dragged over a chair to my desk, the legs scraping
across the linoleum.

"Thought you had to go?"

"Meh." Another shrug. "They'll be fine till I get there. Let's
finish this."

I leaned aside and kissed him. "Thank you." Then I uploaded
the photo that I took outside Chayton Kashk's house and
instructed Google to find similar images. An early Cherokee flag
filled the screen, the white side signaling peace, the red side for
war. "Now the sevens make sense, right?" Without waiting for a
reply, I typed "sacred fire" into the search box.

Levaughn leaned in. "What is that?"

"Not sure yet. It's called The Seven Fires Prophecy." I
skimmed the article. "Oh, okay, it's an Anishinaabe prophecy
that marked life phases for the people of Turtle Island."

Levaughn scratched his five o'clock shadow. "Turtle Island?"

"Guess that's what American Indians used to call North
America back in the day. Anyway, the Seven Fires represents key
spiritual teachings, suggesting that different colors and tradi-
tions come together in mutual respect."

"Okay," he said, unconvinced. "For what, a ceremony?"

"No idea. I haven't gotten that far. Gimme a second." My
gaze shifted back and forth across the screen. "Wow. It's a
prophecy that predates European settlers, even. The Anishinaabe consisted of several tribes, by the way."

Levaughn's eyelids dropped to half-mast.

Since I was losing him—the lack of sleep taking control—I
jumped ahead. "Here we go. With the growing Pan-Indian

Movement of the nineteen sixties and seventies, a philosophy and movement promoting unity among different indigenous American groups, regardless of tribal affiliations, concepts of the Seven Fires Prophecy merged with similar prophetic teachings, and the indigenous people formed a unified environmental, political, and socio-economic voice toward the United States and Canada."

"Well, if that's true—" he brushed dirt off the tips of his dress shoes like he could care less— "then how could Chayton Kashk light the sacred fire?"

"Good question, Detective." I winked. "That's why they pay you the big bucks." Returning my attention to the screen, I read the prophecy of the First Fire...

In the time of the First Fire, the Anishinaabe Nation will rise up and follow the sacred shell of the Midewiwin Lodge. The Midewiwin Lodge will serve as a rallying point for the people, and its traditional ways will be the source of much strength. The Sacred Megis will lead the way to the chosen ground of the Anishinaabe.

You are to look for a turtle-shaped island that is linked to the purification of the earth. You will find such an island at the beginning and end of your journey. There will be seven stopping places along the way. You will know the chosen ground has been reached when you come to a land where food grows on water. If you do not move, you will be destroyed.

"Wow." I nudged Levaughn with my elbow, forcing him to pay attention. "Read that last line. Maybe that's why Chayton traveled between Mass and New Hampshire. He didn't dare stop, or death might take him too soon."

Levaughn kept examining his shoes while I read the Second Fire...

. . .

You will know the Second Fire because at this time the Nation will be camped by a large body of water. In this time the direction of the Sacred Shell will be lost. The Midewiwin will diminish in strength. A boy will be born to point the way back to the traditional ways. He will show the direction to the stepping stones to the future of the Anishinaabe people.

Nodding in a continuous yes, I turned my head toward Levaughn. "Did Chayton believe he was that boy?"

"How the hell should I know?" On the sly, he glimpsed his watch, but I caught it.

"Y'know what? If you don't wanna be here, then go. It's not like I need you for this."

"Aw, come on." He played with the back of my hair. "Don't be like that."

"Whatever." Reining in the anger, I continued on to the Third Fire.

In the Third Fire, the Anishinaabe will find the path to their chosen ground, a land in the west to which they must move their families. This will be the land where food grows upon the waters.

You will know the future of our people by the face the light-skinned race wears. If they come wearing the face of brotherhood, then there will come a time of wonderful change for generations to come. They will bring new knowledge and articles that can be joined with the knowledge of this country. In this way, two nations will join to make a mighty nation. This new nation will be joined by two more so that four will form the mightiest nation of all. You will know the face of the brotherhood if the light-skinned race comes carrying no weapons if they come bearing only their knowledge and a handshake.

"Well, that didn't happen. They obviously underestimated the white man's greed." I flashed a hand before Levaughn pointed out the obvious and this conversation transformed into the same argument as before. "I know, I know. Pot meet kettle. You can stop glaring at me now." I scanned the next paragraph.

Beware if the light-skinned race comes wearing the face of death. You must be careful because the face of brotherhood and the face of death look very much alike. If they come carrying a weapon ... beware. If they come in suffering ... they could fool you. Their hearts may be filled with greed for the riches of this land. If they are indeed your brothers, let them prove it. Do not accept them in total trust. You shall know that the face they wear is one of death if the rivers run with poison and fish become unfit to eat. You shall know them by these many things.

"Wow." I biffed Levaughn's arm. "Did you read that? They predicted the white man might pilfer the land of gold, furs, and anything else of value, bringing with them sickness and disease."

"The Bible has many prophecies too."

Ignoring that remark, I read the Fifth and Sixth Fire.

In the time of the Fifth Fire, there will come a great struggle that will grip the lives of all Native people. At the waning of this Fire, there will come among the people one who holds a promise of great joy and salvation. If the people accept this promise of a new way and abandon the old teachings, then the struggle of the Fifth Fire will be with the people for many generations. The promise that comes will prove to be a false promise. All those who accept this promise will cause the near destruction of the people.

In the time of the Sixth Fire, it will be evident that the promise of the Fifth Fire came in a false way. Those deceived by this promise will take their children away from the teachings of the Elders. Grandsons and granddaughters will turn against the Elders. In this way, the Elders will lose their reason for living ... they will lose their purpose in life. At this time a new sickness will come among the people. The balance of many people will be disturbed. The cup of life will almost become the cup of grief.

"Right again. Y'know, I see why Chayton believed this prophecy. So much of it came true."

"I can too," he said, which totally blew my mind. "But that still didn't give him the right to kill seven people."

And...the cop was back in the room. "I'm not sayin' what he did was right, just that I understand how he might think he could make a difference."

"Really? 'Cause it sounds a lot like you're condoning his behavior."

"Well, I'm not." To lighten the mood, I twisted two fingers together. "Me and the law are like this. I'd never break it."

That got a chuckle out of him. "Yeah, you're the poster child for Citizen of the Year."

Grinning, I turned back to the computer screen, reading the last Fire.

In the time of the Seventh Fire, New People will emerge. They will retrace their steps to find what was left by the trail. Their steps will take them to the Elders who they will ask to guide them on their journey. But many of the Elders will have fallen asleep. They will awaken to this new time with nothing to offer. Some of the Elders will be silent because no one will ask anything of them. The New People will have to be careful in how they approach the Elders. The task of the New People will not be easy.

If the New People will remain strong in their quest, the Water Drum of the Midewiwin Lodge will again sound its voice. There will be a rebirth of the Anishinaabe Nation and a rekindling of old flames. The Sacred Fire will again be lit.

"Did you catch that last line?" Energy surged within me, and the clouds parted, revealing Chayton's motive for the killing spree. "This must be what he meant. It's a rebirth, a rekindling of old flames." This final passage gripped me harder and firmer than all the others...

It is at this time that the light-skinned race will be given a choice between two roads. One road will be green and lush, and very inviting. The other road will be black and charred, and walking it will cut their feet. In the prophecy, the people decide to take neither road, but instead to turn back, to remember and reclaim the wisdom of those who came before them.

If they choose the right road, then the Seventh Fire will light the Eighth and final Fire, an eternal fire of peace, love, brotherhood, and sisterhood. If the light-skinned race makes the wrong choice of the roads, then the destruction which they brought with them to this country will come back at them and cause much suffering and death to all the Earth's people.

"There it is." My whole body numbed. "He was trying to restore peace on earth."

Levaughn rolled his lips. "Murdering seven men and women was sure a strange way to go about it."

"I know, but maybe he thought he had no choice. Maybe he believed the world wouldn't pay attention unless he did something drastic, something so twisted that they'd need to listen." My mother's blood flushed through me, the imprint of my ancestors' suffering bearing down on my soul. "Real change requires sacrifice."

Levaughn exhaled loud enough to make his point, but I ignored him.

"I wonder how the old Cherokee flag relates to the prophecy." My fingers raced across the keyboard, and numerous links appeared.

Levaughn mumbled, "Who's to say he's a hundred-percent Cherokee? Many of us have mixed heritage."

And my eyebrows rose on their own. "Another good point, Detective." I clicked a link called The Rainbow Prophecy...

There will come a day when people of all races, colors, and creeds will put aside their differences. They will come together in love, joining hands in unification, to heal the Earth and all Her children. They will move over the Earth like a great Whirling Rainbow, bringing peace, understanding, and healing everywhere they go. Many creatures thought to be extinct or mythical will resurface at this time; the great trees that perished will return almost overnight. All living things will flourish, drawing sustenance from the breast of our Mother, the Earth.

My eyes pooled with tears while I reveled in the prophecy's beauty, rejoiced in its simplicity, my mother's spirit whispering in my ear, "Hold on to this prophecy, my precious child, for one day, its message will outshine the past."

Levaughn caressed my back, his tenderness and warmth making me even more emotional. "You okay?"

I could only nod.

"You sure?"

I nodded again.

"You can tell me anything, y'know."

I nodded a third time.

"Okay, when you're ready to talk, I'm here."

"I know." With a slight shake of the head, I halted the

production of tears, and swiped my fingers under my eyeliner. "Go." I cleared my throat. "You should get back to the scene."

When he kissed me, my lips trembled, and I held my breath so I wouldn't lose control. Once he left the lab, I locked the door and raced back to my computer, typing in the name of my half-brother, Kajika, in an attempt to find what it meant.

Walks without sound.

Oh. My. God. My eyes bulged. Could the skinwalker be my biological brother?

CHAPTER FORTY-ONE

11:55 a.m.

For hours my research led me down endless rabbit holes, my mind hungering for knowledge about my heritage. But without knowing the exact name of my mother's tribe—many tribes shared reservations—other than she'd fled from New Mexico, I had no way to narrow my search.

Levaughn sauntered back in to the computer lab. "Hey, you. I thought you'd be done by now."

"Why, what time is it?"

Angling the face of his watch toward me, he said, "Almost noon. You about ready to get outta here?"

"I guess." Blood droplets stained the leathered toe of his dress shoe, and I jabbed a chin in its direction. "Is that Chayton's blood?"

"Crap. It's castoff spray from earlier." He propped up his foot on my desk and rubbed the spot with a dry hanky, obsessing over a couple bloodstains. "You find North's purse-snatcher?"

"Yup. Cross-referenced phone numbers with pawn shops around the time of each incident. The moron didn't use a burner, so it didn't take a rocket science to find him." I rolled my lips. "Some sixteen-year-old punk, looking for a way to break up the monotony of his poor, entitled life. You know the drill."

With his leg still raised, his back straightened and he gazed around the room. "Any wet wipes in here?"

"No. Hey, you find anythin' in Chayton's personal effects that points to why he chose Revere Beach and Lake Winnipesauke to dump the bodies? There must be a reason."

Unless, of course, Mayhem gave him a specific blueprint to follow. In which case, I may never uncover the truth.

"Not yet." He scrubbed the bloodstain so hard he practically wore out the leather. "Revere Beach is America's first public beach, if that helps. No clue about the New Hampshire lake."

"For shits and giggles, lemme try something real quick." I typed Lake Winnipesauke + American Indians into the search engine.

One article in particular caught my eye. "It says here, from its southwestern edge at Weirs Beach through Paugus Bay and its neighboring lakes, the great Lake Winnipesaukee eventually connects to the ten-point-five-mile Winnipesaukee River. The waterway flows through the Lakes Region and into Franklin, where it meets two other rivers, the Merrimack and the Pemigewasset. The town where the three rivers converge was an ancient village and gathering spot long before the modern settlement was built."

I glanced up at Levaughn. "Ancient village and gathering spot?" I read ahead. "Oh, also, the Indian Mortar Lot is in Laconia."

His nose crinkled. "The what?"

"It's an historical site that contains a rare petroglyph of a shad—apparently, it's a common local fish—carved into a large boulder. Oh, this is cool, too. It says, the marker also explains how the gouged glacial rock in the middle of this grassy spot was first shaped by water and then by the grinding of corn from American Indians' hands, and how they carved the almost life-sized shad out of a granite rock while they camped along the brook."

Obsessed with learning more, I clicked the next article. This time the story focused on New England, and I read about how for the first fifty years after the pilgrims arrived at Plymouth in sixteen-twenty, the English colonists had a fairly peaceful relationship with the local tribes.

Without the help of the Wampanoag people, the pilgrims wouldn't have survived the first winter. But then, the colonies expanded into Indian territory, and the local tribes grew concerned. As more and more white men arrived from Europe, broken promises became the norm. And after the chief of the Wampanoag died while in captivity, his brother, Metacomet—soon known as King Philip—became determined to drive the colonists out of New England.

King Philip's war devastated both sides, killing six-hundred colonists and around three-thousand American Indians. Many more were captured and shipped off into slavery.

I slapped a hand over my mouth. "Oh my God, Levaughn. Guess what happened to Chief Metacomet?"

He spit on the hanky and lowered it to the bloodstains. "To who?"

"Chief Metacomet became King Philip."

"Okay," he said, more interested in polishing his damn shoe than listening to me. "I'm assuming he was murdered."

"He was beheaded."

That got him to face me. "Say, what now?"

"It gets worse. The colonists displayed his severed head for the next twenty-five years as a warning to other American Indians. The English attacked over half of the ninety-plus towns in New England at some point during the war." I stared at the screen, trying to imagine the scene back then. "Wow. I've never been more ashamed of my race."

"Babe—" Dropping his foot to the floor, he leaned across my desk. "Things happen in war."

"Yeah, but—"

"Look." He sat on the corner of my desk. "Regardless of how Chayton Kashk's people suffered, more violence wasn't the answer."

Chin in my hand, I breathed a heavy sigh. "Still..."

"C'mon." He jumped off the desk and extended an opened hand toward me. "Let's get out of here."

"Need to lock up first. Meet ya at the car in five?"

"Sounds good."

After he left the lab, I logged out of my computer and straightened my desk. Dropped Chuck's file on his empty desk, and hustled through the lobby.

Halfway to the door, the desk sergeant waved the receiver of the phone at me. "Call for you, Daniels."

"Who is it?" I stopped, my tongue playing with the inside of my cheek. "Levaughn's waitin' for me."

"No idea."

My voice raised louder than intended. "Well, isn't it your job to know?"

"I'm not your personal secretary, Daniels." He stared, cold and hard. "You want the call or not?"

"Fine." I ripped the receiver out of his grasp. "Hello?"

A dial tone hummed in my ear.

Passing him the phone, I said, "Was it a man or a woman?"

"No idea."

"Whatever." On my way out the door, I tossed him a salute. "Thanks for your help." Then mumbled under my breath, "Jerkoff."

With both hands, I shoved open the solid glass door. The Crown Vic idled twenty feet away, smoke billowing out its exhaust pipe. I'd made it about ten feet when a crow swooped down out of nowhere and clawed the back of my skull, the force stumbling me forward, nearly knocking me to the ground. I covered my head with both arms.

Sunlight glimmered off Poe's gold ankle band as he hovered a mere six inches above me. His black talons opened in slow motion and out dropped a scroll, striking the toe of my right motorcycle boot dead-center. This bird had perfect aim. I should've stepped over it—one might think I'd learned from experience—but my curiosity overshadowed common sense.

Pulling the twine bow, ivory stationery unfurled, revealing a message from Mayhem. He'd written the death threat in bloody finger-swipes.

Ms. Daniels,

You killed your only ally. Not smart.

See you soon,
Mr. Mayhem

I glared at Poe, and I swore his eyes twinkled with delight. If I didn't straighten out the misunderstanding with Mayhem, everyone I loved was at risk. Levaughn's eyes reflected in the side mirror, and I signaled for him to wait. Spun, and boogied back inside, jogging with a fake smile plastered on my face, silently praying I could get into the computer lab before anyone stopped me.

The key only inserted partway when I stuck it in the lock upside-down. Icy tingles shot up the back of my neck, and I fumbled to get inside and over to my desk before Mayhem made his move.

I logged into the Onion router, then punched in Mayhem's website address. On his message board, I wrote:

Mr. M,

Your psychotic fowl delivered your cryptic scroll. Listen, let me explain. I only broke into your place to retrieve the page you stole from me, but then—

The screen flickered, scattered lines crisscrossing across the screen before the lost connection message popped up, "Oops. Something went wrong."

Dammit! If taken out of context, my partial note made me look even more guilty, like that dead chick in the foyer had tried to stop me from burglarizing the brownstone, so I stabbed her to death, and then covered it up by murdering Mayhem's wife.

Hands trembling, I logged back into the website, wrote:

Mr. M,

I know Poe probably gave you my rosary beads, but—

The connection flickered, flickered, and then died. *Fuck!*

I tried again, but this time, the website address took me to a charcoal-gray page that showed the domain name in the upper-left corner but didn't open the usual message board. Instead, I got a list of related links.

Full body tremors rattled my bones as I stared in horror, my breath heavy and raspy. Mayhem had shut down the site.

This is it. My life's over.

Gaze locked on the screen, I chewed the side of my thumb knuckle, my insides screaming for me to fix this. But how? There's no way Mr. Mayhem wouldn't avenge his wife's death. Oh, dear God, was the girl in the foyer his daughter? Did he think I murdered his entire family?

I dragged my fingers down my cheeks. The more time that passed, the more his thirst for revenge would spiral out of control. How could I stop him? He's a ghost, thanks to me. Why didn't I turn him in when I had the chance?

Black spots danced before my eyes. I shoved my chair away from the desk, the room whirling on its axis. He could get to me anywhere, anytime, anyplace...if the skinwalker didn't kill me first.

ABOUT SUE COLETTA

Member of Mystery Writers of America, Sisters in Crime, and International Thriller Writers, Sue Coletta is a bestselling, award-winning crime writer of psychological thrillers and mysteries. Three years running, Feedspot awarded her Murder Blog as one of the Top 50 Crime Blogs on the Net. Sue's also the communications manager for Forensic Science and the Serial Killer Project and a proud member of the Kill Zone, an award-winning writing blog where she posts every other Monday. When Sue's not reading or writing, you can find her feeding peanuts to her beloved pet crows, who live free.

* * *

Get in touch with Sue:

Website - www.suecoletta.com
Facebook - www.facebook.com/SueColetta1
Facebook - www.facebook.com/SuePhillipsColetta
Twitter - www.twitter.com/SueColetta1
Blog - suecoletta.com/murder-blog
Goodreads - www.goodreads.com/SueColetta
StumbleUpon - www.stumbleupon.com/stumbler/SueColetta1
Pinterest - www.pinterest.com/suecoletta1/
LinkedIn - www.linkedin.com/pub/sue-coletta/a0/1b9/161
Tirgearr Publishing – www.tirpub.com/scoletta

BOOKS BY SUE COLETTA

GRAFTON COUNTY SERIES

MARRED, # 1

When Sage Quintano barely escapes from a brutal serial killer, husband Niko, a homicide detective, insists they move to rural New Hampshire, where he accepts a position as sheriff. Sage buries secrets from that night —secrets she swears to take to her deathbed. Three years pass and Sage's twin sister goes missing. Is the killer trying to lure Sage into a deadly trap to end his reign of terror?

CLEAVED, # 2

Sage Quintano writes about crime. Her husband Niko investigates it. Together they make an unstoppable team. But no one counted on a twisted serial killer, who stalks their sleepy community. Women impaled by deer antlers, bodies encased in oil drums, nursery rhymes, and the Suicide King. What connects these cryptic clues? For Sage and Niko, the truth may be more terrifying than they imagined.

SCATHED, # 3

When a brutal murder rocks Alexandria, Sheriff Niko Quintano receives a letter: Paradox vows to kill again if his riddle isn't solved within 24 hours. Niko turns to his crime writer wife, Sage, for help. But she's dealing with her own private nightmare. A phone call from the past threatens her future. Can Niko and Sage solve the riddle in time, or will the killer win this deadly game of survival?

THE MAYHEM SERIES

WINGS OF MAYHEM, #1

Shawnee Daniels breaks into the home of Jack Delsin who's accused of embezzling money from his employees' retirement fund. Intent on returning their hard-earned cash, she discovers Jack has secrets worth killing over. A deadly game of cat-and-mouse ensues. Can she outrun the killer, prove she's innocent of murder after Jack sets her up, and protect those she loves before he strikes again?

BLESSED MAYHEM, #2

Accompanied by his loyal crow companions, Poe, Allan, and Edgar, Mr. Mayhem's crimes strike fear in the hearts and minds of folks across Massachusetts' North Shore. When Shawnee Daniels–cat burglar extraordinaire and forensic hacker for the police–meets Mayhem in the dark, she piques his curiosity. Sadly for her, she leaves behind an item best left undiscovered. Or is it serendipity by design?

SILENT MAYHEM, #3

A madman is decapitating men and women and dumping their headless corpses on two area beaches. Mr. Mayhem—the most prolific serial killer the North Shore has ever known—claims Shawnee Daniels' life is in danger. He "claims" he wants to help her, but just last year he threatened to murder everyone she loves. Can she find the strength to move forward, or will the truth destroy her?

Printed in Great Britain
by Amazon